PART OF THE GAME

TIM REARDON

ALL THINGS
THAT MATTER
PRESS

Merry Christmas
+
Happy Reading

T. R

This one is for my writing partner, the screenwriter Dan Harlan,
who forces me to keep putting words on paper
and reminds me to kill my "darlings."

Acknowledgments

The author wishes to thank early readers Jim Dekker and Steve McFeely as well as researcher Sean Duffy, volunteer line editor Laura Kelly, and PR magician Tom McKeon.

PRE-GAME

When the new guy, Aram, asked Wayne what was the craziest thing he'd ever seen while working the security monitors, Wayne said, "Fat, naked guy doin' a Hula Hoop."

"That's it?" said Aram, leaning back in his chair now.

"This ain't glamorous work, son," Wayne said and took a peek at monitor six where two guys were arguing over a parking spot down in the garage. As usual, the guy who'd gotten to the spot first kept it, and the other guy sped off, wheels probably squealing on the epoxy surface. Wayne always imagined the sounds when he looked at the silent monitors.

Aram leaned forward now and pointed up at monitor one, which provided an aerial shot of the street and sidewalk in front of the building. "Check it out," he said. "Look at the little kid in the tuxedo."

The guy Aram was pointing at didn't walk like a kid, too cocky, moving down the sidewalk in a kind of swagger. When a woman walked out of the building and crossed his path, though, he certainly seemed small enough to be one. "That's not a tuxedo," said Wayne. "It's just a black suit."

"Isn't that what a tuxedo is?" said Aram.

"Dumbshit," said Wayne. "Tuxedoes have bow ties and cummerbunds."

"Old man," said Aram. "You're still in 1978. You think a tux has to have a ruffled shirt, too? I saw a dude at the Academy Awards wearing a bolo tie with his."

Wayne tapped the control panel and zoomed in on the little guy's face. Definitely not a kid. This was a small Asian man with severe, angular features, a freakin' geometry project of a face, and little strands of hair on each side of his mouth and on his chin, like a child's drawing of a Chinese man.

"Oh," said Aram when Wayne held the zoom. "Dude looked like a little boy on his way to the Oscars."

Wayne panned out so that they could see a medium shot. He wanted Aram to learn the techniques, but he didn't want to have to talk about them, so he just did them and hoped the guy would pick up everything he needed to know. It wasn't brain surgery. In fact, it wasn't any kind of surgery at all, not even oral surgery or plastic surgery. It was just looking at these monitors. Anyone could do it.

The little man on the street was standing with his hand in his pocket, looking around as if he were waiting for someone. Then he pulled something out of his pocket. It looked like a lighter. Wayne was about to look away. People were always lighting cigarettes in Chinatown. But just as he was about to turn to monitor four, the tiny man reached into the inside pocket of his sport coat and pulled out something that didn't look like cigarettes.

"Is that a cigar?" asked Aram.

Wayne knew it was too big to be a cigar. It looked about the size and color of a cardboard toilet paper spool, but that didn't seem right, so he zoomed back in again and watched the man use the lighter to ignite a wick at the end of the thing. Aram was saying, "What the fuck?" while Wayne was thinking, no biggy, Chinatown. These guys were always shooting off fireworks and sparklers and whatnot, but Wayne couldn't think of what the occasion could be.

He panned back out again to get a feel for where the guy was going to put the thing, and he and Aram watched the man walk right up to a delivery truck with Chinese letters on it and throw whatever it was through the driver's side window. Aram said, "What the fuck?" again.

Wayne felt something tighten in his stomach, but he didn't say anything.

A moment later Wayne thought he saw the truck jump just slightly. He couldn't tell if he was imagining the sound or if he could actually hear it from inside the security office. He was almost positive he felt the concussion in his chest, but, again, the visual of the truck jumping and then the smoke coming out of both sides could have created the illusion. He didn't know. It didn't matter.

"Call this in right now," he said to Aram, but never took his eyes off the monitor.

He heard Aram picking up the phone. He watched someone stepping out of the truck. The person emerged through the smoke and staggered to the sidewalk. Wayne could tell it was a man, but he couldn't get an idea of the extent of the injuries, if there were any. Was it just a smoke bomb? When he zoomed back in, he could see the man's face. His eyes were closed, and he was coughing.

Wayne was trying to listen to Aram on the phone and manipulate the camera controls at the same time, and he ended up holding the zoom too long. The guy, whose face was taking up most of the monitor now, opened his eyes for a brief moment. Not just open, but bugging. His mouth formed a ridiculous O. His whole face stretched tight over his skull for a second before he closed his eyes again and sank out of the frame.

When Wayne panned out again, the guy was curled in the fetal position. Blood was pumping out of his chest and spreading across the sidewalk. When Wayne went for an even wider shot, he saw the little man who'd lit the bomb move down the street like one of those Olympic speed walkers to the truck that still had some faint wisps of smoke floating out of the passenger side window. Wayne watched him fold up a knife and place it in his pocket. Then the guy pulled out a handkerchief, covered his mouth with it, and stepped into the truck.

"Jesus," Wayne said to himself. Then, to Aram, "What did the cops say?"

"They're on the way," he said. Wayne could feel him standing behind his chair.

Wayne stared at the monitor and watched the truck move down the street. He could see into the back now. The door was open, and pig carcasses were swinging from the ceiling. For a brief moment, Wayne imagined that he could smell the pork as the truck moved out of camera range. "Did you see the letters on the truck?" he asked.

"It was Chinese letters, man."

"You don't read Chinese?" said Wayne.

"I'm fuckin' Lebanese, dude."

Wayne was thinking of the fat guy and the Hula Hoop now. He was dazed and letting his eyes blur around the edges. "Oh," he said as he watched the blood on the sidewalk spread all the way to the curb.

"The fuck are we supposed to tell the cops?" asked Aram.

"Pig truck, I guess."

FIRST QUARTER ~ SCAMMERS

"The sure way to be cheated is to think one's self more cunning than others."

– Jean de La Fontain

Everyone's a scammer.

Right before all the craziness happened last year, I was sitting on the L Taraval, letting the streetcar take me up past the Parkside Library and the Kentucky Fried Chicken toward Zim's Hamburgers on 19th Avenue. I had my headphones on, but the volume all the way down, so the two suits next to me don't know I'm listening to their conversation.

One of the guys is chubby and bald. He's sweating in his suit jacket, and his moist head's starting to reflect the overhead lights. He's not old, doesn't look more than thirty or thirty-five, but he's not in good shape. He keeps messing with his slacks around the crotch area, trying to get comfortable, but the pants keep riding up higher, showing off more and more of his pasty shins and droopy socks.

"I'm always billing," the guy says to his buddy, who has an amazing pompadour hairdo with some kind of product holding it all together, like a candy-coating. It almost looks like clay-mation hair.

Pompadour nods at the guy, but you can tell he just wants to get to his stop. He looks like he's gazing out the window, but I'm pretty sure he's checking himself out in the reflection, making sure the hair is still in place.

"Y'see," the bald guy says, "If I'm thinking about a case, I'm working on it." He's tugging on the knot of his tie now, still trying to get himself comfy on the hard plastic seat. "And if I'm working, someone's payin'," he says. I don't have the right angle to see it, but the sound of his voice makes me think he's winking.

"What if your plumber tried to pull something like that?" Hairdo says. He's looking at the other guy now. I'm not positive where he's going with this, but I think I have an idea.

"What do y'mean?" the guy says and opens his briefcase. He pulls out a small hand towel and rubs the top of his head with it, changing his dome from semi-gloss to eggshell in one swipe.

Hairdo waits for the man to put the towel away and then says, "What if your plumber says that while he was surfing down at Ocean Beach he was thinking about which snake he wanted to use to unclog the shit in your pipes, so he has to bill you for that hour he spent out on the waves."

The bald guy looks at Pompadour as if the man has handed him a shit sandwich, his facial expression somewhere between amused and disgusted. Eventually, he smiles and says, "I tell him to go fuck himself."

"So it's okay for you, but not okay for the plumber?" says Pompadour, raising his eyebrows, which actually makes his hairline appear to be shifting.

"That's right," the bald guy says. "If I'm on the treadmill for a couple of hours, and I'm thinking about my closing argument, those are billable hours, buddy. Intellectual labor."

"That's billable bullshit," says Pompadour, who then makes a big production out of looking at the other guy's gut sagging over his belt. "Do you mean you're standing on the treadmill? Is it even plugged in?"

I nearly laugh, then drop my eyes back down to the man's bone-white shins.

"Go ahead and be a funny man," says the bald guy. "But I can bill a couple hundred dollars on the streetcar if I'm not wasting my time talking to you." He stops for a moment before he says, "In fact, I might bill this time anyway. Talking to you about billing can go under admin. This is a working commute today."

Pompadour's had enough. He widens his eyes and looks at the bald guy as if he's about to scold a child for shoplifting. "I'd never hire you as my attorney," he says and then he's back looking out the window again.

"You're goddamn right," says the bald guy as he cups the man's shoulder. "You can't afford me."

Everyone's a scammer.

Back in high school, I had what was known as a street agent. I was good at basketball, and there were these guys who used to hang around the gyms and try to make friends with the best players at AAU tournaments. They'd give you new shoes or take you out for a milkshake after the game. Maybe even give you Warriors tickets. They'd basically kiss your ass every which way possible. Some of these guys were in their thirties and forties. I don't even know what their real jobs were or if they had real jobs. But they were always at the big tournaments.

Here's how it works. Real agents—y'know, the guys who represent professional athletes and take their fifteen percent? The Jerry McGuire guys?—there's a lot of 'em. Who wouldn't want to make fifteen percent on a twenty million dollar contract? But there's a finite number of athletes, and all the agents are targeting the same ones. So they're looking to get a leg up on the competition. How do they do it?

Get 'em young.

How do you get 'em young?

If you're an agent, you pay some guy—or, if you're good, a few guys—to find the top young athletes in a certain region and to get to know all the kids who have the look of someone who might eventually get a professional contract. It's like buying futures. The street agent has to have an eye for this sort of thing, and he also has to be a schmoozer to win the kids over. But he can't look like too much of a schmoozer because he'll be dealing with the parents of these kids as well. He's *got to look like someone you can trust. He's got to act like a gym director or a teacher or a mentor. Like he's trying to keep the bad element away from the kid. He can't look like what he really is: a scam artist.*

The hope of the real agent is that the street agent can land him a kid who, in a few years, will be signing a big contract. That's why the agent pays the street agent. In a way, it's like throwing chum over the railing of a fishing boat. You get the fish to start hanging around the bow. Then you throw the line in and hope there's a big one out there. Like in "Jaws" when Roy Scheider tells Richard Dreyfus, "We're gonna need a bigger boat." Or, better yet, it's like paying this guy to go fishing with dynamite. He blows all the fish to the surface, then brings them to you, and you keep the big ones and leave the rest to rot.

My guy was actually giving me an allowance. I knew it was wrong to take the money. But when you're a kid, who's going to say no? Not me.

In fact, I bragged about it until my dad found out.

Then my street agent disappeared. I kept playing basketball, but I never saw the dude again. I asked around for a while, but he'd become a ghost as fast as I eventually would when I got in some trouble not so long after. When I asked my dad where the guy went, he said, "Chuck, your buddy ain't your buddy anymore."

And that was that.

Scammers don't have any real relationships, so it's easy to disappear. No connections. They just pack their shit and find somewhere else to scam.

Sometimes they're allowed to stick around. There's a homeless drunk I know who used to come around the hot dog stand looking for freebies, pretzels that had dropped on the ground, extra cooked hot dogs right before closing, whatever he could get. He wasn't a bad guy, used to be a CPA or something, but didn't have much going for him anymore.

One day he comes up to me all smiles, says his prayers have been answered. "You hear what the Board of Supervisors is voting on?" he says.

I haven't, so he goes, "You ever heard of a concept called a 'wet house'?"

Again, I haven't. He says, "The city wants to buy an apartment building and give the rooms to chronic, homeless alcoholics."

I don't get it.

He must see it on my face, so he's all, "Drunks cost the city a lot of money." And he's nodding now like he's trying to convince me to give him a free dog. "They—we— eat up all sorts of funds for hospital care, ambulance rides, treatment centers, law enforcement costs, all sorts of shit. So they're gonna put us all together in the same place."

"Oh," I say. "Like a big treatment center. That makes some sense, I guess."

"No, man," he says. "I'd never put myself in a program. This place is gonna let us keep drinking. In fact, there'll be an in-house nurse and an attendant to go out and get us our booze."

"You gotta be shittin' me," I say. This doesn't make any sense. This might be

7

the biggest scam of all. You make yourself such a public nuisance that society gives up on trying to cure you, and, instead, the taxpayers just stick you in your own apartment and let you drink yourself to death.

"I shit you not, my friend," he says. "Bunks for drunks. Ain't it grand?"

***

Everyone's a scammer. The nice dad down at the grammar school, who coaches his kid's team every year? You know the guy. Doesn't know much about the game, but he's really generous with his time. He's just making sure his kid's in the starting lineup. Scammer.

The mechanic who tells you that it's not just your brake pads, it's the whole system. Scammer.

The penile enlargement doctor, the group therapist, the self-help guru. Scammers.

The computer salesman, the one who insists on the extra software and the extended warranty. Scammer.

All those rich guys and their corporations donating to political campaigns. Come on, people. Scammers.

The good thing about me. I know all the scams. No one's foolin' me

CHAPTER ONE

After the planes crashed into the buildings in New York, the job market all over the country imploded, especially for folks like Chuck Holiday, a recent Berkeley dropout with a nice jump shot but no other marketable skills. So he took the first career opportunity to pop up: hot dog vender for Stanley's Steamers, his cart stationed right out in front of Macy's Union Square, busy with good-looking ladies, rich, but scrambling for bargains anyway, maybe just for the bragging rights. *See this blouse? Fifty dollars!*

Chuck had been working the last eight months for Stanley Winkler, hot dog aficionado and unbelievable asshole. The man thought he was fooling people with the name of his franchise, making it sound *familiar* so hungry folks wondering if they should chance a sidewalk vendor might think the food was okay. They would read the yellow and black banner above the cart and think, *Oh, I've heard of these before. They must be good.* Like walking through a supermarket and picking up a six pack of Dr. Skipper thinking it was Dr. Pepper. And these fools wouldn't realize that what they'd heard before, what sounded *familiar*, was Stanley Steemers, the carpet cleaning franchise, the yellow vans, not Stanley's Steamers, the steam-heated hot dogs for which Mr. Winkler had Chuck charging shoppers and tourists six bucks a pop, as if they were some kind of imported gourmet sausages. At least the Dr. Pepper knock-off sounded like another soda. Stanley was working with apples and oranges: hot dogs and steam cleaners.

Though Stanley seemed like a misguided scammer, Chuck had to give the man credit. Stanley knew how to make money, knew how to get the most out of his business. San Francisco had put a moratorium on hot dog carts a few years back, so Stanley and a few other lucky bastards had all the carts in the city. And Stanley Winkler had the whole Union Square neighborhood, five carts in all, bringing in a quarter of a million dollars a year, and the hot dogs themselves were just a reason to set up shop. Winkler made his biggest profits on other items, where the markup was nearly obscene. Biggest money-maker? Water. Morons paying three dollars for a little plastic container of water, which he'd bought in bulk for eighteen cents a bottle. The man knew how to make money.

In fact, Chuck wondered if Stanley would be proud of Chuck's own industriousness, his using the hot dog cart as home base for his bookmaking enterprise. Because Stan was such a cheap screw, he actually kept hot dog inventory and checked Chuck's till every day. There were only a couple of ways to skim on this guy. For a while, Chuck was bringing in his own hot dogs from Costco, working the system that way, keeping those profits for himself, but that was a lot of work and it was risky, so Chuck found this other way to supplement the minimum wage that Stan reluctantly paid him.

Chuck Holiday was an entrepreneur in the gambling trade, steadily building his client base and providing betting opportunities for those so inclined to wager on sporting events. He was simply providing a service.

He had just given a customer a hot dog with sauerkraut and two waters when he saw one of his clients approaching the cart.

Larry Bjorkquist was on a hot streak. He'd won hundred dollar bets on six individual games in a row over the past two weeks. No parlays and no doubling down, but still doing pretty well. That being said, the guy didn't want to collect his winnings. He said that if he took the money from Chuck, he'd blow it on coke, which he'd given up years ago but had recently revisited on a whim.

"You finally here to collect?" asked Chuck when Larry, glassy-eyed and chewing aggressively on a toothpick, approached the cart.

"You gotta hold onto it for me for a couple more weeks," he said, putting both hands on the counter and shifting his eyes back and forth from the mini chip bags to the soft pretzels hanging behind the plastic window. "I think I'll get this shit outta my system by then." He wiped at his nose, just a two-fingered, backhand swipe, so quick you might not even notice, before he said, "It's just a phase. Almost done, I think."

"Whatever you want," said Chuck, who'd seen worse than Larry. At least Larry was winning bets. At least he had some luck even as the coke was slowly hollowing out his brain, snort by snort. Most guys who were hooked were trying to win money to buy more, but they'd end up losing bets and doing something stupid, and then ending up in jail or dead. At the very least, Larry knew his weakness. And he had enough discipline to constrain himself from picking up his money, knowing it would soon be in his dealer's pocket.

"I'll tell you what I want," he said, still shifting his eyes around at the various items, letting them rest on the candy rack for a moment before looking back at Chuck. "Soft pretzel with mustard."

"You got it," said Chuck, tearing off a sheet of wax paper and pulling the pretzel off the hook. "Extra salt?"

"Just mustard," said Larry, reaching in his pocket for money but pulling out a handful of gum wrappers, a bus transfer, and some old receipts.

When Chuck reached over the counter to hand Larry his pretzel, Larry looked frightened. "What's wrong?" said Chuck.

"No money," he said. "Can you take it out of my winnings?"

"I try to keep those separate," said Chuck. "Why don't you just take your money, man? Give it to someone you trust to hold onto it until you're straight." He held out the pretzel farther, but Larry was backing away now, shaking his head.

"I don't trust anyone," he said.

Chuck was feeling just the beginnings of a headache rubbing at his temples and between his eyes. He didn't need one of those, not with a pro-am playoff game he was playing in tonight. He could also see a middle-aged couple, they looked European to him, standing a few feet behind Larry, looking at the menu board. He had to hurry this guy up, get him the hell out of here before Stan showed up and got suspicious. "Larry," said Chuck. "Take the pretzel, man. It's on me. It's already got the mustard on it, so I can't do anything with it."

Larry stepped forward and took the pretzel with both hands. "Thanks, dude," he said and took a small bite from the edge, but a whole section broke off, and he stood frozen for a moment with the large segment of pretzel hanging out of his mouth. He looked like a dog who'd just fetched a stick but didn't want to return it to his master. Chuck waited and watched the man control the pretzel using only his mouth. Then he watched the masticated pretzel pass behind the man's Adam's apple before Larry said, "I don't trust no one, and no one trusts me. I'm not even fucking hungry, man."

Chuck took a look at the European couple, who'd turned away from the cart and were headed downstairs to the Macy's food court. The couple probably wasn't *familiar* with the brand name Stanley's Steamers.

Since no one else was waiting, Chuck let his curiosity get the better of him and asked, "Why doesn't anyone trust you, Lar?"

Larry didn't look wired anymore. The corners of his eyes seemed to be turned downward like a sad clown's. "I fucked everything up, Chuck. Why would anyone trust me?"

"Okay," said Chuck, not ready for this to turn into some kind of therapy session. "You'll get it together, bro."

"I don't know if I can," he said. He was backing up, as if he thought Chuck was going to call the cops. He was getting close to the street, traffic whizzing by behind him. He dropped the pretzel to the sidewalk and raised his voice when he said, "I got involved in too much bad shit, too many bad people, Chuck."

His heels were off the edge of the curb now, and Chuck turned his head to check out the traffic. A white van was just shifting into third gear. In the split second that Chuck looked away from him, Larry had stepped backward onto Geary Street and was moving away from the sidewalk, damn close to the traffic. Chuck was actually moving around the cart and looking at the white van now. He started to scream, but when he looked back at Larry, the lunatic was jumping back onto the sidewalk, so Chuck only let out a kind of abbreviated yelp, no words, just a sound, almost like a bark. Chuck caught a glimpse of the driver of the van: bushy mustache, fortyish guy, looking right at Chuck, not even noticing that he'd almost hit Larry. Not even noticing that anything else was going on except Chuck standing next to his hot dog stand.

Before Chuck could even catch his breath, Larry was running back toward him. His hands were flailing now and his eyes were animated again. "Give me my fucking money, Chuck," he said. "Right now."

"Larry," said Chuck. "You gotta wait for my break, dude. I can't do business with you right out here in the middle of the street.

"When's your break?" he said, and he almost sounded threatening now, as if Chuck had been withholding the man's money against his will.

"Someone should be by to relieve me in about fifteen minutes," said Chuck as he took a quick peek into the steamer. He had it set too high, and three of the dogs had split. Stan would not like that. And who the fuck was that guy in the van?

***

Stan pulled up in his BMW right in front of Chuck's cart, the flagship of the Bay Area Concessions cartel. Although Chuck had been with the company for less than a year, Stan liked the way the kid attracted customers, so he stationed him at the Macy's site. Chuck was really tall, he was blond, and he didn't mind chatting up customers, getting them to think maybe they'd come back next time they were in Union Square.

Stan wouldn't want you to get it wrong and think this kid was a winner. He was not. Chuck wouldn't talk about it, but he was definitely a fuck up. Dropped out of Cal. But the kid's dad was a judge; a friend of a friend hooked The Judge up with Stan and got Stan one more cart site in exchange for giving the kid a job.

There was a San Francisco charter prohibiting a hot dog cart expansion, but The Judge knew some folks, and, bingo, Stan gets a chance at another fifty grand a year just for letting this bozo sling hot dogs, which the kid was pretty good at anyway. Not a bad deal. Only thing was, Stan was not allowed to tell the kid how he got the job. The Judge was serious about it, and The Judge was a major pain in the ass. But fifty grand? Shit. Welcome aboard, kid.

"Chuckie-boy," he said as he slammed the door to the BMW and walked back toward the trunk. He used the remote and watched the trunk open in slow-motion. Then he reached inside and brought out the mustard samples. Same exact look as the French's but these were a buck less a bottle. Worth a shot.

"Stan the Man," said the kid without looking up as he was collecting money from a group of high school girls, who were giggling like they were talking to a celebrity instead of Chuck, the dropout.

When the girls walked away saying goodbye and toodles and smiling at Chuck, Stan said, "Jailbait," and winked, then put the mustard sample on the cart counter.

Chuck ignored the jailbait comment and said, "What am I looking at, Stan?"

"Thinkin' about trying a new mustard."

"People complaining about the old one?" Chuck asked, picking the bottle up and examining it now, like he was all of a sudden a condiment expert. "Abe's?"

"No one's complaining about the mustard," said Stan. "But this one's cheaper and probably tastes the same."

"Abe's?" the kid said again, scrunching up his face like the name Abe's was synonymous with shitty mustard.

"Yeah, Abe's" said Stan. "Is there some problem with that?"

"Never heard of it," said the kid, putting it back down on the counter now. "How's it taste?"

"I don't know," said Stan. "Put it on a few dogs today and see if anyone pukes."

"Got it," said the kid, and then Stan looked back behind the cart and noticed a skinny, washed out guy leaning against the front wall of Macy's near the glass doors and looking at Chuck.

"Friend of yours?" said Stan, gesturing with his head to the desperate looking son of a bitch standing behind him.

"Yeah," said Chuck. "He's waiting for my break so I can take him to lunch."

"Take him to lunch?" said Stan. Was the kid serious? "Why don't you buy him a fucking hot dog, son?"

"Jewish," said Chuck. "Said he would only eat here if we served Hebrew National. Kosher."

"Does he know how much Hebrew Nationals cost?" said Stan, pissed off now but wondering if Chuck was making this shit up. The kid would sometimes get a look in his eyes. Stan couldn't quite define it, but it was like the kid was making fun somehow. Like he thought he was better than all this. That attitude coming from a dropout, mind you, whose daddy had to buy him a job. But maybe Stan was wrong. Was the kid even smart enough to have an attitude? "I'd have to charge ten bucks a dog to make any money with fucking Hebrew Nationals."

"You're preaching to the choir," said the kid. "I'm just repeating what the man said."

"Yeah," said Stan and tried to look behind the kid's eyes, see if there was some kind of irony back there, if this kid was a closet ball-buster, but he couldn't tell. Chuck probably just had basketballs bouncing around his brain, playoffs tonight. Stan did like to watch the kid play. He was something of a local legend. Not the kind of guy to be hiding shit behind his eyes from Stan. Not complicated enough. Just an ex-jock slinging hot dogs.

CHAPTER TWO

The Judge was not a man of patience. He'd just hit an eight iron into the tall grass on the fifth hole at the Olympic Club, and he certainly wasn't going to waste any time looking for it. He'd already lost three balls on the first four holes, but that usually wouldn't bother him. He never took the penalty, and he kept a pocket full of new Titleists; he'd become very adept at letting a ball slip out and drop onto a nice piece of grass somewhere in the vicinity of where he thought his ball might have gone.

His problem was that he always closed his eyes and turned his head in disgust after a bad shot as if his doctor was checking for ruptures and had just asked him to cough. With his eyes closed, he wouldn't be able to pick out a marker and would have to guess where the ball ended up. He usually assumed it took a generous bounce.

Today, he made a nice drop and had a good look at the pin through a couple of tall cypresses with only a few low branches. He took out his tour chippo, which some jackass had once told him was an illegal club, and he made a perfect strike at the ball, which landed about eight feet in front of the green, but with the chippo's topspin, rolled onto the dance floor and ended up about four feet from the hole.

When he emerged from the trees, he saw Cunningham sitting in the cart, shaking his head. "You use that illegal club?" he said, shit-eating grin under his bushy mustache, like the kind cops used to wear about twenty years ago, back when they'd smack dirtbags around and no one cared about it.

"How 'bout I wrap it around your skull?" said The Judge, walking past the cart and straight up to the green to putt out.

Cunningham stayed in the cart. He didn't golf, but The Judge insisted that he ride around with him once a week. The Judge never told the man that he had to wear a sport coat and tie, but Cunningham always did, though he never seemed comfortable, even in situations that would require such attire.

After The Judge sank his putt, Cunningham held up the scorecard and said, "What do I give you on that hole, Judge?"

"Gimme what I got," said The Judge, sensing a tone from Cunningham.

"Yessir," said Cunningham, scratching a number on the card and then saying, "What do we got going on this week?'

"Not a whole lot," said The Judge. "I'm gonna go watch Chuck play tonight at Kezar."

"Playoffs?" said Cunningham.

"Got to be," said The Judge, climbing into the cart. "This late in the summer."

"Sounds good," said Cunningham, cruising down the cart path toward the sixth tee. Once he stopped, he used the same stubby pencil to write something in his datebook, which he held on his lap while he was driving. "What about tomorrow?" he said, as The Judge stepped to the back of the cart to get his new driver, a Calloway that was giving him some trouble. Last week he'd thrown the club into the bushes, content to go back to his old driver, an earlier model but more trustworthy. However, Cunningham had parked the cart, walked into the bushes in his slacks and pulled the club out. He cleaned some dirt off the head with the inside of his sport coat and without saying a word placed the club back in the bag. Now The Judge was going to give it another go, see if he could get that extra distance the pro had promised.

"Tomorrow," said The Judge, "is a real estate day for you."

"Okay," said Cunningham. "Which property?"

"The duplex in the Marina," said The Judge. "The one on Francisco."

"What do you need me to do?" said Cunningham, sliding the pencil behind his ear now, probably knowing this wasn't going to be something to be put in writing. "Someone late with the rent?"

"No," said The Judge. "This is more of a tenant's rights issue." He was using a tee to clean some dirt from the grooves in the clubface and listening to the scratching under the sound of his own voice. "Rent control is raping me on that property, Cunningham."

"That the one with the old man in it?" asked Cunningham, squinting through the Plexiglas window of the golf cart.

"The very one," said The Judge. "The motherfucker's been in there for twenty-three years. If he moved out, I could get five times the rent." He put the tee back in his pocket and leaned against the cart. "Maybe ten times," he said. "The four hundred bucks I get out of the guy doesn't even pay for maintenance on the place. It's a fuckin' tragedy that the city protects this son-of-bitch."

The Judge started to walk toward the tee-box, but he stopped and came back. "This goddamn liberal mayor and these chicken-shit supervisors are gonna force me to sell that piece of property that my grandfather built with his own hands. Fucking tragic," he said and walked over to hit the ball.

He was pissed now. Not a good way to play this game, but he didn't care. He was going to let it go with this next swing, really jack one out there, hopefully let his draw carry the sand trap on the right and bring it back to the center of the fairway. Fuck it. Let's see if he could find the sweet spot on this new club.

In order to get the extra power, he let his hands bring his backswing another inch or two above his ear. He simultaneously turned his hips and shoulders just a bit more than he would with his normal swing, a few more inches of torque. Then he let the whole thing uncoil. In that spilt second that the swing was unwrapping itself, he could feel the weight of the club head and the physics of his movement, the gravity working with the force of his body. It was perfect.

And when the club head made contact with the ball, he knew he'd found the sweet spot. The sound alone told him that he'd gotten this one good. It sounded almost distant, not unlike a church bell. And while the vibrations of the bell were still in the air, he heard the whiz of the ball shooting off into its own trajectory toward the spot he'd imagined to the right of the sand trap. It was a moment of grace for The Judge.

But like all things beautiful, it did not last. Before he finished his follow-through, he heard another sound, somewhat like a champagne cork. No. More like the cocking of a gun, but muffled. And it was coming from inside of him. If asked later what came first, the sound or the pain, he would say only that, like the sound, the pain seemed to come from nowhere and everywhere at the same time. At first he thought it was in his chest. Then it seemed to be in his shoulders. Eventually it settled in his upper back, a debilitating sting that became focused but then started to spread again, now into his neck and even the base of his skull.

When he opened his eyes, he realized that he was lying face down in the tee-box. He could feel the cool grass on his cheek. The pain seemed to be subsiding, but he couldn't move. For a moment he thought he was· paralyzed. But he wiggled his toes and fingers and was relieved.

"Judge Holiday," said Cunningham. "You throw your back out?"

That's what it must be. Something got out of line and needed to be shifted back. He'd have to go to a chiropractor or an orthopedic, so that they could get him aligned again. Without lifting his face from the grass, he asked, "Did that clear the sand trap?"

"Yeah," said Cunningham. "It actually never curved back. It went straight over the sand trap, hit the cart path, and bounced up like a super-ball. That ball's long gone, Judge."

"I'm fucking paralyzed here," said The Judge, "and you can't lie to me, tell me it was a great shot?"

"You don't like people lying to you, Judge."

"I guess you're right," he said. "Get me up and over to that cart. I need to get to a doctor."

When they eventually got him into the cart, he was moaning quietly. Every time they hit a bump, he felt like someone had struck him between the shoulders blades with a sledgehammer.

When they reached the parking lot, The Judge said, "Let me just sit here for a minute."

Cunningham said, "What do you want me to do about Evans?"

The Judge was bent forward, his face nearly touching the windshield. He was shaped like a C. "Who the hell is Evans?" he said.

"The old man in the duplex," said Cunningham. "The Francisco property."

"Yeah," he grunted. "We need to get him out." It hurt to talk. Every word was a new jab, an electric shock to his spine.

"Should we offer to buy him out, pay for moving costs?" said Cunningham, stepping out of the cart now to get the clubs and put them in the trunk of the Judge's Mercedes.

"That old shitbag owns another house in Carmel," said the Judge, feeling the anger enter into his back and spread out into his shoulders. "But he pays me like it's 1985. You couldn't get a room in one of those residential hotels in the Tenderloin for what he pays me."

The Judge could hear Cunningham loading the clubs into the car. "If he owns a house," said Cunningham, "he shouldn't be eligible for rent control benefits."

"That's what I thought," said the Judge and ventured to sit up straight, but it wasn't going to happen. It felt like there was a pulley connecting his sternum to his spine, and any movement to straighten would draw the cord tighter and seize his entire body. He let out an involuntary grunt and said, "As long as he calls my property his primary residence, this jack-hole gets all the benefits, like he's some down-on-his-luck geezer." The Judge took a deep breath, which seemed to make his torso contract. "The bastard's a retired doctor."

"Can't you just take the property off the market, say you're moving a family member in?" asked Cunningham, standing next to The Judge now.

"Ten years," said The Judge. "I can't rent the place for ten years if I do that." He'd done all the research. He knew he was fucked. If he'd known all this shit earlier, he never would have bought out his two brothers. "And I still couldn't get rid of Evans," he said. "Since he's over sixty-five, it's against the law to evict him under *any* circumstances. Even if I lost my own home, I couldn't move the guy out. This freeloader with his vacation house in Carmel, he's got me by the balls."

"Maybe you should just sell the place," said Cunningham.

"Who's gonna buy a place with a tenant paying four hundred dollars a month?"

"So whoever buys the place is stuck with this guy?"

"You got it," said The Judge. "So I either have to sell the place for next to nothing and take a big loss, or I keep the place and continue to lose."

"That's hard," said Cunningham.

The Judge had his eyes closed but felt himself tilt to one side.

Cunningham must have been leaning against the cart now when he said, "So I don't know what you want me to say to this guy tomorrow."

The Judge was hurting; it felt like he was in a vice now, like something was broken and couldn't be fixed out here in the parking lot. The real estate bind wouldn't go away on its own, either. The Judge noticed there was a pain in his jaw now and realized that he'd been grinding his teeth since he first heard that muffled pop. "You don't need to say anything to the man," he said to Cunningham.

"You don't want me to go over there?" asked Cunningham.

"I want you to go over there," said The Judge. "But you don't need to *talk* to this guy. Just take care of it." Even as the words were coming out of his mouth, he didn't stop himself. Maybe it was the pain. Maybe it was this pain-in-the-ass, Evans. But The Judge wasn't going to get any more specific. He was just going to let Cunningham figure it out on his own. Whatever it takes.

There was a long pause, and The Judge felt the cart tilt back to a level position. "You want me to take care of the problem?" asked Cunningham.

"Take care of it," said The Judge.

CHAPTER THREE

After high-fives and *Good shit, fellas* and stripping the tape off his swollen ankles, Chuck Holiday passed on a shower and hobbled in his flip-flops straight up the ramp toward the exit of Kezar Pavilion.

It'd been a good crowd, playoffs and all, and through the door's little window, Chuck could see in the foyer a few old time gym rats and junior high dreamers, still hanging around jiving about bad calls and key plays. Chuck was gripping his sneakers in his left hand, and he used them to push open the door to the lobby. When some of the kids noticed him and told him he was the man and that he had hella mad hops and that he took Oakland to school tonight, Chuck saluted with his shoes and kept moving until he heard a new voice coming from the concessions area.

"Shunny, can I shee you over here for a moment?" asked a grey pony-tailed man chewing on the stub of a black cigar. He was wearing an old-school polyester warm-up suit and a brand new pair of two hundred dollar Jordans. He leaned against the concessions counter grinning and wagging a *just for one moment* finger at Chuck.

Chuck thought maybe the guy was a reporter from some local rag who wanted a few post-game comments. Since the San Francisco Summer Pro-Am league had several high profile players this year, including a former NBA all-star and three starters from big market teams, reporters from as far south as Santa Cruz and as far north as Eureka had been offering weekly coverage of the league's developments. But after looking at the man's face, Chuck saw that there was something different about him. He didn't have that tired look Chuck had seen in the eyes of so many tape recorder-wielding members of the scribe tribe. No, this guy looked like he was selling something, but Chuck wasn't sure what.

"I'm in kind of a hurry, bro," said Chuck as he shuffled past and adjusted his duffel bag on his shoulder.

"I got shumthin' you might want to hear," said the man, who then spit his cigar on the floor and got some control over his S's. "I'm a scout."

Chuck Holiday felt his toes slide over the ends of his rubber sandals as he stopped mid-stride and changed direction. His heart jumped back up to fourth quarter speed again, but he kept it cool as he pivoted to a stop in front of the man and said, "What can I do for you?"

For a moment the man didn't say a word. He looked Chuck over like he was picking out a date at the Mustang Ranch, then shook his head and smiled again as he started leafing through the bottom pages on his clipboard. He finally pulled out some newspaper clippings. He held one of them up, then turned it around and presented it to Chuck. "This you?"

In the dim yellow light of the lobby, it was tough to see the picture on the clipping. The print from the reverse side was showing through. But Chuck knew what he was looking at.

It was a quarter-page shot of his high school self: long blond hair, nearly shoulder length; tight left-handed follow-through; floppy socks and knee pads on both legs; cheering section on their feet in the background. Headline: *Holiday for the Bulldogs.*

"Sure looks like me," said Chuck Holiday as he nodded down at the news photo and admired his form: feet hovering above the hardwood, guide hand dancing with the right angle of his follow-through, elbow in, shoulders squared.

When he'd grown five inches in a single summer back when he was fifteen, he'd decided he was going to be a star and that he was going to have an *image* as all true stars did. His idol was his father's favorite player, Larry Bird, but Chuck didn't like the man's image all that much, so he found a different white guy who had some style.

One night he was watching ESPN because they were doing a show on sports legends, and he hit the image jackpot when Pete Maravich dribbled onto the screen with his shaggy hair and funky passes and forty points a game and a shit-load of flash, that 1970's flash you can't find unless you happen to frequent the blacktop three-on-three tourneys and sagging gym leagues at Potrero Hill or Mission Rec. That kind of flash just wasn't around, but this man's nickname was "Pistol Pete," and there wasn't more flash or a cooler nickname than his.

So Chuck Holiday went about building his own image, which was complete by the time the reporter from the *Chronicle* snapped that shot of Chuck at the end of his senior year, hitting the game-winning three-pointer in the NorCal finals. He'd even been given his own nickname. He would have preferred something more like "Pistol," but some joker from one of the weekly papers had started calling him "Goose," as in *loose as a goose.* His mostly black teammates had picked up on it and used it more in the manner of *white as a goose.* Chuck had always thought that his teammates had mixed up geese with swans, black dudes from the city not getting a whole lot of exposure to the exciting world of waterfowl, but that was all right. He'd been loose and white and starring in a black man's game, and he'd loved every minute of it.

"That shot go in?" asked the guy with the ponytail.

"Look at the follow-through," said Chuck. "What do you think?"

"I'll take your word for it," he said and started in at the stack of papers on his clipboard again. While he was still fingering loose programs and stat sheets and rosters, he said, "That was NorCal. How'd you boys do in the state finals?"

"Long Beach Poly put an all-state wrestler on me. I only got off nine shots in the whole game."

The man nodded and pulled out another clipping, which he held like a dirty diaper between his thumb and forefinger. He raised it up as high as he could without standing on his toes, and then he shook it a little bit, just below Chuck's eye level. "What can you tell me about this?" he said. Chuck, again, knew immediately what he was looking at.

The article had been written just about a year after the NorCal game, while Chuck was a freshman starting for the Cal Bears. The headline: *Holiday Suspended.*

"I don't know what you want me to say."

"Why don't you tell me what happened," said the scout as he took out his pen and a little notebook. "Gimme some perspective as to why you'd gone ahead and knocked a guy's eye out."

"Listen, man," said Chuck as he started to turn toward the exit, "I don't talk about it anymore." He couldn't believe he was walking away from a scout, but the incident happened four years ago, and he didn't discuss it anymore, wanted to leave that shit alone, let sleeping dogs lie, bury the dead ... all that.

Chuck was just a couple of long strides away from the door when the man said, "Do you have any interest in getting paid to play basketball professionally?"

Chuck made no movement to cut down the distance between them. He yelled across the lobby, "CBA?"

"I don't think they want you."

"Then who?"

"You ever been to Europe?"

Chuck lumbered back and leaned on the concession counter. The gym rats had stopped their arguing; they were trying to listen in on the conversation. "Let's go back in the gym," said Chuck, and started walking without checking to see if the scout was going to follow him. When he finally sat down in the back row of the lower level so that he could lean his back against the wall, he glanced over and saw the gray ponytail right next to him.

"You want to know about that dude's eye?" he said, extending his legs and letting the insteps of his feet rest on the bench in front of him.

"I need to know," said the scout, "before I bring my recommendations back to management."

"Shit luck," Chuck said and felt his feet pushing harder against the wooden bench now. "Guy's all over me for the whole game, cheap-shots me three, four times in the fourth quarter alone and talking shit the whole time. So when the game's over and people're shaking hands and all that, I give the guy a forearm to the chest. Not to hurt him or anything, just to let him know that when we're down in L.A. for the second game against these clowns, I'm not takin' any shit."

"And that's how he lost his eye?" said the guy, being a wise-ass.

"No, that's not how he lost his eye. The reason the guy lost his eye is there's all sorts of Gatorade or some shit that someone spilled on the floor, and this guy happens to be walking in it when my forearm hits his chest." Chuck took a second to picture the scene in his mind again, to slow it down and watch the absurd details materialize.

"You understand that I'm still not getting it?" said the scout, not being a dick or anything, just curious.

"I know it," said Chuck. "It ain't that simple though. Me and the dude were next to the scorer's table, right? And I guess I put enough pop in the forearm to make him slip in the Gatorade."

The scout nodded and wrote something in the notebook.

"Funny part about it," said Chuck, "When the dude started to slip, he coulda put his hands out to brace himself for the fall. Y'know? Like a normal guy starts to fall and the normal reflex is to put your fuckin' hands out, protect yourself. But guess what this prick does?"

The scout closes the notebook, puts the pencil in the spiral binding, and shrugs.

"He tries to take one more swing at me. You gotta like this guy. His feet were coming out from under him, but he was going down swingin'."

"And he hits his eye on the scorer's table while he's trying to punch you?"

"And that's all there is."

"He's blind in that eye now?"

"Only partially. Stories get blown out of proportion."

"Any legal problems from this?"

"No."

"No trial?"

"No. My dad's a judge. He knew some people."

"What about a civil suit?"

"We settled out of court."

"Good," said the scout, getting up now and straightening his papers. "I'm Ed Fellows. I'll be in touch."

He stuck out his hand to shake and Chuck turned and took it, surprised that the interview was ending. As Chuck stood up, he realized that he'd been pushing down so hard with his feet on the bench that he could still feel the pressure on the soles of his feet even after he lifted them. They felt as if he'd been standing on a ladder all day; the ghost rungs were still haunting him hours later.

"Is that it?" said Chuck, thinking about his feet, wondering if he'd been climbing the ladder up or down.

"For now," said Mr. Fellows.

"What's the name of the team?"

"The Rocks," said Mr. Fellows as he put a new cigar in his mouth and began to twirl it around.

"Are you serious?"

"The Edinburgh Rocks. BBL."

"Should I know what that means?" asked Chuck trying to figure out the B. *Bulgaria ... Belgrade ... Burma?*

"British Basketball League. Thirty-six game schedule, ten players per team, decent salary, off-season jobs, English speaking peoples ... a good gig."

"Why me?" asked Chuck, who knew there were better players in the ProAm league.

"We need to fill seats, and you're the kind of guy we can put on the cover of the media guide. Funny hairdo, mysterious past, goofy knee-pads, that flashy dribbling and passing you do that *I* don't really care for, all that shit sells tickets. And you're a pretty goddamn good player, too."

Chuck wanted to tell the man that Maravich would appreciate the flash. Instead he said, "So what's next?"

"You come out to my car with me, and I'll give you a draft of our basic contract," said Mr. Fellows. "You say your dad's a judge?"

"Used to be," said Chuck. "He does corporate litigation now."

"Well," said Mr. Fellows, "you can have him take a look at the contract if you want before you sign it. I assume you don't have an agent."

Chuck shook his head. He had to bite down to prevent himself from grinning. Agent? This was starting to sound real. Hazel was going to have to take this seriously.

"Have your old man take a gander at it, then sign it or let me know if there's any problems, and we'll talk."

Chuck followed the man through the Kezar doors and out to his car. And as he watched Fellows open his trunk, Chuck started to wiggle his toes, still interested in the ghost rungs beneath his feet, but starting to feel like he was climbing up, definitely climbing up.

CHAPTER FOUR

Hazel lived in an unincorporated section of the town of Colma. Her neighborhood was called Gateway Village, as in *Gateway to the Peninsula*, and it was one of the first towns south of San Francisco, so she occasionally got some big city customers.

She peered through the crack in the curtains as the car pulled in front of her house. This was part of the job. She had to climb inside her clients' brains before she actually met them. She had learned that she could gather important information in the few moments it took the client to park the car in front of her little ranch house and stroll up the walkway to the front door.

This particular client drove a new VW beetle, green, and her vanity plates read VIN-"heart"-JIL. After she got out of her car, Hazel watched as *Jill?* took a slow walk around the vehicle. She stopped once and, with her thumb, rubbed something off the front fender. Then she pulled down the sleeves of her three-quarter length leather jacket and made her way up the concrete path. She navigated a small puddle and stopped once to read the sign propped on the lawn. She seemed to study it, as if she were translating a foreign language, but the sign was pretty straightforward. Big letters: Psychic Readings. Small letters: Tea Leaf, Tarot, Palmistry.

Hazel kept an eye on her as the prospective client, wearing an expensive pair of Italian shoes, stepped lightly. Before she put a foot on the front porch, she took a quick look over her shoulder. To check on her car? To make sure she wasn't being watched?

When *Jill?* finally knocked on the door, Hazel checked herself in the hall mirror. With makeup, she achieved the exotic look that she'd used at work for the past six months. Clients seemed to respond to the extra shadows and colors that accentuated her Asian eyes. She was half Chinese and half Irish, but who wanted an Irish-American fortune teller? People wanted to believe that she was practicing an ancient and mysterious art that had been passed down through genetics, tradition, and supernatural forces, so she never let it slip that her dad was a third generation San Franciscan who worked for the San Francisco Department of Public Works and that her mom was a manager at a Kinkos in the Financial District. Too home spun for those who wanted to believe in the paranormal. She'd sometimes even talk in broken English and stare off at nothing to augment the weirdness.

Her image in the mirror reflected her Asian roots, but from certain angles her Gaelic ancestry betrayed her. Her little ski jump nose, her nearly auburn hair, and the faint trace of freckles above her high cheekbones should have been obvious signs to her curious clientele. However, these people were so eager to believe in the power of the mind and the metaphysical world that most assumed she was born in China, and with *the gift*.

When Hazel opened the door, she continued to evaluate the woman, who looked older at close range—a well-maintained early forty-something year old, who had had at least some work done on her nose and at the corners of her mouth. Good work, nearly undetectable.

"I want to try this," she said. "But it's my first time."

Hazel nodded as she processed the all but faded New Hampshire/Maine inflection. "I help all types of people looking for answers," she said as they lingered in the doorway.

"Good, good," said the woman, who stuck out both of her hands for a feminine two-hand shake. "I'm Jillian."

"Welcome," said Hazel as she felt the lotioned palms and the smooth nails and the thin wedding band. Then she gently pulled Jillian into the house and smelled the CK perfume. She also noted that the haircut was fresh; probably a twice-a-monther. "I do the readings in the back," she said. "Would you like to drink something or to freshen up in the powder room before we start?"

This was a well-kept woman, and Hazel had a feeling that Jillian might be susceptible to the suggestion that she *needed* freshening. Hazel understood that her own face made women very conscious of their appearance. She wasn't vain. She was simply a student of human behavior, and she'd watched women in her presence fumble with compacts and lip gloss enough times to understand that her beauty made certain women uncomfortable. Not resentful as some women get around tall blonds, but just uncomfortable enough to start thinking about the small blemish next to the nose or the eyebrows that had gone unplucked for over a week.

"I'd love to use the restroom, if you don't mind," said Jillian.

"It's right this way. Would you like me to take your coat and bag?"

"Oh, just the coat, please. I need my stuff," she said and pulled off her leather jacket. Underneath, Jillian wore a red silk blouse.

Hazel nodded at a door in the middle of the hallway, and Jillian smiled and handed her the jacket. One of the buttons on the blouse was not properly fastened, and, when Jillian turned toward the bathroom, Hazel caught a glimpse of a lacy red bra under the silk.

After Hazel watched the bathroom door close, she opened the door to the hallway closet and used it as cover as she rifled through the pockets of the jacket. The inside pocket had a ballpoint pen with a hotel logo and a hairdresser's business card emblazoned with half a kiss of lipstick.

When Hazel got to the outside pockets, she found a wad of Kleenex in one and a condom in the other. She took just a moment to read the label. Not a Trojan. Something else. Glow-worm. Glow in the dark condom. Jesus. When she tried to put it back, it slipped and fell to the floor.

The bathroom door clicked open, and Hazel scooped up the condom and crammed it back in the jacket pocket. She was putting the jacket on a hanger, when Jillian peeked around the door.

Hazel could feel herself beginning to perspire, but she spoke evenly. "Right this way," she said and moved past Jillian on her way to the sitting room at the end of the hall. Above the door sat an enlarged upside down Tarot card, about the same size as the Pete Maravich poster that Chuck had taped to the inside of the closet door.

The picture above the sitting room door featured the Two of Swords Reversed: A blindfolded man clutching a sword in each hand and holding them crossed over his chest; a crescent moon floating in the background sky above a calm sea.

Upside down, the magnified card had a surreal effect: hovering water, grounded moon, and the strange blindfolded figure balancing on crossed swords like some kind of medieval acrobat.

Hazel had picked this particular card to greet her customers because it best represented the kinds of people who sought spiritual guidance. The Two of Swords Reversed represents *illusory thinking*, an unwillingness to use intuition or to trust inner resources. The Two of Swords Reversed in a Tarot spread says *I don't know my problems or trouble, and I don't want to face them, either.*

Hazel held the door open as Jillian entered the small room. From where she stood, Hazel could see straight down the hallway through the big window in the front door. When she heard a distant rumble, she paused and told Jillian to sit in the red chair. Then she looked down the hallway, through the window, and saw the single headlight of a motorcycle and a flash of Chuck's windblown blond hair. She smiled, slid into the sitting room, and closed the door behind her.

CHAPTER FIVE

Jogging up the path to the house, Chuck was itching to tell Hazel about Fellows. She'd been bugging him about making some changes. She was four years older than he was. A few weeks back, she'd told him she was hoping to achieve something more in life than being the girlfriend of a part-time hot dog vending bookie who spent the majority of his time playing basketball and watching ESPN.

Chuck had argued that he wasn't just a bookie. "I'm also in sales," he'd said and did his best to sound like he meant it.

"I hope you're not serious," Hazel had replied. "You work at a hot dog stand."

"Yeah," said Chuck, "but I'm learning the business ... inventory and supply and demand and—"

"Stop," Hazel had said. "You're so completely full of shit, I can't stand to hear this anymore. You only do that job because it's convenient for you to meet with all those bozos who want to make bets."

She'd been right, of course. He wasn't learning much about business from Stan Winkler, who paid him to stand behind a cart in front of Macy's and ask "You want sauerkraut with that Polish?"

But he had established *his* business while steaming hot dogs in Union Square. He started out with parlay cards during football season. *Pick four out of four games and make a nice profit.* But hardly anyone ever picked four out of four with the spread. And most people actually tried for six out of six or eight out of eight, trying to make the big money. But it simply didn't happen. Somebody would fumble or miss an extra point attempt or go for it on fourth and two ... whatever. And then Chuck would have another twenty bucks in his wallet, which continued to grow when he expanded his business into a full-service sports book for his friends and their friends and so on. He was making good coin, but he also knew Hazel would probably want out soon if he didn't find a real job.

Well, here it was. A guy named Ed Fellows was thinking about hiring him to play basketball in England. He wanted to throw it out there and see if Hazel'd go for it.

But when he got inside the house, the door to the room where she performed her psychic readings was shut, and when he put his ear to the door, he could hear the psychic murmurings taking place.

From some of the conversation, he could tell that the woman had chosen Tarot Cards, which Chuck found the most interesting. Cool pictures with stories behind them. When Hazel worked with them, he really believed she might have *the gift,* as they called it at trade shows.

Once, when she'd given Chuck a reading, she knew all sorts of shit about his family while she was laying out those cards, private shit that no one was supposed to know. And she even said she knew some stuff about his dad that she wouldn't tell Chuck, that he wouldn't want to know.

And she was obviously hitting the bull's eye with her customer today. Chuck got down low so that he could hear the woman through the crack saying, "Oh, you're good. That's really amazing."

"It's just what the cards are telling me," said Hazel.

"Well," said the woman. "What do they say about my love life?"

"You have to ask a more specific question." Chuck could hear her flipping through the extra cards. "In the Celtic Spread, you have to ask a particular *question* about love. Then I can give you a reading."

"Oh, okay. I guess I just want to know if I should stay in my present relationship. Is it going to make me happy?"

Chuck actually loved eavesdropping on the readings. It could be like sitting in the confessional with the priest as someone unloaded all his screw-ups, which was entertaining. Comforting that other people fucked up too.

After an extra-long silent period, he heard Hazel say, "Six of Cups Reversed." Then he thought he heard her take a deep breath before saying, "What relationship are you asking about, Jillian?"

The woman made a small sound. Not quite a *huh?* because it was more of a squeak, but it conveyed the same message as *huh?* Hazel repeated the question, using different words. "To which man is this question referring?"

"Well, I guess you got me there," said Jillian, and Chuck wondered, as he always did, how Hazel knew. "The question could actually be about either of them."

"Yes," said Hazel. "But I need to know which man so that I can get a clear reading."

"Maybe I'm just trying to have my cake and eat it, too."

"Do you want me to address the question in regards to Vincent or the other man?" said Hazel after a long moment of silence.

"I guess I should—what? Did you say Vincent? That's my husband's name. How did you know Vinnie? Wait a minute. I never told you—"

"It's a gift," said Hazel, as she always did when she shocked a customer.

Then she said some things about the Six of Cups Reversed: *indecision… irresponsibility … lack of growth …* and some more general stuff that could apply to anyone. But she *had* the lady now because of this Vincent or Vinnie thing, so everything else she said sounded like gold.

She moved on to the Two of Wands and The Moon Reversed and the Seven of Pentacles, the whole time Jillian saying things like *Oh, my* and *Is that so?* and *That's what I thought* and finally *Thank you so very much for this.*

Chuck stepped away from the door and into the front room, where he flipped on *Sportscenter*. They were doing a feature on off-season trades, but he wasn't listening. He was waiting for Jillian to leave so he could tell Hazel about the BBL.

Hazel got Jillian's jacket out of the closet, and the woman immediately took some tissues out of her pocket and started dabbing at her eyes. "I'm okay," she said as she turned the door knob and went out. Hazel nodded and closed the door. Then she looked into the front room at Chuck and said, "I told you not to listen to my readings." She walked away, and he got up and chased her.

He grabbed her by the hips from behind; she didn't struggle. He moved one of his big hands over her flat belly and pulled her into the concave area he created by bending his legs and hunching his back. He pulled out the bottom of her tank top with one hand and slid his other hand under the shirt. His long fingers reached nearly from her belly to her side, and he pressed himself closer until he could smell her hair. Then he bent his knees even more so that he could put his mouth on her neck.

She said, "All right. Not now, big boy," and pushed him away with her shoulders and then both hands before she walked toward the back of the house.

"I had some interesting shit happen to me today," he said as he followed her into the sitting room.

She was picking up cards and putting them into old wooden boxes. "Did you sell twenty jumbo dogs or score twenty points?" she said, grinning, as she put the boxes in a chest and then walked past him toward the kitchen.

He followed her. "Better than that." He lifted a leg over a chair and sat backwards, with his chin resting on the seatback. "I think I have a chance at a new job."

Chuck saw her flinch slightly, but she continued filling up a pot with water. She didn't say anything until she'd taken a bag of supermarket brand pasta and a can of green beans out of the cupboard. Then she said, "Did Stan offer to give you a promotion? Make you vice-president of condiments?" She had turned to face him but shifted her eyes downward, maybe feeling she was being a little harsh.

Chuck said, "I actually talked to a scout tonight about playing pro ball."

"Y'mean like for the Warriors?" she asked without any irony.

"No," said Chuck. "It's not the NBA, but it still pays."

"How much?" said Hazel, as she poured the can of green beans into a smaller pot and then put some salt in the not yet boiling water.

"Decent money," said Chuck. "But the thing about this team is it's in England."

Hazel began breaking fistfuls of angel hair and dropping them into the boiling water. After the water foamed up around the pasta, it settled. She waited until it began to boil again before she turned to Chuck. "Well, where does that leave me?"

"What do you mean?" he said. "I want you to come with me. You can set up shop anywhere, right?"

Hazel was stirring the pasta now and staring into the rising steam. "You ever think that maybe I don't want to go to England?"

Chuck looked at her eyes, still colored and elongated by the makeup. She was looking at him now but not giving anything away. Maybe even trying to read his mind, which he thought was going to be tough, because *he* didn't even know what he was thinking. "Take a look at this contract," he said. "See what you think. See if you can get any kind of vibe from it."

Her eyes remained locked on his as she took hold of the contract and walked by instinct to the little round table. She was still watching him as she pulled out a chair and sat down. Finally, her eyes moved to the stapled papers in front of her.

She ran her finger over sentences and numbers. Then she licked the same finger to separate the pages as she scanned each paragraph. Sometimes she backtracked and ran her finger along phrases from previous pages. Then she folded one page over, so that she could examine two pages at the same time. When she finished with the last page, she turned the contract over and folded her small hands on top of it. Then she said, "I know pounds are a little more than dollars, but this doesn't seem to be much of an offer."

"Yeah," said Chuck. "But I think cost of living is a lot less over there, and Mr. Fellows, this scout, said there's a chance I could be getting some endorsement money to go with the contract."

Hazel was up now, pouring water and pasta into a strainer. Once again, her head was in the steam; from the side, with that crazy eye make-up, she looked like some kind of Asian goddess performing a ritual. Chuck wondered if she was trying to read his mind every time there was a lull in their dialogue.

"So the money is actually decent," said Chuck, "if you factor in that it's only four months of games, a couple games a week, and two months of workouts. That's only half a year, and then they say they can set you up with off-season work, or we could come home to see your folks or whatever." Chuck liked the sound of his own voice dribbling through Hazel's defense.

"Couldn't you make that kind of money selling cars or getting a job with the city?" she said. "My dad said he can help you with the civil service exam and —"

"Wait a minute, Hazel," said Chuck as he watched her pouring half a jar of Ragu over the pasta. "We're still young enough to do something cool here, and you want me to take the civil service test? I still wanna play hoops, and these guys're gonna to let me keep doing it and give me some money too."

"Well, I'm older than you, and it'd be nice to know that we have some kind of a stable future ahead of us. And I don't think we can afford to do this anyway. The contract doesn't provide any housing or moving costs. I don't know if we have the money for two of us to get there and get set up."

Chuck absorbed her words as he put plates, forks, and napkins on the table. "If we can get the money together," he said, holding one of the forks up in front of him," I want to try it for one year. See what kind of deal it is, whether we can make it in England. It'll be fun."

"I don't think we have the money."

"If we do," said Chuck, "will you go with me?"

***

In the sitting room behind the drapes, Hazel watched Chuck pull the ventilation grate off the wall and reach inside the duct. He pulled out a canvas bag and put it on the round table in front of her. "Okay," he said.

Hazel opened the bag and started to count the money. Every time she pulled a small bill, she felt her jaw clench, and she slammed the bill down. There was no way they had enough money. By the time she'd arranged the pile into eighteen neat stacks, she said, "Are you kidding me?"

Chuck just shrugged and said, "What?"

"Eighteen hundred dollars? That's all we have?"

Chuck started counting, as if he were going to find a few extra hundred somewhere. "I guess that's it," he said.

"How could that be it?" said Hazel as she began putting rubber bands around the stacks and placing them into the bag.

"The motorcycle," he said and did that half-grin that he'd used on his dad before their falling out.

"Jesus," she said. "All that money on a motorcycle?"

"It's a Harley. And I paid cash." Then he put his hands in his pockets, as if to secure the keys.

And when Hazel shot him her best sneer, he retaliated with, "What about your sister?"

They'd loaned Leslie-Anne five thousand dollars when flooding ruined her Russian River cabin, and Hazel had forgiven the loan without consulting with Chuck, so she didn't have much to say except, "Well, we don't have enough for either of us to go to England unless you start calling the deadbeats. You better get your book."

After they'd tallied up all the recorded bets, they were shocked that eleven people owed Chuck over five hundred dollars, and one had actually accumulated a debt of seven thousand dollars from bets that dated back nearly a year.

"What's the story with *this* guy?" said Hazel as she shook her head and punched the numbers into the calculator again.

"I guess I need to go talk to Brian Curran," said Chuck.

"And all those other people, too," said Hazel. "If you really want to do this." She knew it was going to be quite a challenge. Chuck never rushed anyone for payment and never used muscle to collect. He was the friendly neighborhood bookie, and everyone who played was either a friend or sponsored by a friend, so he'd never had any trouble collecting. However, there was close to fifteen grand here, twelve different guys, and one particular sports fan who was way over his limit, so Chuck was going to have to make the rounds and hope some of them would pay up.

CHAPTER SIX

Brian Curran had moved to the Bay Area a few years back. He'd exhausted his stay in Dorchester, Massachusetts because of a series of crimes including wheelchair theft, statutory rape, dognapping, and the sale of bogus narcotics. His dad was a retired Boston Police captain and kept Brian out of jail, but insisted that his son find a new residence before he embarrassed the family any further.

Since settling in Gateway Village, just outside of San Francisco, Brian had held several jobs ranging from construction laborer for an Irish contractor to deliveryman for a Chinese restaurant. He never kept a job for more than a couple of months. He mainly used them as ways to make contacts that he might be able to use for some kind of easy money pinch later on.

The idea of cheating someone out of something—anything— intrigued Brian; he was always trying to find an angle. He didn't dislike work. He just liked the challenge of a good hustle. It kept life interesting. Californians had it so fuckin' easy that they didn't even seem to care if you burned them out of some of their spare change. It was a nice place to run a con, and he'd been dipping his hands into an assortment of easy scores since he'd arrived.

Just last week, dressed as a tourist, he made the rounds to some local three-card Monte corner games. If the dude was young or skinny or over the hill, Brian would lose two games, and then pummel the little cheat and take all the cash. Who ever heard of a three-card Monte dealer going to the cops because he'd been robbed? There was very little risk.

It wasn't enough of a head game to really qualify as a hustle, but he needed the money. And he earned just enough to go down to Bay Meadows and blow it all on the daily double.

He was having a string of bad luck, but his uncle Troy, who ran a major illegal sports book out of his Marin County home, had always told him, "There's only one thing you can count on in regards to luck: it's never going to stay the same for very long." Brian was waiting for his to change when the phone rang. It was that goofy-looking bookie that Uncle Troy had set him up with. Brian's uncle had a strict policy about accepting bets from family members, but he'd been more than happy to find a local small time bookie to take on his nephew's business. And this ex-jock, Chuck Holiday, lived a couple blocks away from Brian, so it was a perfect match.

Uncle Troy and Holiday did some business together. Apparently, when someone wanted to bet a substantial sum with Holiday, more than five thousand on a single game, Holiday would send the wager over to Uncle Troy, who had the cash to back it. That brought extra business to Brian's uncle. The more games, the better the chances of collecting steady juice. Holiday would get a small percentage of the winnings as a kind of finder's fee.

But although Brian was well aware of the ridiculous odds of ever making any money by wagering on sporting events—he knew his uncle was a rich man—he couldn't help himself. He liked to speculate about games, talk about bets, check his own spread guesses against the professional handicappers, over/unders, parlays, the fuckin' coin toss—everything. It was all interesting to him. And he liked to tell stories about his bets to whoever would listen. Bets would keep him in a bar all day on a Sunday. They'd keep him up late gambling on University of Hawaii home games, the last opportunities of the night because of time zones. He knew he was never going to break the bank, but, boy, did he like trying.

And here was this big goof calling him to ask for payment, like he didn't know Brian was the nephew of Troy Curran. This lanky fucker should probably show a little more respect than to call him on the phone like this and interrupt his studying.

Brian had three books open simultaneously on his lap. One was on dog training, another was more like a brochure about pit bulls, and the last was an old textbook based on the studies of a dude named Pavlov, who'd done some work with dogs. When the phone rang, he lost his place in the Pavlov book and he was red-assed when this punk told him that he'd be coming around to collect on a few bets.

"So why all of a sudden do I lose my credit?" said Brian, as he held his phone out in front of his face and walked down the stairs into his basement.

"Well, it's not really *all of a sudden*," said Holiday in this tone like he was talking to a fuckin' five year old. "You started losing bets almost a year ago. You've won some too, but you're up to, we'll call it, seven thousand dollars in debt right now, and I need to collect. It's part of the business."

Part of the business, like this needle-dick knew anything about business. Brian didn't answer right away. He looked at the two caged pit bulls that were circling his basement.

A few months earlier, Brian had gotten involved with a couple of dudes who were running a restaurant near West Portal Station. Their names were Don and Sid, but Brian called them Dim and Sum, just to fuck with them. These two Chinese guys, trying to be American, had some money and an interest in dogs, particularly dogs that could fight and win them some money.

Brian bullshitted his way through a business proposal that resulted in his taking two thousand dollars to train the dogs plus more cash for all the training equipment and a cut of the winnings. The two clowns acted like Chinese mafia. They dressed in black suits. One was so short he might even be a midget, and the other talked in grunts, trying to be some kind of enforcer. They both wanted street cred, and thought pit bulls were going to put them on the underworld map.

Well, Brian had known a couple of whacked dudes back in Boston who'd trained fight dogs, let them chew on tires and run on cat mills and kill rabbits, all that shit, so he had an idea of what he was doing, but he'd already spent the two thousand by the time Chuck Holiday had him on the phone, and these dogs weren't quite ready. Mean, but not ready for the ring yet, not ready to make any money yet.

"Are you getting this, Brian?" said Holiday, and Brian wondered how long he'd let his mind drift.

"What do mean when you say 'We'll call it seven thousand'," asked Brian in a voice that he thought would piss the guy off.

"Well," said Holiday, "it's not exactly seven, but that might make it easier."

"I don't buy that shit," said Brian. "What's the number?"

"It's actually seven thousand four hundred, but let's just round it to seven and call it even. You've been a good customer," said Holiday, who didn't sound like he knew how to be a bookie. He sounded like a goddamn librarian squabbling over late return fees, not that Brian had spent a whole lot of time in libraries, but this pit bull venture forced him through the door a few weeks back and the vibe of the place was still resonating.

Brian was now sitting on his basement stairs, watching the dogs, tongues lolling, the pads of their feet making soft noises on the slick concrete. Their neck muscles bulged through their white coats. One of them actually looked like he was smiling all the time, like he'd just heard a bad joke but was polite enough to pretend to laugh.

That dog looked a lot like a grinning Uncle Troy, a man who could probably help with Brian's current predicament, but Brian didn't want to ask his uncle for the money. That was the whole point of using a different bookie, but he didn't know where to go with this. He absolutely did not have the money, and he didn't have any way of raising it fast. "That number's not even close to being right," said Brian, who couldn't think of anything else to say.

"Well," said the jerk, and he added a kind of laugh, "I keep pretty good records, but if you want to go over the figures with me, we can sit down and do that."

"Yeah," said Brian. "Let's do that, 'cause I'm pretty sure I doubled down not so long ago and won back most of that money."

"My records show," said the small-time piece of shit, now with a bit of muscle in his voice, "that you doubled down a month ago, but that you lost that bet, and then you made a couple of smaller bets since then."

"Well, fuck that," said Brian. "That ain't right. I want to see whatever it is you got that has all the bets in it." Put the guy on the spot a little bit, see what happens.

There was silence on the line for moment, then, "Do you want to meet somewhere, so I can show you what I have on you?"

Brian didn't like the way he'd said that he *had* something on Brian, but decided he was going to play it cool, not let this fruitcake with the long hair hear the anger in his voice. Instead, he tried to sound like he had something up his sleeve. Scare the bookie a little, make big Chuckie think he's going to get his dick stepped on if he tries anything. "You come over here and we'll straighten it all out," said Brian, as he stuck a pole through the chain-link and poked one of the dogs, who let out a short yelp, then began to growl. Brian didn't have much of an idea of how he was going to straighten anything out, but he knew he wasn't going to pay anything. Even if he had the money, what the fuck was this small-timer going to pull. Nothing. That's what.

CHAPTER SEVEN

Cunningham didn't want to do this. When he'd quit the force a few years back to work for Judge Holiday, it was to get away from all the sickos and the drugs and the violence. The Judge had said he'd be doing surveillance—a great deal of which was of The Judge's kid—security detail, internet searches. That's it. This thing with Evans was *not* in the job description.

Cunningham was sitting in the Marina Lounge on Chestnut, waiting to work up the nerve to walk down to Francisco Street to the kill the old man in Judge Holiday's duplex so that The Judge could rent out the flat for five times the amount Evans was paying. He had the fleeting thought that it would be more appropriate to kill the bureaucrats who came up with the bizarre legislation that handcuffed the landlords and allowed for squatters and deadbeats and scammers, like the doctor who owned a nice piece of property in Carmel and was definitely working the system at The Judge's expense. But, alas, he had neither the time nor the resources for such an endeavor. The doctor had to go.

He'd killed before.

A sting operation ten years back when he was a sergeant working in narcotics. He'd done most of the work to set the whole thing up, recorded these dumbshits making drug deals. He'd figured out who their supplier was. He'd helped his undercover men establish credibility. Then he put together the team that raided the operation in the lower Sunset District on a Thursday morning in December.

It happened fast. Cunningham stood outside the house just around the corner from Java Beach and the Irish Cultural Center and watched the members of his team move up the stairs; then he walked over to the garage. Before he heard the smashing of the front door, the garage door started to rise.

Cunningham crouched down and heard the car's engine spark. The car had been backed in, so he got a good look at the driver. White guy, long greasy hair, cigarette. He was looking directly at Cunningham, who pointed his gun at the man and shook his head. "Don't do it," Cunningham said, even though he knew he wouldn't be heard over the sound of the electric garage door and the car engine.

Before the door was fully up, the driver floored it, and the wheels screeched on the smooth surface of the garage floor. Cunningham got off two rounds before he dived away from the oncoming car. For a split second, he thought he was going to make it to the strip of dead grass next to the driveway, but before he cleared the area, the front bumper hit his left foot. The car's horn was blaring, but Cunningham still thought he heard the crunching of the bones in his ankle. It hurt, but after he hit the grass, he lifted his head and watched the car go straight across 44th Avenue and hit a streetlight in front of a yellow single family home.

Cunningham still had his gun in his hand, but he couldn't walk, so he watched the team come storming down the front stairs and then spread out as they approached the car. Before they reached the midpoint of the street, a stubby Hispanic man wearing a Giants cap opened the passenger side door and came out with his hands in the air. *"Yo abandonar! Yo abandonar!* I quit! I quit!"

The driver had been shot in the head.

Cunningham didn't feel good about killing this guy, but not once did he feel guilty about it. If the scumbag hadn't died, he would've been charged with attempted murder on top of all the drug charges. No, Cunningham was okay with what he'd done that day, but he didn't really want to do it anymore. He'd already lost his wife in a divorce that involved her saying that Cunningham was better friends with his informants than he was with her. His wife had left him, and then, during the drug bust on 44th Avenue, he ended the life of a human being.

Not long after, The Judge offered him the job. When he accepted, he never imagined walking into an old man's house to kill that man. Never. Now he found himself finishing his Jameson at the Marina Lounge, leaving a nice tip, and shuffling out onto Chestnut Street.

He couldn't pick his feet up all the way because he was wearing the *bad guy shoes.* He'd found a pair of beautiful wingtips under the bed in a pot house in the Richmond District once, and walked out of the house holding them as if they were evidence. When he got them home and tried them on, they were at least two sizes too big. So now he laced them up tight and wore them when he was doing odd jobs for The Judge. If something went wrong and the cops had to investigate a crime scene, they would find the footprints of a man who wore a size twelve shoe, not the nine and a half, tops, that Cunningham wore.

He knew that wouldn't exonerate him completely, but he always made sure to leave a couple of footprints somewhere on the premises in the belief that they could cast a reasonable doubt. *If the shoes don't fit, you must acquit.*

When he was outside the duplex on Francisco, he took a deep breath and trudged up the stairs, the shoes making sounds like hooves on the bricks. He had no weapon. This guy was seventy years old. He'd find a weapon in the house. He really wanted this to look like an accident, but he wanted to get an idea of the environment before he decided what *kind* of accident.

He knocked at the door and waited. He heard movement, so he

waited some more. Then he knocked again. This time a woman's voice, eastern European accent, said, "Who is there?"

Cunningham was relieved. It must be the maid. He wasn't going to have to do this today. It would be easy to tell The Judge that someone was there, that he wasn't going to kill *two* people over a couple thousand dollars a month. "My name's Dan," he said. "I work for the landlord."

He heard her muffled voice say something and then he watched the door open slowly. She was young, maybe twenty-two, and she was wearing goofy looking black glasses, novelty glasses. Cunningham didn't say anything for a moment while he looked her up and down. She was gorgeous. Hair in a tight bun. Smokin' body. Wearing a white blouse that was about three sizes too small but buttoned all the way to the top. She wore a navy skirt, sensible looking except for the fact that it only went to mid-thigh. She finished off the look with a pair of clunky black heels.

When he stood silent, she said, "I am the librarian."

"Really?" he said. *What the hell?* "Is the doctor around?"

She hadn't opened the door all the way, and she leaned back into the room while she held the door closed to the width of her body. "He's Dan," he heard her say.

After a moment she looked back at Cunningham and said, "What do you want?"

Cunningham said, "I need to talk to the doctor. I'm here on behalf of the landlord, the owner of this property." He wanted to get a look at the floor plan, the furniture, whether or not there was a back entrance, interior stairs.

The woman leaned back into the room. "He's owner of house," she said.

Cunningham didn't correct her, and after a couple of seconds she opened the door. When he walked in, he saw the doctor sitting on the couch next to another woman, this one in a tiny schoolgirl uniform and a high ponytail.

When he looked at the doctor, the old man's face went through a quick change. It transformed from scared to confused to angry. "Who the hell are you?" he asked without raising his voice.

"Yeah," said Cunningham. "I'm not The Judge. I tried to tell your ... librarian, but she—"

"Well, who are you?" he asked, sitting up on the antique couch now and putting his elbows on his knees.

"I'm Dan," he said. "I work for The Judge."

"Oh," said the old man, who sat back again. "Are you gonna tell?"

Cunningham wasn't sure how to respond until he looked away from the man. He glanced at the schoolgirl, who wasn't as pretty as the librarian, but she was smiling at Cunningham and batting her eye lashes like a cartoon temptress. Then he looked at the coffee table and the console table behind the couch. Both were covered in little, orange plastic bottles.

"We're having a pharm party," said the school girl. Cunningham didn't quite get it. He heard it as "farm party" and had a flash to something very wicked before he looked at the pills on the table and figured it out.

"I guess you are," he said and looked back at the librarian, who was sitting on the arm of a chair now, her eyes glossy and distant, her long legs dangling, and her skirt so high up that Cunningham caught a quick flash of her white panties contrasted against the navy material of the skirt.

When Cunningham looked back at him, the old man said, "I guess I'm busted." He had sad smile on his face, and his hand was on the school girl's thigh. "The Judge probably wouldn't go for this type of activity in one of his properties."

"No, he wouldn't," said Cunningham. Then he walked over and sat next to the librarian. He let himself sink into the soft leather before he said, "But I think we can work something out, so we don't have to involve the police."

CHAPTER EIGHT

Chuck gathered up his betting log and put everything into a yellow backpack, which he slid over his shoulders before he made his way to the front door.

Over the past two years, he'd had to sit down with a few guys who'd made drunken bets they couldn't remember. After he showed these particular boozers his books, they paid. No problem. They were good guys who apologized for being dicks. But this Brian Curran was a different breed. He'd made a whole string of bonehead bets, and now he was playing dumb, making believe there was some kind of misunderstanding.

"I don't know what to expect," Chuck said to Hazel, who was lounging on the front stoop, her bare legs absorbing the sun, the straps of her tank top hanging loose over the sides of her brown shoulders.

"Do you think he's got the money?" asked Hazel, as she sat up and adjusted her straps.

"He doesn't have the money."

"How do you know?"

"I heard it," said Chuck. "It was in his voice, trying to sound like he thought my figures were wrong and getting pissed off that I was bein' a pest. He doesn't have it." Chuck was facing Hazel. Wearing a pair of gym shorts, he knew he didn't look like much of a bookie. He didn't look like the kind of guy who would strong-arm anyone, take a man's finger, break his legs, any of that shit. In short, he didn't look like Troy Curran. However, Chuck's book worked the same as Troy's. When people won, Chuck paid them, and when people lost, Chuck expected to be paid. Not right away always, but after a year and seven thousand dollars, yeah, you had to settle up.

"Then what's the plan?" asked Hazel as she put her hand up in a soft salute to shade the sun's glare coming from behind Chuck.

"It's tricky," he said. "This guy thinks he's some kind of a badass 'cause he's Troy's nephew."

"Why is he betting with *you* if he knows Troy?"

"I guess that's what makes it tricky. It's one of Troy's policies about taking bets from blood relatives. Creates problems when it's time to collect."

"No shit," said Hazel. "So he sticks you with his deadbeat nephew. Thanks a lot, Troy." She shook her head without lowering her salute. Her full lips became a thin line across her face. "These assholes who don't want to pay, they're always the first ones to show up here on a Sunday morning looking to collect after they win."

"I know it," said Chuck. "I took him on as a favor to Troy, and now I'm gettin' screwed."

"Are you sure you should be going over there by yourself?" said Hazel, who stood up on the top step so that she was eye to eye with him.

"Why?" said Chuck. "If he won't pay me, I'm just walking out of there. I'm not gonna try to beat on the guy or anything, so I shouldn't have to worry about him trying to do anything to me, right?"

***

Brian Curran's house was still in Gateway Village, but it was in the older part of town, where the houses were two-story jobs with full basements, built before a developer came in and put up the thousand ranch-style houses that made up the bulk of Gateway.

Curran's house was a rental with a little square lawn in front. It was mostly crab grass, but some early summer showers had turned it into green crab grass with little golden circles, where something seemed to have killed even the weeds, like someone had dipped a basketball in Round-Up and dribbled it across the lawn.

About halfway up the chipped brick stairs, a smell hit him so suddenly that he immediately checked the bottoms of his shoes. Nothing. The house just stunk. It actually worse than dog shit. This was a sweet rancid stink that made Chuck's eyes water. Christ, it made the air thick and hot, like a public high school locker room with broken toilets, bad shit … or dogs. Dogs not eating right, sick dogs.

Chuck hated dogs. They were always running under his long legs, and he was always accidentally stepping on them with his big feet. It was like they were playing this game with him, and then after they lost and felt the bottom of Chuck's shoe, they were pissed off, growling and barking and nipping at his ankles. He hated the fucking things, and they hated him.

So when he stepped up through the odor on that outside staircase, he nearly turned back. He already disliked Brian Curran, and the dog factor was just adding to it. A canine, a goddamn slobbering, hairy beast, was waiting for him on the other side of the door. In fact, there might even be more than one, considering the variety of leashes that hung from a nail to the right. There were strange leashes and spiked, angry collars that looked like they were meant to inflict pain. He could only imagine the kinds of dogs that would wear such a mess of leather and steel.

But he needed to get some money from the owner, and he was, in fact, kind of curious about how Curran was going to play the whole scene, so he continued up the stairs, checking now and then behind him.

And under; he didn't want to step in anything, and he didn't want the son of a bitch sneaking between his legs.

When the door opened, a heavy fume of Lysol mixed with shit and sweat and dog swept over Chuck, but he didn't see any dogs, just the grinning, confused face of Brian Curran with his squinting black Irish eyes. "What can I do for you?" He peered behind Chuck as if he expected to find some clue there as to why Chuck was at his front door.

Curran's tilted question mark eyebrows surprised Chuck. The guy was switching defenses on him, and Chuck stood there silent for a moment, trying to figure out how he wanted to counter this strategy.

He swung his backpack off his shoulder and decided to get right to it. "I just came by to pick up the cash," he said, still trying to figure out what the man was trying to accomplish by pretending that he didn't remember asking to meet.

Curran finally pointed a finger at Chuck and nodded. "That's right!" he said. "This's a good time to get that all straightened out. Why don't you come on in, and we'll figure out how this got all assed-up in the first place."

"Cool," said Chuck, as he stepped into the house. The house that contained at least one dog. *And, by the way, nothing is assed-up.*

"It'll be nice to get this straightened out," said Curran, as he sat down on a couch and pointed at a wooden chair for Chuck. "You kind of threw me for a loop with that phone call. I'm pretty sure I'm just about square, if you check your records again." Curran was having trouble getting comfortable on the couch. He was moving his ass around and fiddling with his shirt over his belt, under which, Chuck noticed the unnatural bulge. Did the son of a bitch have a gun under there?

"I actually double-checked all the records with my assistant this morning," said Chuck, keeping it cool. "We came up with that same figure I gave you over the phone."

"What assistant?" said Curran. "The sideshow chink?"

That came from out of nowhere, and Chuck's reflex was to take one long step forward kick Curran in the teeth. He considered just walking out, but he needed the money. The moment hung, thick and pregnant until Chuck knew he had to respond. "She's half Irish," he said finally. He was immediately ashamed, felt it pressing at his gut. But that's what he'd said; couldn't take it back.

And Curran said, "Good, then at least you can fuck half of her."

"Listen, man," said Chuck, standing up but not losing his temper. Curran was trying to push his buttons, but Chuck wasn't going to bite. "What's the problem here? You want to talk about your bets or —"

"No problem at all," said Curran. "I had a buddy back in Boston liked slopie poontang. Mostly whores. He never lived with none of them or anything like that, but he didn't see anything wrong with bangin' one here and there. Said he liked small butts, had a thing about 'em, and dink chicks seem to—"

"All right," said Chuck. "Whatever point you're trying to make, let's just assume it's been made." He was standing above Brian Curran now, and he had both hands on his hips. He didn't know what had brought him to this ridiculous pose, but he felt like some kind of parody of a superhero, with his hands on the waistband of his baggy shorts, which were hanging down below his knees. "Y'think we can just get down to business here?" he said and folded his arms over his chest.

"Whatever you say, sporto," said Curran, and he was still smiling.

Chuck was becoming more aware of the fact that Curran held the trump. Curran knew that Chuck wasn't going to strong-arm him, and he appeared to have adequate backup stuffed in his pants, so Curran was fucking with him, jerking his chain just to see what would happen.

Chuck was reading this loud and clear, but he couldn't go home without giving it a shot, so he pulled out of his yellow backpack an ordinary spiral notebook and flipped through until he found Brian Curran's name and a series of entries dating back to the previous May. "Did you say that you thought maybe I'd screwed up one of your bets, recorded it wrong?"

"That's a fact," said Curran. "When I got up over three grand, I doubled down on a final four game, won the bet and got the debt down to zilch. You hearing me?"

"Yeah," said Chuck. "So where I have written here that you had Maryland, you really had Duke."

"Now you're getting the picture, champ."

"You don't mind if I double-check that?" Chuck reached into the backpack and removed a blue binder. He opened it to show Curran that it was filled with tiny telephone recorder audiotapes. Was the nephew of a bookie that clueless?

Chuck leafed through a couple of the soft plastic holders and removed a tape. He then unzipped one of the compartments on his backpack and extracted a small tape recorder. Without saying anything, he inserted the tape and played a small section of it twice, so that Curran could clearly hear his voice saying his secret code name, Bosox, and then asking to put everything on Maryland to cover.

"I guess you just got mixed up," said Chuck, and he tried to sound sympathetic, give the guy an out.

"You taped my bets?"

"There's an attachment to my phone," said Chuck. "It tapes every call. Just a safeguard in case someone forgets who he bet on."

"Yeah, a safeguard," said Curran, who was still smiling as if he were amused by his little mistake.

Chuck put his stuff back in the backpack, slid it over his shoulders, and sat on the arm of the couch.

Curran stood up, adjusted his belt again and said, "You got a minute?"

Chuck said, "I got to meet a few more guys, but I guess I have a minute."

"Good," said Curran. "I want to show you something downstairs."

CHAPTER NINE

When Hazel opened the door and saw Troy Curran, with his solid jaw and toothy grin, she thought something must have gone wrong with the nephew. Troy hadn't been by in months, so his appearance on the same day that Chuck was meeting with Brian was unsettling. But she didn't want to show her hand too soon. "How's it going, Mr. Curran," she said and stepped back from the doorway so that he could come inside.

"All goes well, my dear," he said and laughed as if he were telling a joke. He looked right into Hazel's eyes and walked past her into the living room, where the TV was tuned to *SpongeBob*. Hazel knew he'd think she was an idiot for watching cartoons in the middle of the day, but she didn't bother to turn it off. When he sat silently and stared at her, Hazel sat, too, and turned her eyes to the TV. She watched as SpongeBob was being scolded by his boss, Mr. Crabs, for screwing around too much with karate moves and neglecting his job. The scene ended with SpongeBob promising to give up martial arts in order to save his job flipping crabby patties.

When it went to a commercial for something called Blowpens, Hazel turned to Troy, who was still wearing his sunglasses, He'd undone the first few buttons on his Hawaiian shirt. "I heard the good news about the kid," he said.

"Oh, yeah," said Hazel, thinking that he must be talking about the offer to Chuck from that basketball league in England. She was never sure with this thick-necked ball-buster, so she said, "What news is that?"

"What other news is there?" he said and put his hand into his shirt and started to scratch his chest, which was covered in a mat of grey-orange hair.

Hazel could hear the friction of fingernail on skin, scratching away as if he were sitting in his own bathroom. She was afraid he might start clipping his toenails if she didn't say something. "Are you talking about the league in England?"

He pulled his hand out of his shirt and raised it up in a hip-hip-hurray kind of fist. "Of course I'm talking about the BBL," he said. "That's a great opportunity for you two to get the hell out of here and start something nice over there. Those stiffs'll love Chuckie's brand of ball. They've probably never seen a behind-the-back pass before." He started laughing again, and Hazel sensed that something wasn't quite right with the whole conversation.

"Did you come by to congratulate him?" said Hazel. "'Cause he's not here right now."

"You're the mind-reader. Why don't you tell me why I'm here?"

"It doesn't really work that way, Mr. Curran," she said.

She was going to say more, but Curran interrupted with, "I know it don't, sweetheart. I'm just pulling your leg a little bit." Then he moved his eyes down to her legs, which were crossed at the knee. Her impulse was to put bring her leg down, put her feet flush together, and cover her knees and thighs with a magazine. With his red buzz cut and his roaming eyes, Curran reminded her of a clumsy Satan.

She didn't. Instead, she actually started wiggling her toes a bit, so that the heel of her flip-flop started to make a little tapping sound off the bottom of her foot. She had a feeling the man might do some of his thinking with his pecker, and she wanted to have some leverage in case his nephew tried to renege on the debt.

"Since I can't read your mind at this particular moment," she said and leaned back further in her chair, letting her shirt slide up her midriff to show her bellybutton, "you want to tell me what I can do for you." She wanted to sound confident, but after she said it, she thought it came off as rude.

"Little lady," he said, his smile even wider than it had been earlier, the top row of his teeth clamped down to the bottom row, as if he were biting the bullet while someone was sewing up a flesh wound, "I came by to brainstorm some ideas with Chuck Holiday's business partner."

"I'm all ears."

"Honey, you got a lot more than ears, but that discussion's for another time. I got a proposal."

He wasn't being very subtle. In fact, he looked like he might be pitching a tent, but she supposed that could have just been the cut of his funny white pants.

"I don't know a whole lot about business, Mr. Curran, but you can throw it out there, and I'll try to keep up."

She was sitting forward, elbows on her knees, when he said, "I'd like to make you an offer on your sports book."

"I'm not really sure what you mean," she said, though she had a pretty good idea. No harm letting the man think she was ignorant.

"This is not a complex deal, hon," he said. Hazel started thinking about all those stupid movies where some idiot sells his soul to the devil. "With you two going to England, you're not going to keep the business going." He curled his upper lip and nodded. "Right?"

Hazel shrugged and glanced over at SpongeBob, who was using karate moves to make the crabby patties, chopping up tomatoes and lettuce with the sides of his hands and yelling *hi ya!*

"I'd like you to sell me your franchise, send your customers over to me. I give everyone a fair shake. A higher limit on credit. I won't fuck with the spread on Niner games, Vegas odds on everything, just like these boys were betting up at Tahoe or Reno, on the level."

"What kind of offer are you making?"

"For you," he said, "I'd like to make a whole slew of offers, but for the kid's book, we have a simple formula."

"You've done this before?"

"All the time, sweetheart. Your boy's got to get his records together, show me what his customers have bet over the past year. I'll give you a lump sum based on the betters' potential spending, and then you'll also get a monthly percentage of the take, based on what your guys put down. Simple."

"Obviously," she said, "I'll have to talk all this over with Chuck, but it sounds fair—at least at face value."

"It's fair on the ass-side, too, my dear. Any way you look at it."

"Yeah," said Hazel. "It sounds like a win-win, but I don't know if Chuck'll want to do it or not."

"Maybe you're not quite understanding my offer here," he said, with an odd look on his face; curious, contemplating this strange thing that was going down. "You don't have to do any work with this anymore. You and Chuck just get to sit back and collect the—"

"I understand the proposal, Mr. Curran," said Hazel. "It's just that Chuck has his own way of doing things."

"I know. He thinks he's Pistol Pete. But remember, that's part of what got the Goose kicked out of Cal. And now I'm giving him the opportunity to collect a nice lump sum and maintain some income to supplement whatever they plan to pay him over in Edinburgh."

"How did you know it was Edinburgh offering the contract?"

"I'm like you," he said. "I can read people's minds."

SpongeBob was over, and now there was a cartoon animal on the screen that was half-cat and half-dog, heads on both sides of the body, constantly arguing with itself. Hazel wasn't sure what to do. Curran was being playful and serious at the same time. He was making passes at her and offering business proposals, and Chuck still wasn't home.

"I'm not sure when Chuck's gonna be back," she said. "But I can't make any decisions about this without him." She smiled and shrugged. "I can't even show you his books, 'cause he has those with him."

"I got an idea of something you *can* show me while we wait," he said. He rose off the couch, took a step toward Hazel, and removed his sunglasses. He reached under his shirt to adjust his belt, and then he kicked each of his feet out, straightening the cuffs in his pants.

Hazel swallowed hard. She felt the muscles in her stomach contracting; her legs seemed to be paralyzed. She looked out the window to see if Chuck—or anyone—might be approaching. Then she looked back into Curran's eyes.

"My future," he said, suddenly looking as harmless as one of her clients. "Why don't you show me my future with one of your readings?"

***

Troy had been in Holiday's house a couple of times before to drop off envelopes, and he'd spoken with Hazel on each of those occasions, but he'd never ventured to try a palm reading or the crystal ball or whatever the hell the funky chick did in that back room.

But what the hell? She was as good looking a broad as he'd ever seen up close and personal, and sitting across from her while she climbed into his brain was fine with him. He would have preferred a massage, maybe even have the Chinese doll walk barefoot on his back, but that wasn't going to happen, not with Holiday on his way home.

"So what's the premise here with these tea leaves?" he asked.

"It's actually pretty interesting," she told him. "The idea is that your aura permeates everything within three feet of your body, and your aura contains all the information about you, including the future, which exists on a different plane."

"Interesting," said Troy, but he wasn't paying much attention. He was just watching the girl's mouth moving, her lips sending out all this shit about auras.

"Yeah," she said, "and tea leaves seem to be a substance that's really influenced by exposure to someone's aura. So if we expose these leaves to your aura, they'll cluster and symbolically record things about your future."

She sounded like she was doing a routine, like one of those tour guides at Fisherman's Wharf who points out all the things that are supposed to be interesting.

"Interesting," he said again, still watching her mouth, but tempted to take another peek at her tank top.

"Yeah," she said, "so you're going to prepare this cup of tea, and then I'm going to read the cluster."

After ripping open a tea bag, putting the leaves in a cup and pouring water over the leaves, she told him to slosh the water around over a bowl until the cup was empty. He'd swear she was making this shit up as she went. When the cup was nearly empty, she had him turn it upside down over a saucer covered with a napkin. Then it got really whacked-out.

She said, "Now I want you to rotate the cup three revolutions clockwise."

"You're shittin' me," he said, but started to do what he was told.

"You're impregnating the leaves with your aura," she said.

"I'm going to leave that one alone," he said as a storm of dirty lines swept through his mind.

"Now," she said, "pick up the cup by its handle, turn it over, and we'll see what kinds of clusters we have to work with."

"Whatever you say, maharishi," he said and flipped the cup over. When he peeked inside, all he could see was the leafy remains sitting in the bottom of the cup, but the girl took one look and got all excited.

"Oh, good," she said, "lots of symbols."

Troy looked back down but couldn't make heads or tails of the little patches of leaves. He thought one smudge looked a little bit like a boat, but the rest were random, meaningless blobs of wet tea. "Those are symbols?" he said and began to squint and move his face closer to the cup.

"Those are your symbols," she said, and then went on to talk about all the little blobs that did seem to turn into pictures once she told him what they were. It was like when he was a little kid, and he and his buddy were looking up at clouds. Until his friend said he saw a kangaroo, he didn't see anything. Hazel was putting pictures in his mind and then telling him a kind of story about the symbols.

She finished off with a tiny patch hanging onto the side of the cup. When he first looked at it, he thought it looked a bit like the letter Y, with a little speck on the upper left appendage, but she said it was more than that.

"It's a bird perched in a tree," she said, and there it was, sitting right there. If he'd been sitting under it, it would have surely dropped a turd on him. He didn't know how he could have missed it.

"It's a pretty common symbol," she said and picked up the cup, which she wiped out with the napkin she'd used earlier.

"What's the bird mean?" he said, kind of into it now, enjoying the game.

"Well," she said, "it's not just the bird. The tree is important, too."

"Yeah," he said. "Of course." He was aware that he was starting to sound like a moron, but he wanted to hear the end of it. "What's a tree mean?"

"A tree represents family, and a perched bird means that you're waiting to hear from someone, so this indicates that a family member is going to be bringing you some kind of news, a message of some sort, perhaps a request."

He nodded. He couldn't think of anyone who might be trying to get a hold of him, so he said, "When?"

"The position of the leaves in the cup," she said, "tells me that this family member will be contacting you in the next couple of days. It's something important, but that's really all I can tell you. Tea leaves aren't as specific as Tarot."

"No shit?" said Troy, as he sat back in his chair and started trying to figure out what the hell she was all about.

CHAPTER TEN

Brian Curran was surprised that the lanky son-of-a-bitch was going to follow him into the basement. Did Holiday really think that he had a big stash of money down there, that he was going to count out seven large and put it in Chuckie's big hand? That shit simply wasn't going to happen.

The funny thing was that Brian didn't really know exactly what *was* going to happen. He just had the idea that maybe he could use Dim and Sum's dogs to scare Holiday, the Mickey Mouse, jerkwater bookie, who thought he was going to come around like he was collecting for his fucking paper route. Brian had a few lines that he wanted to try out, then he was going to watch for the bookie's reaction and go with the flow from there.

Brian wasn't going to give him any money, but he also wanted to make sure the asshole didn't come around here again. He'd seen enough of Chuck Holiday.

When they stepped through the door and started down the stairs, Brian ducked and said, "Watch it." A beam hung low about halfway down the steps; Brian was used to barking out the warning when he was bringing people down to see his training center. It was like what the dude Pavlov said about his dogs: a conditioned response. Every time Brian passed under that beam, he couldn't help saying *Watch it.* So maybe his dogs were already conditioned to fight. He'd been down there enough to condition *himself*, so maybe the dogs were, too. Shit, if a human could be conditioned that easily, then the dogs must be ready to go.

As Brian got close to the bottom of the stairs, he didn't hear the thumping of Chuck's big feet anymore. He turned around and saw that the bookie had ducked under the beam and frozen just as the steps turned toward the dog cage.

"What's wrong?" said Brian, as he leaned on the cyclone fence and put his hand on the gate latch. "You bump your head?"

"Not a dog fan," said Chuck holding the straps of his backpack just above his chest.

"Everyone loves dogs," said Brian. "Man's best friend, for fuck's sake." The dogs were trotting around the cage in small circles, quick miniature steps, like little wild boars, hungry, pissed off little boars, minus the tusks.

"Yeah … man's best friend," said Chuck. "That's what they say, but I think they're talking about Cocker Spaniels and Golden Retrievers."

"That's not very nice," said Brian, still wondering if the dogs were ready, conditioned to respond. "I think you probably hurt their feelings."

Chuck said, "Sorry, dogs," and started to turn toward the door. "I'm gonna take off now." He paused for a moment and added, "Any chance you can get me that money by the end of the week?" He was talking to Brian, but he never took his eyes off the dogs. His voice sounded robotic, no emotion, like he didn't even know what the words meant.

But Brian knew what they meant, and it was starting to piss him off. He didn't want this shit to drag on, didn't want this two-bit small-timer telling folks on the street that Brian had some bad luck on a few games. He didn't want that out there. He took a moment to get his thoughts together, then started to laugh.

Brian looked down at his hand on the latch. "Well, Chuck, I think you know that's not going to happen. You probably just came over here to show that sweet little thing you got at home that you weren't scared to go shake me up a little bit, rattle my cage," he said and shook the gate, clattering the whole pen and causing the dogs to jump toward the gate and snarl.

The bookie didn't step back, but his chest was rising and falling quickly, his knees were bent, and his hands were out in front of him like he was playing a lazy man-to-man defense.

"I guess we'll just set up some kind of payment plan then," said Holiday, still frozen on the stairs.

"You're not getting this. I'm not paying you, and you're not coming around here anymore asking me for money. Got it?"

"You're not siccing those on me," said Holiday, keeping his hands in front of him and nodding his head toward the dogs. "It'd be too messy for you. Hazel knows I'm over here, and the cops'll be all over your ass in about five minutes, so you can stop fucking with that gate."

"Yeah," said Brian, impressed that Holiday was still standing there trying to be tough, even though he was shaking a little bit. "I've actually considered all that, and I think I'll still be okay if the mutts tear you a new asshole." Brian started nodding. "Y'see, it's pretty obvious self-defense, right? Bookie comes over to rough me up, and I set the dogs loose to protect myself, to save my fucking life from the crazed bookie who came to kill me because I couldn't pay my debt on time. How does that sound?" he asked. *He* thought it sounded great, considering he was pretty much making it up on the spot. "I got a little over my head with my bets, and the next thing I know, this crazy bookie, who got thrown out of college for punching a dude's eye out, is coming after me. The dogs were the only way I could save myself. I like the sound of that. I have a good mind to do it whether you promise to stay out of my face or not. A couple of Chinamen give me these mutts to train for fighting, and I'd like to give 'em some practice today, give 'em a chance to chomp on some hippy white ass."

All the *Chinaman* comments and this last threat of letting loose the dogs just for practice on his—did he hear that right?—*hippy ass*, sent a flurry of images through Chuck's head, rapid-fire images of possibilities. That was one of the reasons he was so effective on the basketball court. He was able to slow down in his mind the fast pace of the game and check out all his options. As he was jumping in the air for a rebound, by the time he got back down on the ground, he knew whether he was going to throw a quick outlet, dribble to the right or left, tip the ball, whatever. He could run it all though his brain that fast. When someone threw the ball to him on a fast break, he knew before he caught it which one of the thousands of options he was going to use.

It started back when he was a little kid. He used to run through scenarios in his mind, sometimes days before they were going to happen. If he knew he was going to get in trouble for grades or curfew, he'd run a dress rehearsal in his mind, so that he'd have all the answers ready when his dad started peppering him with questions. The same thing with fist fights and go-cart races and phone calls to girls. He practiced everything in his mind before it happened.

And that's what he was doing as he faced Brian Curran and his threats. He knew that you're supposed to run downhill if you were being chased by a bear, and that you're supposed to punch a shark in the nose if you happened to run into one out at Baker Beach, but pit bulls were a different story.

When he had his first growth spurt and began hating dogs, he used to imagine kicking a dog as hard as he could, if one had decided to attack him. That was what he was planning to do if the asshole decided to give the dogs some "practice." He was going to kick the living shit out of whichever dog came first, and then he was going to make a run for it. He saw it in his mind, and he was fairly happy with it. Happy enough to say to Curran, "It's little pricks like you that ruin it for everyone. If you'd won a bet, which was very unlikely 'cause you don't know your ass from a hole in the wall, my guess is that you'd want your money, right?"

Curran, who still had his hand on the gate, shrugged.

"But you're too big a fuckin' pussy to pay me when you lose," said Chuck. He felt himself getting more pissed as he spoke. "And you're too big a pussy to go tell your uncle that you're strapped 'cause of your own moron decisions. Troy's your sponsor, man, and you're an embarrassment. Wait 'til people start hearing about this."

When Chuck stopped talking, he felt himself shaking a little bit. To fight it off, he started to shake his head slowly back and forth as he scowled.

Curran's face had changed. His eyes no longer had their trademark squint, and one side of his mouth was starting to twitch up, Elvis-style. He shook the gate again, and something happened. Chuck didn't know if Curran had done it on purpose, but when the gate was rattling, the latch jumped up and held. The dogs froze. All the animals needed to do was push the gate open. Chuck actually thought about making a run for it, but decided that doing so might spark the dogs into some kind of frenzy. So he stayed still, and the dogs held their ground, legs stiff and lolling tongues dripping.

The only sound was their panting.

He saw Curran reach behind him toward a little wooden table with a phone and something round that was shining, reflecting the overhead light. For a moment, he hoped Curran might be reaching for the phone to call his uncle, that he'd decided it wouldn't be so bad to ask old Troy for a favor.

But Chuck knew he was wrong because of the angle of Curran's hand. He hadn't simply reached for the phone. He had his hand held up like he was going to spank a baby or take an oath. Chuck thought of all the idiots rushing the *Animal House* saying in unison with their hands raised, "I, state your name ...."

But Curran didn't begin an oath, and the dogs stayed frozen—until Curran's eyes hit Chuck's. There was a split second when Chuck broke eye contact and zeroed in on Curran's forearm tattoo, a shamrock with some words under it ... *Mighty Craic*? And then Curran brought his hand down hard on what turned out to be a hotel desk bell.

The first dog hit the fence before the after tone of the bell faded. The fence hit Curran and whipped back at the second dog. The one that made it through, the one that looked to be smiling, darted toward Chuck.

As Chuck had rehearsed in his mind, he took one step down and threw all his weight into a left-footed kick, hitting the dog on the side of its head. The moments were coming in a combination of fast-action and slow-motion. The actual kick happened quickly, and he felt the power of the blow when his shoelaces dug into the skin on top of his foot.

Then things slowed down, and he watched the dog drift down the stairs as if it were happening under water. He saw the beast's toothy smile before the animal twisted and bounced into the gate, which was now opening from the force of the second dog.

Chuck was slowing things down even further in his mind. He thought for a second that he was able to watch the second dog with one of his eyes and Curran with his other eye. And as the second dog was approaching the stairs, he saw Curran reaching beneath his belt.

Chuck hadn't rehearsed this part, and his natural reaction was to back up the stairs as quickly as possible without turning his back on either the dog or Curran. After three quick back-pedals, he felt an explosion in the back of his head—*watch it, low beam*—felt his feet leave the surface of the stairs, and then heard the pop of Curran's pistol and the sharp yelp of an animal. There was a brief flash of white light, which flared in his brain, and Chuck couldn't see for a fraction of a second, but he never lost consciousness, as he felt the immediate weight of the dog on his chest and groin, the heavy, dead weight of a motionless pit bull. Then he felt the awkward arc of his own spine, propped up over his backpack, as he lay near the curve of the stairs.

Things sped up again when he grabbed for the dog, which he thought was waiting to rip into him. Then he felt the thick fluid on his hands and heard only the sounds of his own breathing, loud and quick and crackling with phlegm.

He'd felt this kind of syrupy ooze on his fingers before and knew it was blood, but he didn't know whose it was until he rolled the lifeless dog onto the stairs and saw the hole in its side, still pumping a constant flow, thick and dark.

When his brain was able to open up the scene outside of his little bubble on the staircase, he heard ripping and snarling and screaming. The first dog, the one with the ambivalent smile, was tearing Brian Curran to shreds.

Things slowed down again when he reached over the railing to the exposed wall and pulled, through the cobwebs and some dead phone lines, a rusted ball-peen hammer from between the studs. He took three steps at a time around the curve of the staircase, and landed, straddling the dog and Curran, who wasn't struggling anymore.

Chuck was still wearing the backpack, but, with his height, he was able to swing, with good leverage, the hammer into the side of the animal, which had latched on to the area between Curran's neck and shoulder. He could feel the weight of the hammer cracking bones and sinking into soft tissue, but it didn't seem to matter how many times he hit the dog. It wouldn't let go. Finally, after what must have been two or three minutes, its jaws loosened, and its tense body went slack.

While Chuck held the hammer above his head, ready to continue pummeling if the animal showed any sign of life, he rewound the last few moments and felt the throbbing in the back of his head again. He dropped the hammer and put his hand on the golf ball-sized welt near the base of his skull.

The only thing he could figure was that Curran decided to shoot him after he kicked the dog, the one that now lay broken at his feet. But when Chuck fell, Curran's bullet sank into the second dog, which had been in the process of pouncing on Chuck. That second dog had taken Chuck's bullet.

And what was Curran doing with a gun? Chuck had said he was

leaving, so why would the crazy fucker want to shoot him and cause himself more trouble?

It was Chuck's trouble now.

The logical move was to call the cops and explain everything, let them know that the lunatic let the dogs out. But Chuck was pretty sure his hopes of playing for the Rocks would crumble into dust if he got publicly mixed up in a mess like this. He sat on the steps next to the dog with the bullet in its gut, strangely calm. He reached over and rubbed the dog's head between its ears. "That's a good boy," he said.

SECOND QUARTER ~ FUCKUPS

The world is always rolling between our legs.
— John Hodgen (from *Forgiving Buckner*)

Fuckups are all over the place. There's a fuckup on every street corner. But as many as there are, there's really only a few different types.

I guess the most common is the fool. He screws things up because he doesn't know any better. He backs his truck into the fire hydrant. Locks himself out of the apartment. Blows his paycheck on a horse. He doesn't mean any harm, but he's out there, and you don't want to get on a boat with him or hire him to install your sprinkler system or let him set you up with his cousin. It just won't turn out well.

Another type of fuckup is the selfish guy. He'll ruin things because he's so caught up in his own shit that he neglects all the people he cares about. He'll borrow money from his folks because he thinks he's an entrepreneur. Then he'll lose it all on his big plan for bowlers with dirty clothes, the Laundro-Bowl or his cutting edge concept for a new condiment: cran-aise, a combination mayonnaise and cranberry sauce for turkey sandwiches. When the money is gone, he has no intention of paying anyone back because he has convinced himself that an entrepreneur must take risks, and his backers should know that.

Type number three: the lazy fucks. They just don't want to put in the effort to be successful. These guys are equally comfortable hunched over a bar, stretched out on a couch, or passed out on a bed with sheets that haven't been cleaned in months. If they can't find the remote control, they'll watch the same channel all day. They're pretty harmless because they don't really have the energy to do any damage. As long as you don't count on them for anything, you can live with them; but they're fuckups nonetheless.

Then there's me. I don't think I fit into any of those categories, but I'm pretty sure I'm a fuckup.

In all truth, I don't consider myself stupid, selfish, or lazy, but I guess those kinds of people probably don't see themselves in that light either, so maybe I am ... but I doubt it. As I said, I think of myself as a different kind. I've been the captain of my own raft, which I've paddled up shit creek on many occasions. You already know about the stuff that went down when I was at Cal. That's the kind of thing that has happened to me over and over again throughout my life. I end up in really crappy situations, but they're usually only partly my fault.

A few years back, I got talked into going to a cowboy bar down in San Jose. A couple of guys I knew from high school had gotten way into country music and line dancing and a whole bunch of other shit that I really didn't get, but I agreed to go with them anyway. Decided that I'd just have a few beers and watch them ride mechanical bulls or whatever they planned to do.

It didn't really work out that way. One of my buddy's cousins drove five of us down in a brown van that looked a little like Stan's hot dog van. Sliding door on one side. No side windows other than the ones for the driver and the passenger. Two windows in the back. That's it. They're all over the place.

Well, we were only in the bar for an hour before these guys start doing shots of something called a "fried chicken," which was 151 rum with an egg cracked in it. Then the bartender would light it on fire. If you didn't drink it quick, the egg would actually cook. Nasty. But they bought me a few, and I was starting to feel it pretty good, so I decided to stop before things got out of hand.

The others were getting messed up, but I had a ball game the next day, so I decided to get out of there before a fight broke out. I was still on probation at the time, so I couldn't really be a part of anything like that. I would have taken a cab home, but we were all the way down in San Jose, so I figured I'd just go out and lie down in the back of the van. The door was unlocked, so I climbed in and promptly fell asleep.

I thought I was being pretty responsible, but here's the bad part. I don't know how many hours later it was, but I woke up with a foul taste in my mouth. It was dark, but when my eyes started to adjust, I realized that I was still in the van, and the van was in the garage of a house.

When I sat up, I saw that the van was filled with painting gear: tarps and rollers and brushes. There was also a case of Jarritos Mexican soda pop on the floor beneath the seat. This was definitely not the van I'd ridden in to get down to San Jose. It was close, but it wasn't the same vehicle. I guess I'd been drunker than I thought.

I had to get the hell out of there. I didn't have any idea what time it was, but I couldn't stay in this garage, so I quietly climbed out the back and then started to look for an exit strategy. No luck. There was one door that presumably led into the house; the only other option was the main garage door, which led to the outside. I knew I couldn't go into the house. They'd think I was a burglar, and I might get shot. But I was nervous that the garage door would be loud and wake up whoever lived there, and I might get shot anyway. Shit choice.

I felt around the walls until I found the button for the electric garage door. I took a deep breath, prayed that the door was quick — and quiet — and pressed the button. I was standing by the door when it began to move. When it was about a third of the way up, the other door opened, and a Latino man, built like a professional wrestler, looked right into my eyes and said, "Que la cogida?" And then he started running at me.

For some reason I yelled, "Sorry," before I rolled under the door, jumped to my feet and started to run as fast as I could. The guy was screaming a bunch of other Spanish stuff at me, but he couldn't catch me. He had short legs, and I had doubled my lead after half a block.

I'd never seen the neighborhood before. It was morning, and there were actually quite a few people on the street. The lawns were dead, and there were broken down cars everywhere. After about three blocks of running past liquor stores with Spanish signs and groups of kids playing soccer in the streets, I came to the conclusion that I was in Mexico.

When I eventually slowed to a light jog and asked a lady walking a mangy looking dog where I was, she told me East Palo Alto. While I was relieved to still be in the country, it ended up taking me seven hours of buses and trains to get back to San Francisco.

That's the kind of fuckup I am.

CHAPTER ELEVEN

Hazel was relieved when she heard the popping of the Harley pulling into the driveway. She was very interested in Troy Curran's offer, and he'd turned out to be a decent customer—he paid her triple the rate and kept his hands to himself.

"I think that's Chuck now," she said, and rose from her seat in the living room, where Troy Curran had asked if it would be all right to turn off the cartoons and watch a little ESPN while they waited for Chuck.

"I'm glad he's here," Curran said and looked at his watch. Then his eyes narrowed. "But I can't really get into the whole deal with him right now. I'm late for another appointment. It looks like you're going to have to fill him in on the details. It's a sweet deal, doll, so you gotta play it up that way. You know the kid better than me, so you'll figure out a way to explain this to him so he can understand it, right? Be a good deal for everyone."

Hazel nodded, but she wasn't giving Troy her full attention. She was looking behind him, watching Chuck through the picture window.

Chuck wasn't wearing a shirt.

Had he been riding around on his motorcycle with no shirt on? Just a pair of baggy Celtics shorts, his basketball shoes, and a backpack? He'd left wearing a shirt. She knew that. Why had he taken it off?

He moved out of her vision and burst through the front door. His mouth was open and he was shivering, even though it was warm outside. He was also rubbing his hands together really fast, like he was cleaning paint off his fingers, but she didn't see any paint. Just tall, skinny Chuck, standing with his mouth open and his eyes wide, three holes in his face, like a white bowling ball. He wasn't saying anything.

"Mr. Curran's here," said Hazel, and Chuck's bowling ball rolled a half a revolution toward the couch. After he tugged at the waistband of his shorts, he started licking his lips and looking back and forth between Hazel and Troy Curran.

Without warning, Chuck snapped out of whatever state was he was in and said, "What's happ'nin', Troy?" The big smile on his face replaced the thumbhole, his hands not rubbing anymore but giving Curran a ghetto handshakes and holding on like he was really pleased to see him. But Hazel could see that something wasn't quite right. She wanted Troy gone, so she could find out what was going on.

"Mr. Curran has a business proposal for you," said Hazel and nodded at Curran to go ahead and set it up.

"Oh, yeah?" said Chuck, releasing the man's hand and backing into the couch next to Hazel.

"Well," said Curran. "It's pretty simple, but I'd first like to congratulate you on the offer from the Rocks. They had a down year, but they're a top-notch organization over there. That's a feather in your cap, son."

"Word got out, I guess," said Chuck. When he leaned back, Hazel noticed a rust colored spot on the white part of the waistband of his shorts. The drawstring, which was hanging out, was sprinkled with the same color.

"People around the game like to talk," said Curran.

"Yeah, they do," said Chuck. "Thanks. It could be a good opportunity for me," he said, but he didn't sound like himself. Something was missing. His swagger, maybe. "Surprised you've heard of 'em." He put his hand on Hazel's thigh and added, "And this'll be good for Hazel, too. It'll be nice for both of us." Then he crossed his ankle over his knee and put his arm around Hazel.

"Indeed," said Curran. "And I'd like to get you off to a good start over there by offering you a deal that could get you some nice cash, and you won't have to do much to get it."

"Those are my favorite kinds of deals," said Chuck, who seemed much more relaxed than he had when he came in. But Hazel looked down and saw red sprinkles on the toe of Chuck's shoe and around the edge of the sole. Something was wrong. She pushed his foot off his knee and stood up.

"Can I get anyone anything," she said, looking at Curran, who was still standing.

"No, hon," said Curran. "I really do have to get going." He took a pair of old-fashioned sunglasses out of his breast pocket; they looked right on him for some reason. Then he said, "Chuck, I'm going to let your girl here fill you in on the details, but the gist of the thing is I'd like to buy your clients when you leave for England. It'd be pretty tough to run your book overseas, and I'll give you a good offer for all your friends' business." Then he clapped his hands once and opened them like he was setting free a bird.

"Buy my clients?" said Chuck. "Can you do that? Buy people?"

"Sure you can, Chuck," said Curran. "Who's going to stop us?"

"I guess you're right," said Chuck. "My guys're still going to want to bet when I'm gone. Why not?"

"Yeah," said Curran. "Why not?"

"Is my little list of guys worth much to you?"

"*You* know how easy this job is, especially for me. My boys take the bets over the phone and Claudel does the collections side of things for me. I just count the money. I sit home and count money, Chuck. It's not a bad gig. But your book's not for me anyway."

"You're giving my guys to Claudel Shanks?"

"No, no, no, champ. Claudel works for *me*. I can't have him doing his own business on the side. Conflict of interest. I'm actually going to set my nephew up with your book," said Curran, and Hazel was sure she saw Chuck stiffen. Then she glanced back at Curran, who looked to her like some kind of B-movie producer, selling his story ideas about giant killer-centipedes and prom nights gone bad.

"He's a bit of a big-mouth, young Brian is, makes a lot of dumbass mistakes," said Curran. "But I think he could run book if he kept things small and had my backing. He wouldn't have to answer to me or anything, but I think I could keep him out of trouble if I knew what he was doing."

Hazel watched as Chuck nodded and scratched his chin but didn't say anything.

"You don't have to make any decisions right now, son," said Curran. "I'll be around. I'd like to invite you and your business associate here over for a nice dinner at my house. You've been there, right?"

"Yeah," said Chuck. "Nice place, view of Mount Tamalpais."

"Yes," said Curran. "We'll have a few drinks, and we can take a look at your numbers and see how much your franchise is worth. You like lamb?"

Chuck nodded again and looked at Hazel, who couldn't stop stealing looks at Chuck's feet.

That fucking Brian Curran must've tried something. She knew it. But how in the hell do you get blood on your shoes? What has to happen to get blood on your shoes?

From out of nowhere, Curran asked, "You always ride around on that motorbike with no shirt on, young man?" He winked at Hazel.

"Nice day today," said Chuck. "When do you think you want us to come over?"

Curran smiled. "Don't you play for the championship over at Kezar on Friday?"

"We do," said Chuck.

"We could celebrate your victory with a late dinner. Does that sound all right for you?" he said and looked at Hazel, who shrugged and smiled at Chuck.

"Sounds great," she said and nodded to Curran, and then to Chuck, whose hand was now on Curran's back, leading him to the front door. He clearly wanted the man out. Hazel could feel it, and she wanted him out, too.

"That'll be great," she said again as she started to see things in her mind, not quite pictures, but blurred flashes. Flashes of bloodiness, not anything defined, nebulous shapes and colors, mostly red. She knew something bad had happened. She felt it creeping inside of her whole body; she wanted to scrape out the insides of her veins, scour the unclean thoughts that had penetrated her, chilling her and making her shiver in the warmth of the sun-drenched entryway.

"If I don't see you at the game," said Curran, "I'll see you at my place afterward. Bring all your stuff, and we'll see if we can put together a nice package for you kids. You've done a good job, Chuck, setting up your clientele. My nephew better appreciate it." He gave them his biggest smile, adjusted his sunglasses, and walked out the door.

After Chuck closed the door and locked it, his face turned into the white bowling ball again, three holes in the middle of the pale, sickly skin. "I hate dogs," he said.

CHAPTER TWELVE

When Don and Sid turned the van onto Brian Curran's street, they watched a very tall white man run out of the house. The man had stopped to take off his pack and pull his stained T-shirt over his head as he ran. Then he'd jammed the shirt in his pack, slipped the pack over his shoulder, jumped onto a motorcycle, and drove off past them. Both men stared through the windshield at his long white hair blowing in the wind; he wore no helmet.

Sid, who was much shorter than Don, five-four to his friend's five-eight, said in Mandarin, "That's the tallest man I've ever seen."

"Yes." Don wasn't much for words.

"Was he bleeding?" asked Sid. They'd been working on their English for most of the day, good for business to understand the food orders and say *Have a good one* or *Come again,* but they were tired of it.

"No" said Don, shaking his head matter-of-factly.

"Was the blood just on the shirt?"

"Yes," said Don, as he took off his seatbelt and opened the driver's side door to the van.

Sid jumped from the high seat of the van onto the sidewalk. After he'd closed the door and straightened his thin black tie, he shuffled, in black leather shoes, around the van and followed Don across the street. He wasn't sure what to expect after seeing the ghost riding off on a motorcycle.

Now they were in the house. Sid didn't have to duck on the stairway to the basement; he was able to observe the scene without obstruction. "Motherfucker," he said in English as he stood on the steps and watched Don tiptoe through the mess. "What is this?" he said and started to scratch at his scalp, a nervous habit that had been plaguing him ever since idiot Brian Curran had talked him into this dog business. "Big money," he'd said and laid out the plan: Curran would train the dogs if Don and Sid would get the American Pit Bull Terriers and the training equipment: a chain link pen, a tire on a rope, a treadmill, leashes and collars and chains, food, many, many things that cost them a great deal of money out of the restaurant business account.

Aside from the money, Sid enjoyed being part of it. These dogs and chains and guns and Curran and the eventual fights were all turning him into an American badass, someone not to be fucked with. And now Curran had somehow screwed it up. Now the dog business was over, and their restaurant was struggling.

Sid watched as Don leaned over the mutilated Curran and looked into his face. The man's eyes were still open; he looked happily surprised, like he'd just won a contest he'd forgotten he'd entered, like he didn't know that some of his neck and most of his shoulder were hanging from the dog's teeth. "Dead," said Don. Then he continued to act as medical examiner as he looked over the two dogs. Dead. Dead.

Sid did a better job of thinking when he talked, so he started conjecturing, still using the Chinese language to keep from confusing himself. "These dogs turned on Curran, so he shot them?"

Don shook his head.

The pit bull near Curran didn't have a bullet hole in it like the one on the stairs. Instead, it had tiny craters all over its body. How could dog kill a man after it had been beaten that way? Or how could a man shoot a dog after the dog has eaten his neck? Makes no sense. Bad theory.

Sid decided to have another go at it. "Curran shot one dog, so the other dog got mad and killed Curran."

Don looked up at Sid, who was now sitting on the steps next to the dog with a hole in its side. He shook his head again and swatted at some flies that were buzzing around his hair. "You think the other dog committed suicide after he killed Curran?"

Good point, Sid realized. How did the other dog get killed? He looked at the scene again and thought about his investment, broken now forever. He'd never liked Curran. Something was not right about him.

"Maybe the giant on the motorcycle hated Brian Curran, and he came in and killed our dogs."

Don had come out of the pen and was crouching next to the dog, the one with its mouth open, lying next to Curran. Don was petting the dog when he looked up at Sid and shrugged. "Could be," he said.

"But why did that dog turn on Curran?"

"Maybe the dogs were not trained right," said Don, who was now in the pen, walking around the treadmill, kicking the tire, and then walking back out toward the blood. "Maybe he was telling us lies that he knew how to make dogs fight."

"Motherfucker," said Sid. "He called us Dim and Sum. I would have liked to see him get his neck chewed on by the American Pit Bull Terrier."

Don nodded and said, "But we lost lots of money. We can't get it back from a dead man."

"From whom do we get it, then?"

"The man with the motorcycle. He did something here. He needs to refund us for the money we spent on the dogs."

"You know where to look for him?" Sid scratched his scalp again.

"No. But maybe we can find something in this house that will help us find him."

CHAPTER THIRTEEN

Chuck was on his third bottle of beer. He'd finished recounting to Hazel what had happened at Brian Curran's, and now they sat silently at the kitchen table, looking at each other but not knowing what to say. All Chuck could think about were the Rocks and Mr. Fellows and his *second chance* ... rolling, rolling, rolling out of bounds, time running out, here comes the buzzer.

Hazel finally said, "I guess we should call the cops. There's a dead body, and we know about it. You're supposed to call the cops in that situation, right?"

Chuck stood and walked to the refrigerator, where he took out two more beers. He opened them and put one in front of Hazel, who was still nursing her first.

"Yeah," he said. "The only thing is, we call the cops, it's coming out why I was over there."

"Why does it have to? Why not just tell them you were going over to see a friend?"

"Yeah, a friend who sicced his dogs on me and shot at me."

Hazel took a big swallow and narrowed her eyes. "Couldn't we come up with a story that would keep all that out of it, something that doesn't have anything to do with gambling debts?" When Chuck didn't respond, she took another drink and set the bottle back on the table. "All we have to do is think about what the cops are going to see, and then make up something that fits the scene." She paused for a moment and nodded at him. "It's what I do, Chuck. I look at those tea leaves and make up a story to go with the little wet blotches. It's my job, making up stories to go with pictures."

"I thought you had *the gift*," he said, wiping the beer from his chin with the same hand that was holding the longneck bottle. He was angry now and taking it out on her. Shit like this shouldn't happen to a guy twice. Gatorade on the floor, fucking dogs in the basement.

"The gift isn't there twenty-four-seven, you jerk," she said, and, with two fingers, pulled her hair behind her ear. "Sometimes I get a customer, and I don't see anything. The lady just has bad psychic energy, a weak aura, whatever, but I can't say that to her, right? I have to pretend that I'm seeing something or I don't get paid."

Chuck was interested. "How often does that happen?"

"Occasionally," she said, as the hair slid out again from behind her ear and swung in front of her eye. She didn't push it away. "It's happens enough where I've gotten good at making stuff up, okay?"

"Okay," he said. "So do you want me to tell you what the scene looked like when I left? And you can make up what happened?"

"I think I better see it myself, so we can cover all the details."

Chuck stood up and walked behind her. He put his hands on her shoulders and said, "I don't think you should see it, Hazel."

She didn't answer. She took the last swallow of her first beer, put it down and reached for the second. She took a sip, then said, "I think I can handle it, Chuck."

***

As they were walking up the front steps of Brian Curran's house, Hazel stopped and said, "Maybe you're right. This place feels bad to me. And the smell is horrible."

The smell was still awful, but different. The dog odor was there, but now he thought he could smell bleach mixed in with it. It was bad, more shocking, he guessed, than anything else. "We're here now," he said. "Why don't we just get it over with, get our story, call the cops and hope Troy Curran and Mr. Fellows still want to do business with us."

They were at the front door, which was slightly open. Hazel peeked in and said, "I could understand that Troy might not want to do the deal if his nephew's dead, but why would Mr. Fellows back down?"

Chuck leaned on the wall near the doorbell and said, "I'm a fucking wild card, Hazel. Fellows is putting his ass on the line for me as it is, but if I'm involved in something where a dude gets killed, or if he finds out that I'm a bookie, he's gonna drop me. Why take a risk on a guy like me?"

"There won't be a risk," said Hazel as she pushed through the door. "Where's the basement?"

Chuck followed her and showed her the stairs, told her to watch her head, even though she wasn't tall enough for the beam to be a problem. She was a few steps in front of him, diving right in instead of testing the water with her toes. Before Chuck made the turn and ducked the beam, he saw her at the bottom of the stairs; he couldn't see much else except for Hazel and the last few stairs. She was standing with her feet together and her hands and shoulders raised in a kind of *what the fuck?*

He stopped and crouched down to scan the basement. It wasn't the same place. No dog pen. No chains. No tire. No treadmill. No dogs. No ball-peen hammer.

And no Brian Curran.

The whole place had been hosed down; it was still wet with water and bleach and cleansers. It'd been scrubbed, no traces of anything left behind. He couldn't even see any dog hair in the spots of floor that were beginning to dry.

Hazel turned around and she raised a single eyebrow.

"They must have just left," he said. "It's still wet."

"Who?"

Chuck moved to sit on the stairs near where the pit bull had been shot a few hours before. "I have no idea," he said, as he stretched his legs out and rubbed his knees.

"Well," she said, "let's come up with some ideas, so we can figure out our situation."

"I guess someone could have heard the gunshot. But we were down here, and he had a little gun; it didn't sound like much more than a firecracker."

She sat on the bottom step now and turned her body toward him, her knees together and her feet folded beneath her. "Okay," she said. "But even if a neighbor heard, would they come over here and clean up the mess?"

Chuck shook his head. "Neither would the cops. They'd be here taking pictures and blood samples, all kinds of shit. They'd be yellow-taping the whole street."

"So not a neighbor and not a cop … who?"

"I actually have a couple of guesses," said Chuck. "One, it could have been Troy. He leaves our place, goes over to visit his nephew, tell him about the deal with Chuck Holiday, invite him to the fuckin' dinner on Friday, but there's Brian, lying in blood with dead dogs all over the place, so he calls some of his boys, cleans the place up, and gets the body out of here."

"But why? Wouldn't he want it to be investigated, so he could find out how it happened?"

"I've got an idea that Troy would want to conduct his own investigation and have him and Claudel Shanks administer their own kind of justice. Remember, Brian was Troy's brother's kid, and I think Troy was supposed to be taking care of him out here."

"Oh," said Hazel, letting her hair cover her eyes again, trying not to let Chuck see how scared she was. But he knew it, because he was scared himself. He got along with Claudel Shanks, but he also knew that Claudel did what he was told to do.

"The other possibility's the Chinese dudes that own the pit bulls came to check on their animals, and they walk in and see all the shit that went down, and even though they didn't do it, they decide they don't want anyone tracing it back to them, so they clean it up and hope it goes away."

Hazel asked, "They paid Brian Curran to train their dogs?"

"I think that's what Curran said."

"But what if they think someone came in here and killed Curran and the dogs?" said Hazel, squinting her eyes, looking like she was trying to figure it all out.

"It might've looked that way to someone who came in here and saw the scene, all that blood. But it would still look funny, 'cause one of the dogs got Curran."

"Yeah," said Hazel, still squinting, really working her mind, maybe trying to see the whole thing in some kind of psychic way. "But it's also pretty obvious that someone else was down here. It couldn't have just been Brian and the dogs, because there'd be a last man—or dog—standing."

"That's right," he said, wondering if she'd close her eyes, maybe have a vision of who the fuck took the bodies.

"Then if it's the Chinese guys or Troy, they're gonna be looking for that other person, who happens to be *you*."

"But they got no way of knowing it's me," he said, hoping he was right, trying to sound confident but hearing a trace of doubt in his voice.

"Let's hope not. But you had to have left traces of yourself all over the place, right? Finger prints, DNA, all that stuff."

"This isn't TV. Whoever cleaned it up probably washed away any traces of me. We might have gotten lucky."

"I feel like that should be reassuring," she said. "But it's just not."

CHAPTER FOURTEEN

When Claudel Shanks was playing minor league baseball, he was listed in the media guide as standing five feet nine inches tall and weighing two hundred pounds, but that wasn't right. Even in his spikes, Claudel wasn't more than five-eight, and in the years since he blew out his knee and started working for Troy Curran, he'd beefed up to nearly two hundred and fifty pounds. From far away, he looked like a black cube on wheels, his little steps creating the illusion that he was gliding down the sidewalk, his tweener afro—in between the seventies Harlem Globetrotters' look and the tight cuts of today—bouncing a little as he walked.

There were no brothers in sight. He was in Golden Gate Heights on the west side of Twin Peaks, sitting in his old Cadillac and checking the San Francisco address he'd written in his notebook. He rolled down his window and stuck his head out, peering up at the house. Lots of stairs. The place must have fifty motherfuckin' stairs. He thought about taking off his leather jacket, but didn't want to ruin his look.

He reached into the back seat and pulled out an Adirondack, a thirty-five incher, thin on the handle and thick and heavy at the barrel. Before he'd screwed up his knee going into the visitor's dugout after a pop foul, he'd ordered a case of bats, nice Adirondacks, expensive, comped by the club. And even though the hitting coach said they were top heavy, Claudel could still get around on a ninety mile an hour fastball. That's what got him into professional baseball: a quick bat, so quick through the zone he could really wait on junk ballers and rip line-drives right back up the middle, undress these single A junkers with their circle-change bullshit and split-finger cheese. He maybe didn't look like a hitter because of his build, but he was hitting .327 when he tore the ACL. Shit, he'd had a shot at moving up, making some big money if his luck hadn't gone bad.

But he still had the case of Adirondacks. And he still had a quick bat.

He checked out the manicured lawn and the flowerbeds against the base of the house before his ascent up the brick stairs. He had one hand on the railing and, with his other hand, he was using the bat as a walking stick. When he felt the sweat on his thighs under his pressed slacks, he made a mental note not to make house calls in this neighborhood anymore. Catch the motherfuckers coming out of work instead.

He tapped three times on the door with the knob of the bat and waited, smiling at the peephole, trying to look like a Jehovah's Witness. The bat was behind his back. After a few moments, he heard someone fiddling with the chain, then he watched the door open a few inches.

Without removing the smile from his face, still keeping it professional, he kicked the door open with his good leg, ripping the chain off the wall, and stepped inside, where a dude in his mid-forties, a handsome white man with thick wavy hair, was sitting on his ass on some nice parquet floor, like the Boston garden and shit. The dude was looking up with blue-ass eyes and he's got his arms crossed in front of him, like he's some kind of Power Ranger or shit, or, better yet, Claudel decides, like he's on a plane about to crash and this is what the stewardess with the nice ass and too much makeup told him to do in case of a water landing.

Claudel almost felt sorry for the dude, but business was business. Before the guy could get in any more Power Ranger defense positions, Claudel said, "Hey, now." That was something he'd picked up from a TV character; he couldn't even remember what show anymore, but he liked the way it sounded, and decided to make it his calling card. "Hey, now," he said again. He had the bat out in front of him and swung quickly and efficiently at the man's knee. One swing was enough, a short, compact chop, the way Billy Madlock used to do it with the Pirates in the late seventies. Claudel heard the pop, and he knew the man must've heard it, too.

Now came the shitty part. The man howling, and Claudel had to wait until he was done to let the man know what this was all about. And here comes the nice-looking wife out of the kitchen. She has a look like Jackie O, or Mary Tyler Moore back when she was Dick Van Dyke's wife and wore those tight little pants. And she's trying to scream, but no sound's coming out. Probably seeing the first real live black man in her whole life, he thinks, and here he is right in her own house, and he's holding a baseball bat.

"Stay right there, baby," said Claudel. "Else I'm gonna give your man another poke." She leaned against the wall and crossed her hands over her chest. *Was she a Power Ranger, too?*

"What do you want?" said the man, sounding almost like a little kid, curled up in a fetal type position and holding his knee. Claudel knew that wasn't gonna help it none. Nothing really helps until they give you the painkillers.

"I'm just here to deliver a message," said Claudel and took a quick look over at Mary Tyler Moore, making sure she wasn't going for the phone. "Your boy, Eric?"

The man said, "What about him?" at the same time a breathy little cry escaped from the woman.

"Yeah, well," said Claudel. "Shit, he owe a lot a money to my boss, dig?" He liked to use words like *dig*, like he was a bad guy on *Shaft*. Bad guys had more character back then. Now, most of the criminals he saw got all types of body armor and heavy artillery, and no one says shit like *dig* anymore.

"For what?"

"The kid likes to bet NBA games," said Claudel, looking over at the lady again and smiling. She did look nice. Good sized tits rising and falling with her scared breathing. "But you can't bet them games. It always come down to free throws or some scrub hittin' a trey in garbage time ... you get killed bettin' them games."

"So you're a ... bookie," said the lady in her breathy voice, like she's workin' a one nine hundred number or some shit, trying to hold it together, but coming off sexy by accident.

"No ma'am," said Claudel. "I provide a collection service, and if y'all can't come up with the cash by the end of the week, people gonna lose more than a knee cap, also called the patella, hooked up by the ACL and the MCL, ligaments, joints, tendons, muscles. Complex shit, tough to put back together."

She looked at her husband and then back at Claudel. "Why did you let a teenager bet on sports games?" she said, sounding like she scolding a fourth grader.

"I ain't his parents," said Claudel. "You two supposed to be in charge." He pointed the bat at her and then at her husband, who had his face in the carpet, maybe even crying.

***

Back in the Cadillac, Claudel lit a joint and pushed in a Wilson Picket disc, wanted to unwind with some real R&B, funky acts like the very Wicked Wilson Picket and Otis Redding and Sam and Dave, and the white-black fusion bands like Sly and the Family Stone and War, dudes using horns and badass rhythm sections and Negro girls singin' backup ... dudes with some soul.

It pissed him off that nobody was making that kind of music anymore. Kool and the Gang and Earth, Wind, and Fire put together some good shit in the seventies and eighties, but that was the end of it. Rap came along and fucked it up, and so did Whitney and Toni and Mariah and their bullshit power ballads. No funk, no Aretha grooves, just the same old vocal acrobatics, soulless shit.

But Wilson had it, and he was doing *Mustang Sally* when Claudel took a nice easy hit and flipped open his phone to call up Troy Curran, let the man know he'd notified the kid's old man and expected to be paid by Friday.

Troy answered with this new thing he'd been doing, obnoxious as fuck. "Speak," he said in his deep, throaty drill sergeant voice

So Claudel gave it right back to him. "Hey, now," he said.

"What's the status of that job, Claudel?"

"I don't think we gonna have no problems with little Eric's old man," said Claudel, thinking of the fear in that dad's eyes and the nice looking wife. Dude didn't want Claudel anywhere near Mary Tyler Moore.

"Thanks for taking care of it," said Troy, sounding like Claudel was doing something above and beyond, doing the man a personal favor or some shit. This is the job, man. But then Troy kept going. "I got something else I want you to do before you come back over the bridge," he said. "I need you to get yourself over to Gateway and check in on my nephew."

"Troy … TC … T-Rex," said Claudel, letting the nicknames slide off his tongue like R&B lyrics. "Why you wanna make me go over there? You know me and him ain't tight."

"Yeah, yeah," said Troy. "Fuck all that. You're a couple of bitches as far as I'm concerned."

The man was not sounding too patient anymore. "Okay, boss. I'm headed over to Gateway. Tell me what shit you want done."

"You gettin' *paid* enough?" asked Troy.

Claudel could feel it coming. "You do me right," he said.

"Then lose the attitude, will you? I'll find someone else, someone who'll use a gun instead of a fucking baseball bat."

"Hey, now," said Claudel, trying to get the man off this kick, but he wasn't through.

"You could try to be more like my man Andrew, polite and appreciative."

Andrew Tupps was Troy's new bodyguard. South African body-builder and nigger-hater to the core. "Yeah," said Claudel. "Tupps, he good people, a great lover of African culture. You think he digs Wilson Picket?"

"What the fuck you talkin' about, Shanks?"

"No matter," said Claudel. "What can I do for you over in Gateway?"

"Go by Brian's place and see what he's up to. He's not answering his phone, and I need to talk to the boy."

"I ain't going down in that stinky basement with them hellhounds," said Claudel, using the old bluesman, Robert Johnson's, *hellhound,* like in *Hellhounds on My Tail,* R&B having its roots in the Delta blues.

"You don't need to do any of that," said Troy. "Just find him and tell him I need him over here in Marin on Friday evening. I have an excellent business opportunity for the young man."

CHAPTER FIFTEEN

Don and Sid sat in the office of their West Portal restaurant *The Singing Sow*. On the front window was a picture of a chubby pig rubbing her belly. No Chinese food here. San Francisco had enough Chinese and Thai and Korean restaurants, so Don and Sid opened a barbeque joint, simple honest food, big portions, and fair prices. American food. People didn't have to know that the owners weren't any more American than pot stickers. All they had to know was that they were served up hot sausages and chicken and pulled pork and baby back ribs.

Sitting across from Don, who had a plate of barbequed pork ribs resting on his lap and a grease-slicked face to go with it, Sid could hear the clinking of activity in the kitchen. He had Brian Curran's phone and was clicking through the contacts. He'd been making calls all afternoon, and he was only up to G.

He'd used the same greeting the first twenty or so times, and it'd been effective; Sid was sure that the people he'd spoken to were not responsible for the deaths of his two dogs.

He dialed the next number, Randy Green. When a man answered, "Green's Plumbing," Sid said, "You left something over at Brian Curran's house."

"Huh?"

Sid had gotten that response a lot already, but repeated his statement, just to be sure. "You left something over at Brian Curran's house. You have anything you want to say about that?"

"Listen, I don't know who the fuck Brian Curran is, and I don't know what the fuck—"

Sid hung up. This wasn't his man.

Sid was mostly going on instinct, but his thought was that whoever had taken part in the gruesome scene in the basement would give himself away with his voice, his response, his lack of response—something.

"Not the man?" said Don, who was licking his fingers one by one, getting ready to start on the next slab.

"No. But I'll find him, and we'll get our investment money back. I assure you," he said, trying to sound like one of the tough Italians on the HBO program, where, when someone said *I assure you*, he meant it, and took care of the business. Sid was ready to take care of business. He was ready to become a player, and he was going to test out his new *balls*, as the Americans would say, on whoever killed the dogs and cost him all that money.

Don took a big bite out of a fresh rib and dropped the bone back on the plate. "How are you going to get anyone to admit it?" he said, chewing with his back teeth so that he could be heard.

"I will be able to tell from whatever the man says to me when I mention Brian Curran."

"Okay. Then how are you going to get the person to give you the money? What if the person doesn't have the money and can't get it?"

"If the person has the money, I'll get it from him. And if he does not have it, I will kill him. Then people will know not to play games with us."

"What people?" Don asked, putting his plate on the desk then standing up a bit to slide it beyond his own reach.

"People on the street. People who are going to start knowing about us and having fear of us."

Don pulled the plate back; the temptation was too much. As he reached for another rib, he said, "After the people fear us," he paused to dislodge something that had stuck between his teeth, "what will we get then?"

"Respect," said Sid. That was what he wanted from America, even if he had to acquire it by force. "And once a man has respect, he will end up on top, Don. We end up on top." He returned his attention to Brian's contacts.

Don asked the question Sid knew was coming. "On top of what, Sid?"

There were no more G's, so Sid clicked to the next interesting entry: Holiday bookie. Did this listing state the man's job? The others didn't say Flemming doctor or Green plumber.

But there it was: bookie.

But people ran into problems with bookies, and could even get themselves killed. Had this bookie had problems with Brian Curran? Sid tried to put the name together with the image of the tall man on the motorcycle. They seemed to fit for some reason, but the man did not look like a bookie. Weren't bookies old men with felt hats and pencils behind their ears? Cigars?

Don asked again, "On top of what, Sid?"

"It's an expression, man. Shit," he said, and began to dial Chuck Holiday's number.

***

Earlier in the day Chuck had called Stan Winkler and quit his job selling hot dogs, not out of overconfidence about the BBL gig, but because he was sick of it, and he didn't have time to be screwing with sauerkraut and soft pretzels this week. He had the game Friday, the Troy Curran dinner afterward, and the Mr. Fellows meeting Saturday. He didn't need to be fucking around with hot dogs.

He was watching *Cool Hand Luke* on television: Paul Newman putting down fifty eggs while George Kennedy rubbed his bloated belly, getting ready to collect on the bet, nobody believing the little guy could chow down that many in one sitting.

Chuck smiled, admiring the cool of Paul Newman. The phone rang, the betting line. Chuck pulled out a notebook and a pen and answered, laughing to himself at the thought that maybe it was someone who wanted to bet against Luke.

Before he could even say *hello*, he heard a voice say, "You left something over at Brian Curran's house."

Chuck could hear the accent. Chinese? Korean? Something Asian, but he didn't recognize the voice, and didn't have any Asian betters. The mention of Brian Curran stopped his breathing for a moment. He didn't respond, wanted to let it play out in his mind first. It only took a few seconds for him to rerun the part where Brian Curran talked about the Chinese dudes who'd paid him to train the dogs. This had to be one of them, looking for someone to blame.

"You left something over at Brian Curran's house," said the voice again, this time sounding pissed off.

"Who is this?" said Chuck, pretending that the question didn't mean anything to him.

"What were you doing at Brian Curran's house?"

"Who *is* this?" said Chuck, sounding unconcerned, like one of his buddies was on the line, fucking with him, trying to get him to bite. But he knew he was going to have to talk to this dude and find out what he knew and what he wanted.

"What business do you have with Brian Curran?"

"Are we gonna play question Ping-Pong here, or're you gonna tell me who I'm talking to?"

"Do you know where Brian Curran is right now?"

Chuck felt his throat tighten. He thought about Hazel, who was in the back room with a client. This was real, and he was putting her in danger. "Who gave you this number?" He could tell that the person was covering the mouthpiece with his hand and talking to someone else in the room, so Chuck waited and felt the tightness in his throat spread to his chest and arms. Hazel's safety was beginning to slip away from him, and he didn't have a plan.

When the man came back on the line, he said, "We know where you live," and hung up.

Chuck was still holding the receiver in his hand when Hazel and an old woman wearing a red beret came out holding hands, the client saying how glad she was that she had Hazel to keep things in perspective, whatever that meant.

He watched Hazel escort the woman out and then turn toward him. "Who're you talking to?" she said, pointing to the phone, which was still in his hand.

"I think you better go stay with your sister for a few days."

CHAPTER SIXTEEN

Claudel Shanks sat in his Cadillac in front of Brian Curran's house. He pulled the roach out of the ashtray, lit it, pinched it between his thumb and forefinger, and took a nice easy hit. Long and smooth, a kind of tired, lazy hit of the ganja called Chocolate Thai that actually smelled like hot cocoa and mellowed his shit out right quick.

He was trying to figure out what the fuck had happened to Brian Curran, whose house had been trashed, probably by someone looking for something. And what happened to them dogs and all that fencing and chains and shit down in the basement? Where'd it all go?

Claudel took another hit and pushed in the Godfather of Soul, James barking out some grunts and hoots and shit. The Chocolate Thai starting to take effect, and Claudel laughed, picturing the hardest working man in show business cuttin' the stage up, looking double jointed and showing those big teeth and sweating. Hey, now!

He pulled the car out into traffic and decided to head back to San Rafael. He'd call Troy when he got to the bridge. No sense in getting the man all uptight and having to listen to him piss and moan on the phone the whole way back to Marin County. No, he'd wait a bit, let James finish a few more tracks, then give the boss some insights into what went down at the kid's place, let the man know that the nephew's not around, and it looked like some bad shit happened up in there. He had a few guesses about who might be involved. He was just turning up the volume when, hey, whoa. There was Chuck Holiday's place, his Harley parked in the driveway. Claudel pulled over in front of the little house with its basketball hoop hanging above the garage.

That dude could flat out play, had serious handles for a big man. He'd made a nice-ass move the other night against Oakland's team and got a standing ovation. It looked like something a guy would try to do playing H-O-R-S-E in his backyard.

Chuck also had a nice looking lady, he recalled. She could read your mind and shit. Time to go see those two good people.

He took one more hit and listened to the rest of *I Feel Good* before he eased out of the Cadillac and strolled past the Psychic Readings sign. When he got to the door, he gave a fun, semi-stoned knock to the backbeat of an old Isley Brothers tune, but he maybe carried it on a bit too long, because the chick, Hazel, had a funny look on her face, squinting her Chinese eyes, when she opened the door.

Claudel smiled and said, "Hey, now!"

Chuck heard a man's voice and looked over Hazel's shoulder, but he couldn't see a face, only huge black arms wrapped around her waist. He could also hear a deep baritone laugh, smooth and easy, the way he imagined Barry White might laugh if he ever thought something was funny. He knew it had to be Claudel Shanks, ex-minor leaguer who used to play ball on Sundays in the semi-pro league at Big Rec in Golden Gate Park.

Chuck's dad used to take him to watch the games when Chuck was a kid. The Judge always liked baseball better than hoops, so they'd watch a lot of games during the summer, mostly over-the-hill ballplayers and kids trying to make names for themselves. But there was also Claudel Shanks, not old yet, but hobbled by a knee injury. The guy couldn't run anymore, but he could hit the crap out of the ball. Chuck used to stand up when Claudel was up at bat to make sure he could see the ball when it went sailing over the center fielder's head and out toward the concrete stairs in center field.

"Goose," Claudel said. He'd watched Chuck play in the Pro-Am League at Kezar. He'd become a fan of the game. He liked the pace more than baseball, and he liked that more black chicks came to the games. And he was one of the few who still used the old nickname. "What up, my brotha?" He moved toward Chuck, still with one of his arms around Hazel.

Chuck reached for Claudel's hand and said, "Same old shit, Claudel." He smelled something he thought must have been pot, but with the scent of a Hershey Bar or a Kit Kat. Maybe Claudel'd gotten the munchies after smoking a few bowls.

"Well, it's good to see you, man," said Claudel.

"It's good to be seen. What're you doing in Gateway? Looking to play a little one-on-one?"

"Naw, man." Claudel laughed. "Just doin' some business for Curran. He want me to check up on the asshole nephew, few blocks away."

"Did you already go over there?" Chuck asked, flashing back to the bloody scene with the dogs, even though he knew it was all gone, hosed out, probably by the Chinese guys.

"Matter of fact, I did," said Claudel, making his way over to the couch.

Chuck looked at the TV; Hazel was watching SpongeBob.

Then he watched Claudel sit down, taking up two cushions on the couch, his feet barely touching the ground.

Chuck had an idea that might work to take care of the Chinese dudes *and* Troy, but his plan wasn't quite a plan yet. The timing had to be just right. He wanted to finish the business deal with Troy before anything else. He knew what he wanted to happen, but the details of how to get there were still floating around in his brain, waiting to meet each other. Now it looked like he was going to have to play his hand and see if Claudel wanted to go along with him.

Hazel was in the kitchen, and Chuck was still standing when he said, "How's the nephew doing?"

Claudel didn't look away from the cartoon. "Whose nephew?" he said as he started to laugh and point a stubby finger at SpongeBob driving around in an underwater boat with a fat lady fish.

"Troy Curran's nephew, Brian. You said you went over to check up on him."

Claudel looked away from SpongeBob, who was crashing the boat. "Yeah," he said. "Brian's not around, and his pad's been done over."

"What do you mean?" asked Chuck.

"Somebody looking for something. Pulled all the drawers out, knocked over tables and chairs and shit." Claudel stared at Chuck and shifted both of his feet to the floor. "You know somethin' about it?"

"I know something about it," said Chuck as he sat down in the chair opposite Claudel. SpongeBob was making himself into all sorts of other shapes, making himself look like the starfish, only keeping his own eyes and daffy grin. Chuck watched the underwater scene, wondering if mobsters still put guys in concrete galoshes and dropped them in the big drink.

"Give it up, Goose," said Claudel. "What happened to Brian?"

Chuck paused, wanting to get it right, but before he could speak, there was a knock at the door, followed by the sound of Hazel flip-flopping down the hall.

CHAPTER SEVENTEEN

Hazel opened the door to two angry-looking Chinese men, both wearing black suits with white shirts and thin black ties. One of them had a tiny reptilian face, twitchy and nervous. In the brief moment before they barged past her, Hazel thought they looked like Chinese Blues Brothers.

As the men peered into the living room, Hazel looked over their heads and watched Chuck's face change. He looked like he was capable of doing bad things. Were these men the reason why Chuck wanted her to get her stuff packed and ready to go stay with her sister? She'd never seen such a look of intensity on Chuck's face, not even during playoffs. This was a different kind of game—for both of them.

Claudel broke the silence by pointing at the new arrivals and chuckling like an old boat motor starting up.

Hazel stood behind the visitors, so she could only imagine their serious faces.

No one moved.

Then the small one turned to Hazel and said something in Chinese, which caused Claudel to laugh again.

Hazel smiled—she couldn't help it with Claudel's laughing in the background—and said, "I'm sorry. I don't speak Chinese."

The other man turned to face Hazel; both men were staring at her. The smaller one spoke again, in English. "My friend, he want palm read."

"Friend" appeared surprised, but shrugged at Hazel, who looked over his head at Chuck, who was standing behind him, expressionless once more. He nodded, so Hazel said, "Okay, let's go in the back."

***

Chuck wasn't going to allow Hazel to be alone with the stranger for very long. While the little one was looking down the hallway, Chuck whispered to Claudel, "Gotta frisk 'im."

Claudel didn't hear him right, and said. without whispering, "No, I don't gotta piss, but I think I'll get goin' now.

Chuck peeked over at the little guy, who was still standing with his arms folded over his chest, trying to look bad, but not making it; he was just too fucking small. Chuck assumed he was the guy who spoke to him on the phone, but he didn't know how much English the little dude had. So Chuck decided to try again with Claudel, just in case the guy pulled out some kind of ninja star or something. "We gotta search this dude," he said to Claudel, probably loud enough for the little ninja to hear. He put on his most serious look, hoping to make his message clear to Claudel, whose eyes were bloodshot and glassy.

Claudel had been getting ready to leave. He was moving slowly, almost seemed to be drifting across the room, but when he got about halfway, things changed. The Chinese man started to reach for something in his pants, and Claudel's slow, fluid movement became quick and powerful. With one hand, he snatched the man's wrist, and, with the other, grabbed him by the back of the neck and started to lift him off the ground. The captive swung a few times with his free hand, but Claudel didn't seem to feel the spastic blows. "You want to search the motherfucker 'fore he take my eye out with one a' those baby fists?"

"Yeah," said Chuck, staying cool as he walked over and patted the man down. Nothing exotic, but he did have a gun. Here for a palm reading. "Do you mind holding him while I go check on Hazel?" He was already moving toward the hallway and looking at the gun; it was the first time he'd ever touched one.

Claudel said, "I may hold the motherfucker by his nuts, he don't stop swingin'."

Chuck stopped and walked back into the living room. Claudel was sitting on the couch and holding the dude in a headlock.

"Can I let him go now," asked Claudel.

"Just one minute. Do you know how to take the safety off this thing?"

"Who you plannin' on shooting?"

"Nobody," said Chuck. "But I don't know if this other dude's holding a gun on Hazel or something, so I want to have some security if I need it."

"Give it here." Claudel took the gun with his free hand and started to adjust something. The Chinese guy took a grab for the gun. Claudel didn't pull it away from the man's outstretched hand. He simply squeezed the man's head tighter under his arm, his black bicep stretching over the man's cheek.

Chuck heard a little grunt and watched the man's hand release its hold on the gun. Claudel said, "Good to go," and handed the weapon back to Chuck.

"All I gotta do is pull the trigger?" asked Chuck, practicing a little bit, raising the gun and pointing it at the Chinese man.

"That's right," said Claudel. "Good to go. Now go point that thing somewhere else."

Chuck held the gun in front of him and walked straight to the door, ready to start barking orders at the man with Hazel. He opened the door quickly and poked the gun in first. When his head followed, he scanned the room, and then he let out a long breath. Hazel was holding the man's hand and running her finger along the network of lines, saying something about the man's business—a restaurant—when Chuck interrupted the reading by tapping the gun against the guy's temple, something he thought Clint Eastwood might do.

Hazel was still holding the man's hand when she said, "Whose is that?"

"The little guy's."

"What're *you* doing with it?"

"I thought this one might be trying to pull something in here."

"He's cool," said Hazel and nodded at the man, who nodded at Chuck. Then she looked at Chuck and asked, "You ever fire one of those before?"

Chuck shrugged and shook his head.

"How's it feel?"

He turned the gun back and forth in his hand, then bobbed it up and down as if he were going to guess its weight. "Not bad."

CHAPTER EIGHTEEN

Troy sat on a cushioned wicker couch on his front porch in San Rafael, enjoying the panoramic view of Mount Tamalpais, as the sun dipped below the jagged peak in western Marin County. He was sipping ice tea—he'd mostly given up booze years ago—and reading a paperback mystery when security man Andrew Tupps and Troy's wife Gabby walked onto the deck. Gabby sat next to her husband.

Troy placed his book on the end table and smiled at her.

"So what's the story with this dinner tomorrow?" she asked as she flipped her black hair behind her shoulders.

Troy took a long drink from his iced tea, then placed it on the table next to the book. "Just a business dinner." He didn't like to get into too much detail. She knew where he got his money, but she didn't need to know all the particulars. What she needed to do was keep the house nice and stay in good shape.

"Well, who's coming?" she asked and crossed her long brown legs at the knee. She was wearing a sundress with a slit up the side, and Troy could see her leg all the way up to the edge of her underwear. He shot a quick glance at Andrew Tupps, but he wasn't taking any notice, being a good team player, looking out at the sunset and keeping his mouth shut.

"A few people," said Troy. "Guy named Holiday and my nephew and Holiday's girl." He let it hang for a minute while he pictured Hazel in his mind. She didn't have Gabby's legs, but what a face.

"What about Claudel?"

"Count on him, too. The big fella doesn't like to miss a meal."

Tupps, who hadn't seemed to be paying attention, laughed. Troy understood that Tupps didn't have anything personal against Claudel. He just didn't like black people. He'd once told Troy that he thought they were dirty. He didn't like the way they talked, smelled, walked … everything about blacks pissed him off.

"Is Holiday the really tall guy with the blond hair?" asked Gabby as she reached over Troy, brushing her breasts against the side of his face. She grabbed his tea and took a sip, holding a piece of ice between her lips for a moment before dropping it back into the glass.

"Yeah," he said. "You met him before. Asian girlfriend. They run a shitty little book outta Gateway Village, take care of Brian's bets over there."

Gabby nodded. She glanced at Andrew Tupps, with his T-shirt about five sizes too small stretched across his ridiculously massive back.

"My nephew leave any messages with you?" he asked.

Gabby closed her eyes and tilted her head toward the darkening sky. "Not that I can think of," she said. "No, I can't remember the last time I talked to him. Why?"

"I need to talk to him, so's I can get him over here tomorrow night. I got Claudel over there looking for him now."

"Your *nephew* is probably out committing some crime," she said. "Stealing purses from old ladies or ripping off a lemonade stand or something."

"All right," said Troy. "Enough of that shit. He's my brother's kid, and we're gonna get him straightened out, give him a little book to work by himself. Spending money, something to do when he wakes up in the morning. That's how I got started."

"Yeah, Troy, baby, but he's not you. I think he might be too dumb and too mean."

"He ain't dumb," said Troy. "And meanness can work for you in this business. Now if that fuckin' Shanks ever reports in, we can set this thing up with Holiday, give Brian a chance to prove himself, and everybody'll be happy."

"What about Claudel? Do you think he'll be happy?"

"What *about* Claudel?" he said. "Fuck Claudel."

Tupps laughed again. His hands were on the rail and his shoulders were moving with his laughter when he repeated, "Yes. Fuck Claudel."

Gabby was looking at the big body builder again when she said, "I just thought that Claudel'd maybe want his own book, too, y'know?"

Troy gave Gabby a look, trying to get her to realize she was talking too much, making a fucking idiot out of herself in front of Tupps. "Claudel's just a blood from the 'hood," he said. "He'd fuck up an operation like this in about a week." Troy knew he was pleasing his muscle in the T-shirt, so he kept on. "Guy like Claudel might be able to run crack in the projects, fuck up his own people and make some coin, but being a bookie's a little more complicated." He was starting to enjoy himself, like playing a character in the movies. "Claudel Shanks is happy to be driving around in his pimp-mobile, listening to little Stevie Wonder, another blind, happy brotha."

Tupps turned around and said, "Stevie Wonder," with a laugh. Troy wondered if the South African would get a kick out of hearing *Ebony and Ivory … together in perfect harmony …*

***

Claudel was still sweating. He'd had some fun taking the Chinese punks out to their car. He held the gun on the other while he dragged the little guy by one of his feet all the way across the front lawn. It wasn't much harder than pulling a bag of catcher's gear across a baseball diamond. He didn't mean to hurt him, but he wanted to humiliate him, teach him a lesson. It really was an accident when Claudel let the man hit his little head on Hazel's sign out near the sidewalk.

But Claudel didn't say sorry. He told the taller one to drive, and he stuffed the little one through the window into the back. In the process, a shoe came off in Claudel's hand. For a moment, he thought about throwing it in, but he changed his mind and held onto it.

Now he leaned against the kitchen counter, with the tiny black shoe in front of him. It looked like a knickknack from a gift shop. Claudel shifted his eyes over to Chuck and Hazel, who were hunched over the kitchen table, looking like they'd just done a motherfuckin' marathon, even though Claudel had done all the heavy lifting. "So you saw the asshole get eaten up by pit bulls?" said Claudel, shaking his head and wondering how did this clean dude get mixed up in all this dirty shit?

"He didn't get eaten," said Chuck. "The dog just jumped up and locked onto his throat."

"And you beat that motherfucker off with a hammer? That's some shit, Goose. *Serious.*"

"Yeah, but it looks like our friends from the Orient want to be reimbursed for their loss, and they think I owe 'em for all the cash they were gonna make off those fight dogs. Somehow, they know I was in the house when all that shit went down, and they want me to pay, one way or another."

Claudel knew it was more than that. He'd seen these kind of ghetto Asians trying to cut their teeth on the street. "Naw, man. It ain't just the money they was interested in. They thought the dogs gonna make 'em thugs. Can't you see that little Jackie Chan-Bruce Lee motherfucker wannabe a persuader? He wanna be a street cowboy, a hardboiled egg. It ain't the money. The man wanna be a heavy, and now you give him a reason to flex his muscles, prove himself on you, get street cred."

"Okay," said Chuck. "I can understand where maybe they'd be like that, but I think I got a way to get rid of 'em so they'll leave me alone, only I need you to call your boss for me and tell him a little lie."

"Now why I wanna do somethin' like that to a man signs my paychecks?" Claudel said, smiling, interested. "And what does Troy Curran have to do with the two Chinese cowboys?"

"You get actual *paychecks*?"

"Figure of speech. But he the man pays me is what I'm sayin'."

"Okay, that's what I thought," said Chuck, kind of smiling and shaking his head a bit, like he's got something cooking. "You know my deal with the BBL?"

Claudel nodded. It sounded like a sweet deal, someone paying you to do something you like to do for free.

"Well, Troy Curran knows about it, too, and he wants to buy my business since it looks like I'll be moving to England."

"Yeah. I heard he do that occasionally, but that don't have nothin' to do with the Chinamens."

"Forget about them for a minute," Chuck said. "I want to get back to this deal with Curran and my franchise. Y'know what he wants to do with it, with the list of my betters?"

"Yeah," said Claudel and laughed. "He wanna take all they money."

"No, he doesn't." Chuck put on a serious face and said, "He wants to give the business to his nephew, let *him* make the easy money." He waited a moment and gave Claudel a smirk, squinting his eyes and saying, "Not *you*, Claudel, who worked for the man for years, but that little asshole, who sicced his dogs on me. That's who Troy wants to bestow this great gift on. He'd like to hand all this free money over to a dead fight-dog trainer."

Catching on to the man's game, Claudel said, "Chuck Holiday, you think you gonna work me into a lava 'cause the man don't wanna cut me a slice of the melon? Shit. Papa Curran never give his nigga no gifts before. Why start now?"

Chuck narrowed his eyes even more, and Claudel felt himself trying to look like he didn't give a shit, but he was also trying to figure out whether or not he really *did* give a shit. It was true that Curran had never offered him anything beyond his current job breaking kneecaps, but that was his job. It was what he did. Nothin' wrong with it.

But maybe this was a turning point. Maybe Goose had something up his sleeve, could make it so he didn't have to be Troy Curran's line-doggie no more.

Brian Curran, even when he was alive, couldn't run no sports book operation.

"Motherfucker," said Claudel as he opened the refrigerator and took out a bottle of beer. Before he opened it, he asked, "So what's this little lie you want me to tell Mr. Curran?"

CHAPTER NINETEEN

They were still on the front porch when Gabby Cortez-Curran put her hand on her husband's thigh and said, "Honey, I think I'm going downtown to do some shopping."

"Grocery or clothes?" he said without looking up from his book.

"I just want to pick up a few things. There's a sale—"

"Groceries or more clothes?" he said, putting his thumb in the middle of the book and closing it on his lap.

Gabby was getting fed up. *More* clothes, he says, like she'd married him to expand her wardrobe. But she didn't have time to stir the pot right now, so she said, "If you don't want me to go …."

Troy stared out at the silhouette of the mountain against the sky, now fading into a deep post-sunset blue. His cell phone rang, and he answered it before he could respond to Gabby.

"Speak," he yelled, and kept staring at the mountain.

Gabby stood up and peered into the house through the window at the waiting Andrew Tupps lingering in the half-light of the foyer.

"It's about fucking time," Troy said, then listened to whatever the caller had to say. Probably Claudel *reporting in.*

Leaning against a console table inside the house, Tupps was swinging a set of keys around his finger, his lips gathered together in a whistler's pucker. When he and Gabby made eye contact, he shrugged and made a big production out of checking his watch. Gabby smiled and looked back at Troy, who was closing up his phone.

"What's going on?" she said as she looked at her husband and tried to imagine him with Andrew Tupps's body, Troy's little carrot head perched on top of that mountain of abs and pectorals and whatever else there was bulging under Tupps's tan skin.

Troy gave her a fraction of a smile, looked at the phone in his hand and said, "Claudel." Then he shook his head and asked, "Why's he so down on my nephew?"

Gabby didn't feel like getting into it. Nobody liked the little prick. But Andrew was waiting, and she didn't have time to list all of Brian Curran's flaws. "Claudel doesn't like many people," she said.

"That right? I thought he was an easy-rollin' eight ball."

"I don't know," said Gabby. She wanted to get out of there, but she was also curious about what was going on with Claudel. "Are all them gonna be here tomorrow night?"

"I hope so," he said. "Claudel says he must've just missed Brian, 'cause the dishwasher was still running when he got inside the house.

The kid's gotta be around somewhere. Claudel left him a note and told him it was important that Brian *get his Archie Bunker cracker ass* over here for the dinner." Then Troy half-smiled again. "What the hell's wrong with Archie Bunker?"

"Before my time," said Gabby. "He's the guy from *Heat of the Night*, right?"

"Yeah," said Troy, with a look of surprise, his thin red eyebrows arched up like he couldn't believe his ears. "Good knowledge," he said. "Sometimes you surprise me, Sugarpop. You never heard of the *Rockford Files* or *Starsky and Hutch*, but you know that Archie was on *Heat of the Night*. You know more than you let on. You're a funny gal, huh?"

"I know a lot of things," she said. And she did. Like the fact that Troy wasn't as big an asshole as his nephew, but he was still a rotten egg. He was her husband and gave her an allowance, but how could she trust a man like that? A man who'd tell Claudel to go out and crack people's knees up.

She looked down at Troy, then over his shoulder and saw Andrew still waiting, inspecting his tricep, in the hallway. Troy followed her glance. "What's he doin' in there?"

"He's gonna drive me down to Fourth Street."

"He's my security man, not your fuckin' driver, Gabby."

***

Andrew Tupps was driving so hard that Gabby thought the bed would break or that she would get hurt this time. They were in the Crescent Moon Motel, just off Highway 101 near the Central San Rafael Exit. Andrew was being methodical, thrusting as if he were pumping iron, doing his squats in time to that same heavy metal thumping that he blasted in the in-law apartment under Gabby's house that Andrew had converted into a workout room.

The sheets were cool, and Gabby was thinking about how this wasn't anything like having sex with Troy, who'd already be lathered into a heavy sweat by the time he'd wrestled off his own pajamas. The sheets were always drenched by the time he finished one of his marathon sessions, during which she'd give up during the first five minutes, knowing that he'd never quite find the right spot, while he'd continue on, working to find his rhythm, always an inspired effort, although mostly ineffectual.

Sex with Andrew was different. They were both in great shape and hardly perspired at all. Simple and efficient, the missionary position got them both there every time. Ten or fifteen minutes, a quick shower, and back to the house, no one the wiser, almost like one of those abbreviated workout videos on TV, like *Eight Minute Abs* or *Buns of Steel*, just fit it into your day whenever you have a chance, and feel good when you do.

So she didn't understand what was going on this time. They'd found the right rhythm quickly, and she'd already finished and was almost positive that he had, too, but he kept going. And now it was starting to hurt.

"Hey," she said, no longer out of breath.

He immediately rolled off her and covered his face with his hand, his huge chest was heaving.

"What're y'doin', Andrew?" she asked, trying to get him to look at her, but he rolled over and faced the wall.

"What's going on?" she asked.

"I'm angry."

"What?" she said, trying figure out how the man all of sudden in the middle of sex got angry.

"I'm angry that I have to share you with Mr. Curran."

"What?" she said again, not sure how she was supposed to feel about what he'd said. Flattered? Scared?

"I'm in love with you, Gabby." He rolled back over to face her.

"What?"

"Why is that hard for you to understand?" He jumped out of the bed and stood naked in front of her, like he was posing for a sculpture class at the junior college.

"Don't you love me back?"

"What?" she said for the fourth time and realized she should probably say something else. "Where's this coming from, Andrew?" She pulled the sheet up to her chin, suddenly self-conscious about her nakedness. "And could you please put some pants on?"

CHAPTER TWENTY

Cunningham had taken to mixing his Jameson with 7 Up and driving around town, sipping right out of the can, not trying to get drunk, but pouring enough in to take the edge off. He found a parking spot near Kezar Stadium and walked up the block to The Judge's. He took one more drink before he dropped the can in a public garbage can on Carl Street, pretty close to the house, but definitely out of view. The Judge didn't like Cunningham drinking. He'd once told Cunningham to clean it up or go back to making heroin busts in the Tenderloin and doing illegal searches on gangbangers up in Hunter's Point. So Cunningham started cutting the booze with a little soda. He actually liked the taste; it was pretty refreshing when the 7 Up was still cold.

When he got to the house, he walked around and knocked on the side door. He didn't like to go through the front door because he'd have to talk with Cleo, who was a nice lady, but Cunningham preferred the first Mrs. H. She had a wicked sense of humor and could shut The Judge up with a couple of well-timed zingers when she had a mind to do it. Cleo just wanted to give him things: coffee, a slice of angel food cake, a cigar, new socks. She just liked to give people stuff, and he wasn't all that comfortable taking anything except his paychecks from either of the Holidays.

When The Judge answered the door, he was hunched over a bit, holding three television remote controls. "You know anything about cable TV?" he asked and stepped aside to make room for Cunningham to move past him into the den.

"I lost my remote control about a month ago, so I don't watch TV anymore."

The Judge frowned. "What the hell do you do when you're at home?" He started clicking one of the remotes at the TV, but the channel was stuck on ice skating.

"My wife left all her paperbacks. I been going through two or three books a week."

The Judge dropped the remote controls on top of the TV and sat down on one of the leather chairs. "What're you gonna do when you've read all the books?"

"I guess I'll start looking for my remote control again," said Cunningham. "How's the back?'

"Chiropractor got everything aligned," he said. "You take care of the Evans situation?"

"In a manner of speaking." Cunningham started to smile, but he was able to get his lips under control before he said, "I made a deal with the old man."

"Dan," said The Judge, "tell me you've taken care of the situation."

Cunningham thought back to the doctor's flat. How the pills had gone so well with the Jameson, given him a nice full-body buzz, loosened him up for when Marta, the librarian, took him into the other room. The two of them had a nice little connection. Maybe it was the pills. Maybe not. But they'd been hanging out since they met at the doctor's. She was waiting out in the van even while he checked in with The Judge. "If you can be a little patient," he said, "I can have the doctor out of there in thirty days. Does that work for you?"

"You're telling me he agreed to vacate the apartment?"

"He just needs thirty days."

Cleo poked her head into the room. "Oh," she said. "I didn't know you were here, Dan."

"I came in the side door."

"I'm glad you're here. I have something for you." She slipped back out and Cunningham could hear her feet tapping up the stairs.

"Why does she always wanna give me stuff?" he asked.

"Beats me," said The Judge. "All she gives me is a pain in the ass."

"Oh, yeah?" By doing what, making you dinner? Doing your laundry? What?"

"Spending my money, wise guy. That's how she inflicts pain in my ass."

Cleo returned the room just as The Judge finished his sentence. "Please don't use that kind of language in the house, sweetie," she said, and held up a big white cowboy hat, the kind Cunningham had seen country singer Brad Paisley wear. "I bought the hat for this one over here," she said, gesturing with it toward The Judge. "But his head is too darn big, so I thought you might get some use out of it, Dan."

Cunningham looked over at The Judge. He couldn't picture him in a cowboy hat. The man sometimes wore a visor when he golfed, but Cunningham couldn't picture him in any other kind. Beret? Sombrero? Ship's Captain's hat? No way.

"It's called a Stetson," said Cleo. "Top of the line."

"Oh," said Cunningham. "I could definitely get some use out of that hat. It's beautiful." He walked over to Cleo and let her put it on his head. Then he tilted it down a bit until he could feel it close to his eyebrows. He winked at The Judge and then said to Cleo, "What do you think?"

"Brilliant," she said, smiling as she left the room.

"You know how much that cost?" said The Judge.

"A lot," said Cunningham. "It's a Stetson, for God's sake."

"And you're keeping it?"

"You know how Cleo gets if I refuse a gift," said Cunningham, looking out in the hall for a mirror. He couldn't find one, so he came back into the den and studied his reflection in the window. Not bad. When he wore a baseball cap, people said he looked like the old ball player Bill Buckner. But with the cowboy hat on and a bit more grey in his mustache, he had a different look, maybe a little like Sam Elliot in one of his cowboy roles.

The Judge shook his head. "You know you look ridiculous?"

"Ridiculous like a fox," Cunningham said and pushed the hat up with one finger, like he'd seen so many cowboys do in the movies. It felt natural.

"Okay, back to business. How'd you get the doctor out?"

"I didn't have to use violence. I reasoned with the man. We came to a gentleman's agreement."

"I want that quack out of that apartment in thirty days."

"He'll be out," Cunningham assured him.

"You don't want to tell me how this is going to happen?"

"You really want know?"

"Just get him the fuck out."

Cunningham wasn't really listening. He was wondering what Marta was going to think of his new Stetson.

"Keep me posted on anything else going on this week," he said.

The Judge grabbed his datebook off the big mahogany desk. As he was flipping through it, he said, "You've been doing good work keeping an eye on the kid." Then he took an envelope out of the inside pocket of his jacket and handed it to Cunningham.

Cunningham put it in his own inside pocket. "Much obliged, partner," he said, sliding his fingers along the brim of the hat.

CHAPTER TWENTY-ONE

"Why do you want to go to your dad's?" asked Hazel as she hopped on the back of Chuck's motorcycle and wrapped her arms around his waist.

He yelled over the rumble of the engine, "I just wanna ask him for something before we try this other thing with Troy and Claudel and the Chinese."

Hazel had noticed that Chuck had taken to referring to the two men who had stopped by the house simply as "the Chinese," as if the entire country was out to get them.

"I'm just starting to get a little nervous about all this," he said and turned partially around. She let go of his waist and leaned back. She was wearing her helmet and tilting her head to the side so that she could see the top of his face over his shoulder. "If everything doesn't work out just right with the setup, things could get dangerous."

"How?"

"Even though the Chinese are clowns, they could be dangerous. Maybe Claudel's right and they just want to hurt me to prove they're tough. Who knows?"

Hazel wondered if Chuck was talking about some specific danger or if he just had a *bad feeling*. "What do you think's going happen?" She took off the helmet, not liking that Chuck's voice sounded muffled.

"There's just a lot of *what ifs*," he said. "Like what if Claudel's not as good at acting as he is at swinging a bat? And what if the Chinese guys come back to settle up before things get going? And what if Troy somehow finds out about Brian before he pays us for the franchise tomorrow after the game? Y'think he'll wanna buy it anyway?"

Hazel *had* thought about all these things. Running a sports book was risky. Rummaging through women's purses while they were in the bathroom before a psychic reading was risky. That was part of the game. All the risks they'd been taking since they'd been together were just *part of the game.*

But seeing Chuck with the gun the day before had been something different. That was taking things to a different level, and it was tough to figure out if it was worth it. "I don't know what to think anymore," she said. "I kinda got it in my head that going to England would be great for us, getting away from this place, seeing something different ...." She was tired of trying to see his face over his shoulder, so she got off the bike and held the helmet like a football under her arm, standing on the curb and looking him in the eye. "What're you gonna ask your dad for?"

"Money."

***

Chuck's dad and his second wife lived in a small, elegant Victorian flat in Cole Valley, between the northern half of Twin Peaks and the western edge of Haight-Ashbury. Chuck had grown up in the Avenues; he still wasn't quite used to his father living so close to Jerry Garcia's old stomping grounds.

Outside the house, a long-haired girl was sitting in the passenger seat of a van. Chuck couldn't get a good look at her; she had her seat pushed way back and her head was against the headrest. In his mind, the van didn't seem to fit with the neighborhood.

When Chuck knocked on the front door of the big house, he was half hoping that The Judge wouldn't be home, but when he heard the sounds of someone fiddling with the lock, he looked at Hazel and took a deep breath.

Chuck's stepmother, Cleo, opened the door and smiled. "What a wonderful surprise," she said in a stage voice, apparently to alert Chuck's dad. "Come on in—and bring your little friend."

"Thanks," said Chuck. "C'mon, little friend." He grabbed Hazel's hand.

From the small anteroom, Chuck could see his father watching TV in the den. "Fuck these Russian judges," he said and waved Chuck and Hazel into the room as if he'd been expecting them.

Chuck heard the side door shut. He could feel a slight chill in the room, but he didn't get a look at whoever had been visiting.

"You're watching women's figure skating, Dad?"

"Cable's out."

Chuck's father seemed to like Hazel a lot more than he liked Chuck, who knew that Hazel was aware of that when she said, "It's okay to get in touch with your feminine side, Judge. The experts say almost everyone has some gay tendencies."

"Aw, Hazel," said The Judge. "Why do y'have to give an old man grief? I thought you people were supposed to show respect for elders?"

"My dad's Irish, Judge, and I think he'd appreciate my giving you a little grief for this," she said, then pretended to be interested in the television. "What's on next? Martha Stewart?"

"Yeah, well, that's pretty funny, but the reason I'm watching this is I'm being patriotic here. Something about which your generation doesn't have a clue."

Hazel winked at Chuck and said, "You got us there. *Your* generation still had the American Dream to fall in love with." Then she walked up and put her hands on The Judge's shoulders. "We're just struggling to get by, living day by day, paycheck to paycheck."

The Judge looked up at Hazel and said, "Well, that's what you get when you live with this guy over here who sells wieners for a living."

Chuck had heard enough and thought this was a good time to jump in. "Dad, I got a pretty good job offer the other day. I don't have to sell hot dogs anymore."

"What about your *other* entrepreneurial endeavors?" asked his father, arching an eyebrow, then letting his mouth droop.

"I'm not sure what you're talking about," Chuck said, realizing for the first time that his father somehow knew about his *other job*. It didn't surprise him. Ever since he was a kid, he'd never been able to get away with anything. It was as if the old man had informants all over the city. Maybe he still did. "But listen," Chuck said, trying to take the discussion back to his BBL offer before his dad started talking about illegal gambling and the penal code, "this is a good job. Only thing is, I gotta move outta the city."

"I hope you're not thinking of moving back east because I—"

"Dad, the job is playing professional basketball in England."

Hazel still stood behind Chuck's father, her hands on his shoulders; the old man was breathing easy, watching the TV again. An Asian ice skater was crying as her scores were posted. Her coach sat next to her whispering in her ear, but she kept crying. The camera actually moved in for a close up; all the viewers could see was her face, tears streaming down, until the coach moved in front of her and blocked the camera.

"You think you can handle it this time?" asked The Judge.

"What do y'mean *this time*?"

"Charles, the last time you left home and had to deal with responsibility ... let's just say things didn't work out as well as they could have."

"Dad," said Chuck, "I've been living on my own now for more than a year. You kicked me out to teach me a lesson—or because you were embarrassed, whatever, and I've been taking responsibility ever since." Chuck knew that was a stretch, especially since The Judge somehow seemed to know he was a bookie. "Now I'm ready to take advantage of this opportunity."

The Judge put his hand on Hazel's and rose to his feet. He was about an inch shorter than Chuck, but still towered over Hazel, who was standing at his side looking at Chuck. Her head was just above The Judge's massive belly, which began its expanse beneath his chest and extended far beyond his beltline. It wasn't flab. It was a rock hard mound of flesh that he'd carried around like a sack of cement mix for the past five years or so, and it wasn't going away. Chuck hoped he'd already be in England when his dad had the heart attack which was bound to happen. He didn't want to be there to see it. He could imagine his father telling Cleo that Chuck had caused the heart attack by screwing up the Cal scholarship. *That was the beginning of the end,* he could hear his father whining as Cleo fluffed his pillow and gave him his heart medication.

No, he wanted no part of that, but he did notice that his dad was starting to look a little older, hunched. "What's going on with your back," said Chuck, nodding at his dad's posture.

"Wrenched it on the golf course. But I'm all right. Went to the chiropractor." Then he looked at Hazel and said, "If I'd known you were coming over, I would have had you stick some needles in my back. I hear that'll take the pain away quick."

"If I knew you were hurt, I would have brought my kit," she said and smiled.

"You really do that shit?"

"No, Judge," she said and crossed her arms. "And I don't know karate, either."

The Judge looked at his son. "So, are you here to say goodbye?"

"Yeah. And to ask for a favor."

Hazel stood next to Chuck as if to suggest that the favor was for both of them. To a certain extent, it was.

If The Judge would float them a loan, they might be able to walk away from Troy's proposal, let the Chinese think they'd scared him out of town, and play dumb about the Brian Curran incident. With some cash, they could split and not look back.

"What can I do you for?" asked The Judge, keeping his blank expression.

"Well, we'd," Chuck switched to *we* now, since Hazel seemed to be helping the cause, "we'd like you to take a look at this contract." He pulled the folded pages from his back pocket. "Then, if it seems to be on the up and up, we wanted to see if maybe there was a chance you could loan us some money to get us started over there. We'd pay you back as soon as I've gotten a couple of regular paychecks."

Even though Chuck was taller than his father, he still felt as though he were looking up at him as he handed his dad the contract.

Chuck and Hazel shared the leather ottoman and watched an old episode of *I Dream of Jeannie* on Channel 44, Chuck wondering why the astronaut didn't retire to some tropical island and let the magic chick keep granting him wishes. The premise was more ridiculous than the folks on *Gilligan's Island* not being able to build a boat, or the *Bewitched* dude not letting his wife use her powers.

By the end of the show, The Judge was reviewing the opening page again. Then he looked up over his reading glasses and said, "It's all legal, but it's not the kind of thing that's going to make you a rich man. You do understand the exchange rate?"

"We got all that, Dad," Chuck said. "We just need a few dollars to get set up. The salary'll be enough for us to live and maybe save some."

"Yes, I understand that, Chuck." He pushed up his glasses with his free hand and rested them on top of his head. "But you probably know what I have to say."

Chuck stood up. "No, Dad, I don't know what you have to say."

"Now, Chuck, when we parted ways after your incident, I thought I was clear that you were going to be on your own. You said you wanted to be a big boy and stop going to school, so I told you go ahead."

He stopped, and Chuck remembered the yelling that had happened that day, The Judge telling him he should stay in school even though he wasn't playing basketball, and Chuck telling his dad that the only reason he was going to school was to play. And more yelling, followed by Chuck grabbing some of his stuff, telling his dad to fuck off, and walking out of the house.

"So that's your decision?" asked Chuck, pride making him unable to look his father in the eye anymore.

"That's it."

CHAPTER TWENTY-TWO

Ten minutes later, The Judge, his address book resting on his lap, sat in the big leather chair in his den. He held a glass of scotch in one hand and leafed through the address book with his other. When he got to Bill Fellows's number, he reached for the phone and started to punch it in. Cleo came to see if he wanted something to eat, and he told her to take a hike.

Fellows picked up on the first ring. "Go ahead."

"Bill," said The Judge. "Holiday here."

"What can I do for you?"

"I just spoke with Chuck, and I took a look at that contract."

"Everything's okay, right? That's the best I could do."

"It's not a whole lot. And it doesn't provide any dough to get him set up over there, airfare, lodging, things like that."

"It's the standard contract we give these kids unless we're dealing with some kinda superstar," said Fellows. "This ain't the NBA, y'know."

"No, I get that. But I don't understand how they can afford to fly over there before they even get a paycheck."

"Judge, this is the best I can do for you," said Fellows. Then he added, "My bet is most of these kids' parents give 'em money to get started until they get their salaries."

"Yeah, okay," The Judge said and hung up. He wouldn't do that, though, would not write the boy a check. That'd defeat the purpose. Chuckie needed to do this on his own, prove to himself that he could take some responsibility for his decisions. Sure, he'd helped out a little bit with Fellows and this BBL thing, but Chuck didn't know that, so the lesson would still be intact. The boy could take something positive from the experience. And get away from the gamblers. They'd suck the life out of him.

***

Chuck and Hazel sat across from each other at one of the patio tables at Park Chow on Ninth Avenue, just a stone's throw from Golden Gate Park. From where they were, Chuck could keep an eye on the Harley and enjoy the summer sunshine while they drank beer and tried to figure out what they were going to do next.

Hazel was wearing cat's eye sunglasses and had her hair up in a high ponytail. The brown skin of her neck contrasted with her white V-neck T-shirt. She was leaning back dangerously in her chair, rolling up the sleeves of her shirt to give her upper arms a chance at some sun.

Chuck was sitting in the shade, looking out at the foot traffic, an eclectic swarm of young women in tube tops and Doc Martins, old men waiting for the fog in their tweed coats, couples with ice cream cones and shopping bags, gays and straights, tourists, neighborhood bums, and street musicians. They all had something in common: when they walked past, their eyes lingered on Hazel. Some were subtle. Some were obvious. But none of them missed her. Some did a double take. Guys walking in pairs would elbow each other and crane their necks to get a better look. Even the pretty girls couldn't help running their eyes over Hazel as they walked by.

And he, chicken-shit college dropout, small-time bookie, was about to put this woman that men would fight over and women envied in danger. And he was going to have to rely on a plan that would require Claudel Shanks to keep Brian Curran's death a secret for at least twenty-four hours. It was also going to require Claudel to do some acting, which Chuck kind of suspected the man would enjoy. Give him a chance to try out his dramatic side on his boss, who'd rather set up his deadbeat nephew with a nice job than help out his right hand man, who'd been loyal forever. But Claudel had said that it was cool, that if the man didn't want to help him out, then he didn't have to help out the man.

Chuck took a sip of his beer and asked Hazel, "You think Claudel's up to this?"

She put both hands above her head to adjust her hair, first working the rubber band, then squeezing the ponytail and running her fists over it as if she were wringing it out. "I think so. But you never know with him."

"What do y'mean?"

"I mean he smokes weed all the time, Chuck. That's what I mean."

"So you think he'll screw something up 'cause he's stoned?"

"It could happen," she said, wiping the condensation from her beer bottle with a cocktail napkin.

"So do y'think we should say fuck it and tell Troy the whole truth, get it out in the open and see how he responds to the fact that I went over to Brian's house to collect on his gambling debt, and, after his dogs and him were dead, I walked away, and now the body's gone? And then you want me to say, and, oh, yeah, do you still want to purchase my client list so I can afford to go play basketball in Europe? Is that how you think this should go?"

"You're funny when you're nervous, Chuck. I don't believe I've ever seen you nervous, but I do now, and you're kinda funny."

"Why do y'think I'm nervous?"

"Because you're getting kinda hyper, saying things that don't sound like you." She tilted her head as if to say *Can't you see it?* "I don't think you should tell Troy anything. Let him buy your book and let *him* take care of the Chinese guys like you said'll happen if everything works right."

Chuck didn't answer.

"I'm just pointing out that Claudel has to be sharp if this is gonna work," she said and gave him a tilted little smile with her shrug, the rolled sleeves of her T-shirt beginning to unravel at the shoulders.

"It doesn't work, we could be in serious trouble," he said, and reached for her hand. Then after trying to pinpoint something that'd give her away—a nervous tick of some sort, sweat on her upper lip, a shaking knee, anything—he said, "Y'know what else we can do?"

"Tell me."

"We could gather up all the cash we can get our hands on, enough to get a couple of plane tickets to London and a few weeks' rent." He smiled and nodded, trying to convince himself that it was a possibility. "And we could take a couple of easy jobs over there so we can get by until the season starts."

"That's what you wanna do?"

He nodded. "We'll leave Troy Curran and the Chinese behind us and just take off," he said. "I don't think anyone's gonna follow us to England. We could leave the whole fuckin' mess behind us, get on with it, y'know?"

"Just leave it all behind, huh?"

"Why wouldn't we?"

She pushed her sunglasses on top of her head. "Why wouldn't we?" she repeated as she leaned back even further in her chair, balancing on the back legs and closing her eyes against the sun.

"So is that what you wanna do?" he said, thinking he'd do whatever she wanted at this point, feeling like he owed it to her.

"We established a lucrative business," she said, leaning forward and squeezing his hand. "We provided a service for people who enjoy the excitement of a good wager. There's nothing immoral about that, even if it's against the law. It's like the difference between selling weed and running a bar. Why is the bar owner a respectable businessman and the pot slinger a pariah? The law?" She frowned. "Bunch of legislators sit around and decide what's best for their campaign contributors. That's bullshit. We know we haven't done anything morally wrong, right? The churches are running bingo. Knights of Columbus have raffles. And I don't even want to get into these day traders." She sighed, tired of talking, tired of reasoning with herself.

Chuck had never thought about it as a moral issue. It started out with parley cards, guys just wanting a little something to keep the games interesting. The people who got in trouble did it to themselves. Chuck shook his head. No, they hadn't done anything wrong.

"We never strong-armed anyone," she said. "Never let people get themselves in too deep. It was an honest business, Chuck. And I really wouldn't feel right about walking away without getting something out of it first. We earned it."

"Yes, we did. We did a lot of work. Worked our asses off." He let a real smile take over his face, and immediately his brain started working on the plan again, trying to think of a way to get the Chinese over to Troy Curran's house, make them disappear.

CHAPTER TWENTY-THREE

Sid sat on a short wooden stool—short enough that his feet could reach the ground—next to the Singing Sow's main refrigerator. Don, as usual, was bent over a butcher block, sampling the day's entrees from a tin tray, dipping different kinds of meat in a puddle of reddish brown barbeque sauce.

They still wore their suits, but Sid's tie hung out the pocket of his coat. He lifted his heels off the hard floor, first one, then the other. Something sticky was either on the floor or on his shoes. He kept pressing down his heels, then pulling them up, listening to the sound it produced—something like old Velcro, right before it loses its stick. Over and over he made the movement, trying to work out his next move with Holiday, how best to teach the bookie and his black friend not to fuck with Sid Toy. He wasn't scared of either of them. He wanted someone to pay for his lost investment, and he wanted people to know that he'd been paid. He wanted a story to go with his compensation. At the moment, the only story he had was that a fat black man had held him up in the air and taken his gun. Then the fat man had kicked him out on the street and stuffed him in the van. The story couldn't end that way, not if he was going to make a name for himself. He needed to press some people, get shit done.

"We are going back there, and I'm getting my gun and my money from Holiday," said Sid in Chinese as he continued to drum the floor with his heels, first the thump and then the slow zip as he lifted the shoe and felt the light adhesion of the stickiness.

"Okay," said Don, hammering the chicken leg he was holding down on the tray like a gavel. "But you better be careful around the black man. He looked like he has eaten men like us."

"He's a piece of shit is what he is," said Sid. "And he'll be sorry that he disrespected us."

Don walked over to one of the two oversized sinks, nodding at the dishwashers. They moved out of the way, and Don turned the water to cold. Then he soaped his hands and washed them quickly, splashed some water on his face, and used the bottom of one of the dishwashers' smocks to dry himself. He unlocked the padlock and used both hands to open the door to the walk-in refrigerator. When it was open just enough so that its contents were visible to only the two of them, the door still shielding the inside from the two dishwashers' view, Don said to Sid, "And what are we planning on doing with this?"

Without shifting on his stool, Sid turned his head and stared at the heap in the back corner of the refrigerator, at the blue vinyl tarp from Brian Curran's garage wrapped around the maimed body of Brian Curran, one of his sneakers poking through a tear and bloody hair sticking out the top. "Will he start to smell soon?" asked Sid. All the employees who worked in the back were illegals, and only a rare few would use the walk-in. He knew they would keep their mouths shut. But he did worry about the smell.

"Should have used the freezer," said Don, leaning against the big door.

"No room with all those fucking pigs," Sid told him, thinking back to their Chinatown heist of the previous week. He'd taken care of the driver, then drove away in the pork distributor's truck with a load of pigs hanging from ropes in the cargo area. He'd been testing himself, checking his courage by committing crimes on the spur of the moment in broad daylight, proving that the bigger the balls, the easier it was to get away with the swag. But now he was stuck with all those pigs, heavy motherfuckers now filling his freezer.

"Why don't we get rid of him?" asked Don, pointing at Curran's body.

"I think we may be able to use him," Sid said and walked past the plastic jugs of barbeque sauce and boxes of hot links toward the blue heap in the corner.

"Use him for what?"

***

Chuck and Hazel stood on the sidewalk looking at the pig on the front window of the restaurant. Chuck's hand was on her shoulder, and she held on to the bottom of his T-shirt. Chuck saw their reflection in the window, and hesitated for a moment as he noticed that his head was lined up perfectly to fit on the body of the swine on the window. They moved closer and peered inside where a white man with a long blonde goatee but no mustache was taking orders behind the counter, and three men were sitting at small tables finishing up barbeque platters, mountains of oily napkins scattered about their tables.

"Are you sure this is the place?" asked Chuck, surprised that he wasn't standing in front of Chinese restaurant.

Hazel took a business card out of her pocket and held it up. *Singing Sow* with a miniature version of the pig drawing from the window printed on it. Beneath the pig were two names: Don Ng and Sid Toy. Chuck guessed the little lizard-faced one was Sid Toy, maybe because he was almost small enough to be a toy, a little Chinese action figure with a gun.

"How did you get this?" He flipped the card over as if there might be some answer to his question on the back.

"The guy gave it to me."

"The guy who had his palm read?"

"Yeah. He was impressed that I knew he was in the restaurant business, and he grabbed the card and put it on the table, like he wanted to prove to me that *I* was for real."

"Funny. How *did* you know? You have a vision?"

"No, I was too nervous. I thought something bad was going to happen because stoned Claudel was out there with you and the little guy, and I was alone in the back room with this other one."

"I know," he said, stepping away from the window now and leading her down to the next storefront, a used bookstore with bins set up on the sidewalk. He didn't want Don and Sid to show up and try something before Chuck got a chance to talk to them. "I'm sorry I put you in there with that guy. I just wanted to split 'em up. But how did you know he worked in a restaurant if you weren't feeling any vibes?"

"I wouldn't say that. I was getting plenty of vibes from him. Big pores, like he works near a lot of heat and steam, and he smelled like food, not like he just ate some but like he'd been working with food. It's a different smell. I don't know why, but it is. And he had what looked like meat under his finger nails and burn marks on his hands." She shrugged and said, "I don't know. I just took a guess and got it right. Then I had the guy."

***

When they eventually got to the counter, the man with the blonde goatee didn't say anything. He nodded, waiting for an order.

"We'd like to talk to the owners," said Hazel.

"How do you know *I'm* not the owner," he said with a wink.

Hazel looked at Chuck for a second, then turned back and said, "'Cause you look like an idiot. Now where's the boss?"

The man behind the counter opened his mouth quickly, as if to speak, but stopped and looked almost like he was going to cry. Silently, he turned and pushed through the greasy doors next to the order window.

"What was that all about?" said Chuck.

"If these guys're gonna play tough with us, I'll play along. It's kinda fun," she said and turned her head when Don and Sid slammed through the door.

The smaller man stepped forward and said, "You come to pay me my money?" Then he started to laugh and looked from Hazel to Chuck and then back to Hazel again. "Or you going to work it off in the kitchen?" he said. This time he didn't laugh. He darted his lizard eyes at Chuck and licked his lips, then let the sneer turn into a greedy, lustful smile that he directed at Hazel. "I can think of ways that she can work off your debt, Holiday."

Chuck felt a chill start below his ears and shoot quickly down his neck and into his shoulders and spine. He said quickly, maybe too quickly, "I think I gotta better way." Then he moved in front of Hazel so that she was out of the man's view. "I don't have the cash for you, man. To tell you the truth, I don't really even think I owe it to you. Your man, Curran, fucked up and got himself killed, and the dogs just happened to get in the way. In fact, Brian Curran's the one who shot that dog. The other one," he actually felt the hammer in his hand when he let the image of the dog scamper into his brain, "he was just collateral damage." Chuck thought about telling it all, but when he saw the two men shaking their heads, he knew it wouldn't matter. "I know you don't care. You want to be paid, and you think I'm the guy who should have to do it."

Both men smiled and said nothing.

"But I can't do that," he said. "I'm just not in a position to hand over any money right now." The little man's face twitched, and he looked like a lizard again. Chuck didn't wait for more threats. He said, "But I'll tell y'what I wanna do. I wanna make you an offer that'll turn into a lot more money than those dogs're worth, and it'll set you up with a good little side income."

"Tell me," said the little guy, speaking in the first person singular, cutting the other fella out of it.

"You boys understand I'm a bookie, right?"

"I know what you do."

Chuck tried to get a read from the man's response, but his little face and dry reply didn't give anything away. All Chuck was thinking about was Claudel's stoned assessment of Don Ng and Sid Toy: that they wanted to establish themselves on the street, wanted to build a reputation as tough guys, street thugs. Claudel saw them as a couple of small-timers who wanted to make a step up. Chuck was going to try to use that now.

"Well, I'm going out of business," he said. "And my boss is looking for someone to run my book. I told him about you two, and he said he'd like to set up a meeting, see if we could work out a deal, maybe you bring him a few more customers."

The small man's eyes lit up, although he looked like he was trying to hold his lips in a half sneer. "You offering us a business proposition?"

"That's exactly what I'm doing."

"To run a gambling operation?"

"Yes."

"I think we might be able to deal, Holiday."

CHAPTER TWENTY-FOUR

Friday. Game night. But Claudel wasn't thinking much about Goose's championship game. He was thinking about Troy Curran and regular money coming in and nice clothes and good food and why in the fuck was he gon' put that on the line for a dude he don't even know that good?

He guessed it was because Goose had a plan that sounded like it could work. Claudel knew he had to take some risks in life if he wanted to make it, and here was risk, looking him square in the eye.

He slipped in one of the side doors of Kezar and sat a few rows behind the scorer's table. When he checked the scoreboard, they were halfway through the third quarter and Chuck's boys were down by six. It was a timeout, and Goose was sitting on the bench with his head down, shaggy hair hanging in front of his face.

Claudel tapped the kid next to him, a teenager with a puffy down jacket and a ski cap in the summertime. "How's the Goose doin'?" he asked.

"Huh?" said the kid, checking out Claudel's leather jacket, then looking back at his eyes.

"The white dude for San Francisco."

"Oh, yeah," said the kid, smiling now. "He hit a coupla treys in the first quarter, but hasn't done much since. He got good handles, though."

"Yeah," said Claudel then watched Chuck get off the bench and walk back onto the court with his team. Kid didn't look himself. He was bent over holding the bottoms of his shorts, and it was only the third quarter. But he was always fooling people. Just when they thought he was done, he could find some way to win. Claudel'd seen him do it all year to teams not expecting it, so he'd just wait and see what the man had left.

Claudel saw Troy on the other side of the gym, sitting with Andrew Tupps. Looked like Troy was doing all the talking and Tupps was being the typical yes-man, sitting there in his polo shirt, nearly ripping out of it like the fuckin' Incredible Hulk and shit. Only Hulk didn't hate brothers like this motherfucker. How could he? How could a green dude look down on a black dude?

***

Chuck was in good shape, but he hadn't slept the last couple of nights; his mind was constantly working, trying to figure out a way to sneak through the Troy-Don-Sid triple team, how to get Don and Sid off his back about the dogs, and how to get Troy to buy the business for Brian, even though Brian was dead. On top of that, he had to keep Hazel safe and keep Mr. Fellows from finding out about the business. The whole thing was sucking his energy.

Hoops had been pushed so far back on his priority list that he was reduced to letting instinct carry him through the game—and, he hoped, past the game to Troy Curran's house, where things might get hairy.

Just before he moved to set a pick, he glanced past the inbounder and saw Mr. Fellows a few rows back. The Rocks deal was dependent upon only Chuck's signature at that point, so he wasn't worried over having a mediocre game. What troubled him was that Fellows was sitting right in front of The Judge, and it looked like his dad was saying something to him. Chuck had only a split second to register that scene before he had to get back to setting a pick, but he couldn't stem the flood of thoughts that were rising in his already saturated brain. Could it be a coincidence, his dad sitting so close to Fellows? Maybe someone introduced them and they were talking about the Rocks, The Judge probably asking all sorts of bullshit questions and, hey, he rolled out of the screen and caught the inbound pass.

**

Two minutes left in the fourth, and Chuck knew it was over. They were down by twelve and couldn't stop the six-foot-ten center from East Palo Alto. All they could do was foul him and hope he missed his free throws, but he didn't.

Chuck hit a couple of jumpers in the last thirty seconds, too little too late, but his team kept fouling even with eight seconds left, down by seven.

When they lined up for the foul shots, Chuck was exhausted. Sweat was running into his eyes, but he took a peek into the stands and found Hazel sitting with Claudel, both of them dressed for the dinner at Troy's, both trusting Chuck to come through, to make their lives better. He felt the tiredness in his bones now, his legs almost paralyzed with it, but he went through the motions until the buzzer sounded, then shook hands with his teammates, and wandered through players and spectators and the press toward the locker room.

When he got to the ramp leading to the showers, he heard his name and looked up to see the Chinese leaning over the railing. "You play lousy defense," said Don, his thick fingers gripping the railing.

"Yeah," said Sid. "Why you can't stop the big guy?"

"Too big," said Chuck. "What're you guys doin' here?"

Sid said, "We want to know about the deal, when it's going to happen."

"Listen," said Chuck, sliding close to the wall so that he couldn't be seen from the other side of the gym. Chuck couldn't let Troy see him talking to the Chinese. He had to end this conversation quickly. "I told you guys I had a meeting tonight, and that I'd set up *your* meeting as soon as I took care of some other business."

"We think we should come with you tonight," said Sid.

"It can't happen that way," said Chuck, looking behind him now to make sure Troy hadn't wandered over to his side of the gym.

"You going to see the man tonight?" asked Sid.

"Yeah, but—"

"Then we should go with you."

"Fellas," said Chuck, realizing that he didn't have control, was driving on ice, breaks locked, steering wheel useless, sliding off the cliff, nothing to do but let go of the steering wheel, "You wanna come tonight? Come along. In fact," he threw his hands up, "you wanna follow me around, come on into the locker room and take a shower with me. You can soap my back. Follow me all over the fucking city. I don't care." He became aware that he was waving his arms around, drawing attention to himself, so he clasped his hands together and said, "But I don't think this deal's gonna work if you guys show up tonight. It's a dinner, fellas. My boss isn't gonna want to do any business with people who don't respect his home and his privacy."

Sid was leaning over the handrail, his arms hanging down, the rail up under his armpits and his chin resting on the metal. He looked like a puppet, Chuck decided, smiling down and saying, "But we're very eager to start the deal." He stood up and opened his jacket quickly, just enough for Chuck to see a new gun sticking out of his belt.

"Yeah," said Chuck. "But if you want it to ever get off the ground, you're gonna have to listen to me and do this my way." "Get off the ground?" asked Don.

"Yeah," said Chuck. "Get the business up and running."

"Running?"

"You wanna start making money?"

"We do," said Sid.

"Then let me talk to the man tonight and set up a meeting for you. Let's do this by the book and make everyone happy."

"What book?" said Don, smirking.

Chuck realized that the bastard was fucking with him, but he took a deep breath and said, "I'll call you tomorrow and let you know when you're supposed to meet my boss, okay?"

"Tonight," said Sid.

"Or we'll come and find you and kill you," said Don, who made a point to show Chuck that he had a gun as well.

"And do things to the girl," said Sid, showing just the tip of his little tongue and then flicking it out like a toad catching flies.

HALFTIME

"Every great mistake has a halfway moment, a split second when it can be recalled and perhaps remedied."

- Pearl S. Buck

"Some people are so fond of ill luck that they run halfway to meet it."

-Douglas William Jerrold

"The fundamental problem with program maintenance is that fixing a defect has a substantial chance of introducing another."
– Frederick P. Brooks, Jr., software engineer and author

In "Pulp Fiction" John Travolta accidentally shoots a guy sitting in the back seat of his car. Travolta and Samuel L. Jackson have blood all over 'em, and the car's a mess. They don't know what to do, so their boss calls in a guy known as "a cleaner." That turns out to be Harvey Keitel in a little cameo role. He's got a thin mustache, and he's wearing a tuxedo because he was coming from some swanky event or something when he got the call. He says, "I'm Winston Wolfe. I solve problems." Mr. Wolfe's the cleaner.

He doesn't come in with any ingenious plan. He just keeps everyone calm and tells them how to clean up and dispose of the body. Nothing all that inventive, but effective.

I could've used a cleaner back when I was in sixth grade and was trying to expand my newspaper delivery enterprise. I worked for the San Francisco Progress, a three-times-a-week rag that was actually free, but the paperboys still collected door-to-door back then, and some people would pay a monthly fee, either because they wanted to help out the paperboy or they knew the paperboy's parents or they wanted to keep the paper in print.

After having the route for about a year, the paperboy who had the adjoining route quit, so I told the district manager that I'd like to throw that kid's papers, too, work a double loop, make double the pay. The paperboys got a monthly check plus a percentage of the money they could collect from any generous customers.

Once I had the two routes, it was pretty tough to deliver all the papers and still make it to school on time, and I eventually got tired of running around trying to get them all delivered, especially since only about fifteen people in the combined two routes would actually pay. I don't remember when I got the idea, but I eventually started to deliver the papers only to those fifteen people who paid. I figured the folks who didn't pay probably didn't care about getting the Progress anyway. They either got the Chronicle or the afternoon Examiner, and didn't care about my paper.

The challenge centered around all the extra papers.

There was a public junior high school right in the middle of the two routes. A thick hedge ran all the way around the perimeter of the big buildings. On the first day I decided not to deliver the papers, I took a big stack and dropped it in between the building and the hedge. When I leaned over the hedge and looked down, the papers fit snugly in the small crease between the building and the hedge. Perfect. I even stepped back ten feet and looked at the hedge from the street. No sign of the papers.

I was only in the sixth grade at the time, so I didn't have much foresight. I did that same routine for about a month and a half before I realized I'd run out of space. Every available inch of the hedge line was jammed with newspapers. It was only then that I began to fully analyze the plan. For example, why didn't I throw the papers in the dumpster in the middle of the campus? That way, they'd get taken away once a week and my plan could last forever. And what was going to happen when the gardener finally got around to trimming the hedges? Surely he'd see the thousands of newspapers while he was clipping branches, and somebody'd eventually trace them back to me.

I needed a cleaner.

Mr. Wolfe did not live in my neighborhood, so I had to go to Toby Wagner. He was in my class at Saint Aloysius Grammar School, and he lived right around the corner from the public junior high on my route.

When I told Toby my predicament, he said, "What's the big deal?"

"My dad's gonna kill me if I get busted for this."

"Then let's get rid of the papers," he said and looked at me like I was an idiot.

Because I was already a wiseass, I said, "What should we do, make ten thousand paper hats? Or how about a giant paper-mache blimp?"

Toby used to light firecrackers and put them in his G.I. Joe's pants. He also liked to hold his finger in a candle's flame just to see how long he could do it. Years later he was arrested for selling illegal fireworks.

"Let's just burn 'em," he said. Of course.

So we got up at about five fifteen in the morning and started taking the stacks of old papers out from behind the hedges. We'd stolen a shopping cart, which helped us with time. By six, we had nearly filled up an entire dumpster. Toby had matches and lighter fluid.

It was surprising how fast the contents of the dumpster were on fire, and even more surprising how high the flames got.

I have to admit that for about a minute I just stared at it. It was still dark, and I could see every ember floating up into the sky. I could feel the heat from twenty yards away. The flames just kept getting higher until they reached the branches of the old pine tree that was leaning over the dumpster. For a moment I thought we should try to put it out, but there was just no way. And after the first of the branches started to glow, we actually heard the sirens approaching, so we ran as fast as we could out the back entrance of the school into an alley that led to the main road.

All I could think of while I was at school that day was that I hoped the firemen saved the tree but lost all those newspapers.

When I turned the corner to walk onto my street on the way home that afternoon when school let out, I saw two trucks parked outside my house. One was a Progress newspaper truck and the other was a fire truck. I hid behind the mailbox at the corner and waited for the drivers of the trucks to leave. They both walked out at the same time. They were talking and shook hands before they went to their vehicles.

I waited for both trucks to drive past me before I began my long walk to the house. I heard the muffled voice of my dad from outside the front door. He was never home in the afternoon. This was not good.

When I opened the door, I saw my mom and dad standing in the living room. I could tell my mom had been crying, but she didn't talk.

My dad said, "Hey, buddy. Good day at school?"

I knew I was busted. There was no way to talk my way out of this one. So I just said, "I'm sorry."

"Oh, good. So you know you almost burned down the whole neighborhood this morning?"

"I didn't think—"

"No, you didn't," he said. "You dumb shit."

That was all I needed to hear. I knew a good beating was coming, but I didn't want it at that moment, so I took off. I ran out of the house and didn't get the belt until later that night.

I guess I should have thanked my dad for keeping me out of Juvenile Hall, but part of me thinks things might have turned out better for me if I'd done some hard time. Maybe I would have learned that trying to fix one mistake can sometimes lead to more

CHAPTER TWENTY-FIVE

The stereo was turned down, but Chuck could still hear the faint sounds of Aretha Franklin feeling like a natural woman. He had put on a pair of light khaki slacks and a Hawaiian print shirt, but he was still sweating even after a cold locker room shower.

He'd let Hazel sit in the front seat, but now he was regretting it. There wasn't much leg room in the back, and his knees were butterflied against the door and a center ashtray. When he'd slid into the car, he had to move a baseball bat off the seat, and he was still holding it, feeling the smoothness of the wood on the barrel, tracing the burnt-in insignia with his thumb, as they pulled out of the Kezar parking lot.

"Dude was big," said Claudel, with one big hand guiding the Cadillac onto Stanyon Street.

Chuck was still thinking about Sid and his tongue. "Huh?"

"Dude that scored all the points," said Claudel. "Big motherfucker."

"Yeah," said Chuck. "Y'think he had thirty?"

"At least."

"Why didn't you guys zone 'em?" Hazel asked, craning her neck to look around at Chuck.

"You don't really play zone in this league," he said. "It's considered to be sort of gutless play." He put the bat on the seat next to him. "This league is more about one-on-one moves, trying to take your guy to the hoop, mano y mano."

"Well, you might have been able to win with a zone," she said. "You could have pinched him with two guys. Isn't it more important to win than to be worried about being considered gutless?"

"Winning's important," he said, not really in the mood to pursue the conversation. He'd been on the winning side of a lot of basketball games, but he'd always been concerned about *how* he won. Style was important. Winning something with flair was much more fun than simply winning.

But Hazel was right. When flair could cost him something important, it didn't seem as important. Maybe he should take a more straightforward approach to his current predicament and come clean to everyone. Tell Troy about Brian's death, pay Don and Sid and be rid of them forever, and be honest with Fellows—let the scout know what he'd been doing for money the past two years, then let Fellows decide whether he still wanted him or not. It didn't have much style, but Hazel would be safe, and Claudel could keep his job, and Troy might even want to buy the business anyway.

"It's not too late to change our strategy for this thing," said Chuck.

Hazel got up on her knees and turned all the way around so that she was facing Chuck. Claudel started looking in the rearview mirror, shifting his eyes from the mirror to the road and back again as he turned the car onto Park Presidio and headed toward the Golden Gate Bridge. Neither of them said anything.

Chuck said, "I could come clean with Troy about his nephew, see if he wants to do the deal anyway."

"Why you wanna do that?" asked Claudel, looking in the rearview too long and running over the lane divider bumps before he shifted his eyes back to the road and steered the big car back between the lines.

"I dunno," he said. "It might just be easier. No games. Just get it out in the open."

"That's right," said Claudel. "*No games.* You ain't gonna be playin' no games for that England league 'less you stick with the plan, get your money, and get rid of them Chinese dudes."

"You think those guys deserve it?"

"Who?" said Claudel. "The Chinese assholes? Hell, yeah. Motherfuckers came into your crib with guns, man. You think they worried about your well-being? Uh-uh. No fuckin' way, Goose. I told you what these dudes is up to, making a name on the street. Dead Chuck Holiday'll give 'em a name."

Hazel looked at Chuck with sad eyes. "You don't wanna be responsible for what's gonna happen to those guys, do you?"

"Rather not have it on my conscience," he said.

"So you don't really see them as a threat to us?"

Chuck thought back to Sid's tongue flicking. "I guess I do."

"Then don't drop this," said Claudel. "We got a good thing here. Good guys get what they need. Bad guys get what they deserve."

"We're the good guys?" asked Chuck. "Small time bookie and a guy who breaks people's knees?"

"That's right," said Claudel. "We just doin' our jobs. Ain't no meanness in what we do. So let's make sure we all set on what we gonna say tonight."

"The only thing you have to talk about is the fact that you got a message from Brian Curran on your cell phone, and make sure you're specific about his mentioning the Chinese," said Chuck. "We gotta plant that seed right away."

"So you think I should tell him as soon as we walk in the door?"

Chuck looked at his watch. It was eight-thirty. "Right away. We don't wanna look like we're messing around. It's pretty late, and my hope is Troy will go on with the meeting anyway." Chuck looked at Hazel, who was nodding. "I got all my books here and Hazel's done all the numbers, so I assume it's a simple deal."

"It is," said Claudel. "He got a formula for buyin' dudes out. He'll take your total numbers for the past two years and give you a good percentage of that. Then you gonna get some juice every month after. You'll still be on the payroll even though you don't do shit."

"But that's gonna be your cut for helping us out here," said Chuck as they made their way up the Waldo Grade toward the winding freeway of south Marin County.

"That's my cut," said Claudel and smiled at Chuck in the rearview. "So long as this all works, else I'll be lookin' for a job. If Troy figures this shit out, we in deep."

"How can he figure it out?" asked Hazel.

"Shit happens, right? That's what white folks say, and they right," Claudel said "Never know what kinda shit might go down."

The sun had set. Chuck looked through the fading orange of the evening at the outlines of the houseboats that lined the bay harbor. Beyond the harbor, he could see the silhouette of Angel Island rising up out of the black water, the murky bay with its algae film hiding the shadowy movements beneath.

"Well," he said, "can you anticipate something specific that you think might happen?"

"Naw, Goose. It ain't like that," said Claudel. "I'm just sayin' be ready. And, oh, yeah, I almost forgot. We gotta keep a eye on Troy's man Tupps."

Hazel asked, "Why?"

"He the Incredible Hulk, only he hate niggas."

CHAPTER TWENTY-SIX

Troy left with two minutes left in the fourth quarter, wondering why Holiday never got his game going. He looked like he'd been sick or something. Troy had lost a couple hundred dollars in a friendly bet with the bartender at Finnegan's Wake, two blocks east of the arena. But that didn't matter. He was going to get this deal together tonight for his nephew, which would make older brother Frank happy. Sure, Frank would rather have Brian in a nice city job, but he also knew that Brian couldn't do it. He had a wild hair up his ass and couldn't clip it for the life of him. Running sports bets would at least keep him out of major trouble. He wouldn't do any time if he got caught. The cops had bigger fish to fry. It was Troy's gift to his brother, keeping the kid out of trouble.

In the kitchen, Gabby was chopping things for a salad, exotic colored bell peppers, some kind of tropical fruit—mangos maybe—red onions, a bunch of other shit he wouldn't necessarily think went together, like walnuts and crumbled up blue cheese. She'd finally become quite a cook, taking a class over at the junior college and clipping recipes out of magazines. Troy would have been satisfied with meat and potatoes every night, but he didn't mind trying out new stuff.

He walked up to her and put his hands around her waist. She was wearing a white sleeveless sundress with large pink flowers blooming all over her body. "How's it comin'?" he asked and leaned forward so that his face was close to hers.

"It's comin' baby," she said and turned her cheek away. "C'mon, let me finish this." She wiggled her hips out of his grasp.

"How's Mr. Tupps doing with the meat?" The security man had immediately taken to Gabby, and helped her in the kitchen to put together her strange concoctions, experiments the two of them cooked up sometimes, but most of the time not bad.

Tupps was working the outdoor grill, doing lamb chops, but Gabby'd also bought some prawns to serve as appetizers, and Tupps was preparing them as well, brushing on a marinade that smelled like some kind of citrus and vinegar mix.

"They should be here pretty soon," said Troy.

"Oh," said Tupps, just realizing that Troy was behind him. "Well, these only take a minute," he said and motioned with the brush toward the lines of prawns. "And I already have the chops going on low heat, so we'll be ready whenever it's time."

"Good. Good," said Troy, happy he had such excellent help, this man he hired for security, who drives his wife around and helps her with the cooking. Like a nice little family, they were. "We'll all eat in the dining room, I guess."

"That'll be good," said Tupps. "But don't put me next to Shanks, okay?"

"Wouldn't think of it. You sit next to Gabby."

***

Before Chuck rang the doorbell, he took a quick look at Hazel, whose mouth was moving, just slightly. Probably rehearsing lines. And Claudel was tugging at his leather jacket and smiling at the door like he'd just opted for curtain number three and didn't even care what the prize was, just that he'd taken the risk of the unknown.

When the door started to open and Troy Curran's red buzz cut came into view, Chuck was startled by Claudel barking out, "Hey, now," and pushing through the door like he owned the place. The man was either not nervous at all or doing a great job of acting like it.

"Claudel," said Troy, watching the big man roll by. "What's the word?"

"The word's barbeque, boss," said Claudel. "What're we cookin'?"

"Chops," said Troy over his shoulder as he welcomed Chuck and Hazel into the house, shaking Chuck's hand and putting an arm around Hazel's waist.

"Pork or lamb?" Claudel called out as he moved out of sight into the kitchen, but Troy didn't answer.

"Fuckin' guy," said Troy, shaking his head and smiling as if Claudel were a funny little boy, who hadn't learned his manners yet.

"Claudel," said Hazel with a shrug, as if that explained it all.

"You guys close?" asked Troy.

"He goes to all the games," said Chuck. "So we see each other now and then."

"He's got some strange ways," said Troy. "But he gets the job done."

Troy led them through kitchen and out onto the circular back deck, and then excused himself. Claudel was already sitting on a wrought iron chair, and Gabby was leaning against the railing next to a guy who had to be the Incredible Hulk Claudel had mentioned. He was wearing a white, short-sleeved mock turtleneck and a pair of black lightweight slacks. He was bulging out of the shirt, but the pants were loose and baggy. The effect was that the man looked like a buffed up Aladdin, minus the pointy shoes.

"How's it?" he said and extended his hand.

Chuck took it and said, "Good."

"Andrew Tupps."

Chuck picked up the accent, which he'd first thought was Australian but now realized was probably South African, like the golfer, Nick Price.

"Chuck Holiday," he said, waiting for the man to start crushing the bones in his hand. "And this is my girlfriend, Hazel."

Tupps nodded at Hazel and gave her an easy smile. "Have you met Mrs. Curran?" he said and motioned toward Troy's wife, who was still leaning against the railing. She could have been posing for a fashion magazine; she was good-looking enough to pull it off. She was a still-shot, except for her eyes, which were moving up and down Hazel, who was shaking her head. No, they hadn't met.

"*I've* met Mrs. Curran," said Chuck, stepping forward and expecting her to do the same, but she kept her pose, so he stopped short and waved his hand toward Hazel. "This is Hazel," he said.

"Troy's mother's middle name is Hazel," said Gabby.

Hazel smiled.

"And there was that old TV show with the ugly maid named Hazel. You ever see that show?"

"Can't say that I have," said Hazel, and then, after a pause, just long enough for things to feel uncomfortable, she added, "Probably before my time."

Gabby tightened her grip on the railing, but before she could say anything, Troy was back, asking, "So, where's my nephew?"

Claudel looked down at his watch and said, "Should be here. I definitely gave him the right time."

Chuck shook his head, giving his best *who knows?* look. "I haven't talked to him in a while," he said and looked at Hazel so he wouldn't have to look into anyone else's eyes. He knew he was a lousy liar, so he was going to say as little as possible and let things take their course.

After a few minutes of small talk, some about Brian, some about the Lakers, and some about Chuck's game, Claudel's phone rang. "Excuse me," he said and walked over to the far curve of the deck, which looked out on the garden, orange and red flowers growing right up to a smaller lower deck surrounding a sunken hot tub.

They stopped talking to look at Claudel, who was yelling, "Huh? Slow down now." He was doing a good job so far. Chuck wondering who Claudel got to make the call.

Then Claudel turned toward the group and frowned, still holding the phone up to his ear, saying, "You breakin' up, man." Then he stopped and listened, making a face like it hurt to listen that hard. "The Chinamen?" he said then looked at Hazel and shook his free hand in a gesture meant to imply *no offense.* "I ain't getting' all that," he said, his face showing anger. "Look, you gotta—" He looked at Troy. "I lost him."

"Who?" said Troy, just as another set of marinated prawns sizzled onto the grill, Tupps adjusting them with tongs.

"Man, that was Brian," said Claudel. "But I couldn't get him."

"What does that mean?" asked Troy.

"It means I couldn't get him," said Claudel. "His phone was breaking up and dudes was yellin' at him in the background. Shit, I think that boy in trouble."

"What do you think you heard?" asked Troy.

"Here's what I *know* I heard," said Claudel. "And I'm doing a quote here." He looked at Hazel and nodded another *no offense*. "He say, 'The Chinamen's pissed.'"

Chuck was starting to pick up on some of Claudel's theater tricks: opening his eyes real wide for surprise, tightening his lips for concern, tilting his eyebrows for confusion. Almost too much, but it seemed to work.

"Do you know who these Chinese people might be?" asked Troy.

"Only Chinese dudes I know about," said Claudel, "is the dudes own the dogs, man, the mothafuckin' pit bulls they want trained."

"Any idea why they might be pissed at my nephew?"

"You know your nephew," said Claudel and looked around the deck for confirmation.

"You hear anything else?" asked Troy.

"Nothin' I could get hold of."

"Well, what do you think we should do?"

Claudel shrugged and looked down at the phone in his hand. "Eat that food y'all cooked up. Do the business with your man, Holiday. And I'll keep waitin' for the boy to call back and tell us where he's at."

Troy looked concerned, but he nodded.

Chuck liked the way things were going, and he felt that he was doing a nice job of hiding his excitement. He even tried Claudel's little trick of giving the tight-lipped concerned look before he said, "Whatever you guys wanna do."

CHAPTER TWENTY-SEVEN

There was definitely something going on between Andrew Tupps and Gabby Curran, Hazel thought. Didn't need to have *the gift* to see the steam between them. While at the dinner table, she had a hunch that if she'd looked under the table, she'd have seen Mrs. Curran's hand down his pants. They sat a little too close, stole looks during conversations, brushed up against each other in passing.

Not that Hazel could blame her. Anyone had to be better than Troy Curran. There was just something twisted and smarmy about the man, not to mention his age. Gabby looked older than Hazel but nowhere near Troy's age. His slick clothes couldn't hide his veiny nose and sagging neck, which was what Hazel was staring at as Troy was leafing through the paperwork in front of him.

Hazel, Chuck, and Troy had retired to Troy's office, which looked like something out of a James Bond movie. What appeared to be a linen closet, complete with towels and sheets, was actually a false front that could be pushed open into an office filled with oak furniture and leather chairs, not unlike Judge Holiday's den. To Hazel, the secrecy seemed a bit elaborate for a bookie, but, since he obviously had the money, why not?

They sat at a round felt table, which probably doubled as a card table for high stakes poker games. Troy's hands were moving like a dealer's, shuffling papers, banging on the calculator, and taking notes with a ball point pen that he kept in an empty coffee mug when he wasn't writing.

Chuck and Hazel answered questions and helped Troy find information, but otherwise sat still and waited for the offer.

After Troy had spent nearly two hours and gone through the prior three months of bets twice, he wrote down a figure on a piece of notebook paper, ripped it out of the book, and slid it over to Chuck.

Chuck looked at the number and pushed the paper toward Hazel, who was wondering why Troy couldn't just say the number, but this was fine. It would give her time to react before she had to say something. When she looked down and saw $45,000, she said, "And this reflects next year's projected earnings, which you're willing to give us as a flat fee to run the book for as long as you want, like buying a franchise?"

"It does," Curran said, his voice flat, no emotion, like he was playing poker, maybe holding something big but didn't want to scare off the other betters too soon.

Hazel looked at Chuck and knew what he was thinking. They'd run the figures the day before and projected over fifty-two grand for next year, based on the previous two years' earnings. But she wasn't sure what Chuck wanted to do. It was a lowball bid, but it would still get them to England, with plenty left over.

She pushed the piece of paper back to Chuck, who said to Curran, "We had it figured a little higher."

Troy nodded. "Of course you did, son. But you probably didn't account for any attrition."

Chuck looked at Hazel but didn't change his expression. She lifted her eyebrows and turned to Troy Curran without saying a word, although she had an idea where Curran was going, even if he wasn't using quite the right word.

"Attrition," he repeated and scratched more numbers on another piece of notebook paper. "Every time I make one of these deals, I lose ten or fifteen percent because guys don't want a new casino. They want to stick with their own guy, or they don't want to bet at all." He waved the paper in the air. "It's a fact. Losing my nephew alone'll cost the franchise thousands. You got any other guys on that list might stop betting 'cause Chuck Holiday ain't the provider anymore?"

Chuck paused a moment, then grabbed at his book and started looking through the names. After nearly a minute, he said, "About ten, fifteen percent." He looked up at Curran and nodded.

"People forget about the attrition," said Curran, as he pushed the piece of paper with the number on it back in front of Chuck. "Couple years back, I wanted to buy up this little punk's book he was running out at USF, Catholic kids blowing their student loans on NFL Sundays. But the shifty little fucker wants me to pay a hundred percent of the projection, even though we both knew damn well that half his clientele's gonna be graduating and moving back to fucking Fresno and Bakersfield and Cleveland."

"So what happened?" asked Hazel, smiling a little, enjoying this quick glimpse into Curran's world, and feeling certain that they were going to close the deal.

"I told him he could stick it up his ass," said Curran, with a big toothy Hollywood grin. "I don't need any more business, but it's hard to turn down easy money when the price is right." He turned serious, showing the rows of lines in his forehead, and said, "This here's a nice deal for you kids."

"Do you mind if Hazel and I talk it over for a minute?" asked Chuck, looking relaxed and confident. Hazel suspected he'd even forgotten about Brian and Don and Sid, at least for a moment.

Of course, if Curran had only arrived at her house a few hours earlier the week before and made his proposal, Chuck wouldn't have ever gone to Brian's house to collect on his debt. Never would have seen those dogs. She and Chuck could have just tacked Brian's seven grand onto Curran's asking price. They would have never met Don and Sid and would probably be looking for an apartment in Edinburgh right now.

"Take as long as you want," said Curran as he rose from his seat and moved toward the door. "I'm goin' down to the back deck to enjoy a cigar and see about my nephew."

When the door closed, Chuck and Hazel were left alone with the mess of scattered pages and scribbled notes. Chuck picked up the scrap with the number forty-five thousand written on it, and held it with both hands. Then he held it in one hand at arm's length and studied it like a farsighted old man. Then he held it in both hands again, turned it upside down, and gazed at it at as if he were looking into a crystal ball.

"C'mon," said Hazel. "Quit messing around. What do you wanna do?"

Chuck grinned and said, "Take his money and get the hell outta here."

"How do you feel about it," asked Hazel, her hands folded on the table as if she were about to say grace.

"About selling the business to Curran?"

"Yeah."

"We need the money, right?"

"Yeah."

"Then I feel good."

What she wanted to know was how he felt about misleading Curran, letting the man think that Brian Curran would be running the business. But she didn't want to ask him. Chuck was right. They needed this money, and Curran had it, and the business would still be profitable. "Then let's do it and hope Claudel hasn't screwed up his end of things."

Chuck said, "Listen, I *do* feel a little crappy that his nephew is dead, and we can't tell him yet, but I don't see that it makes that big a difference." He stood up, ducking the small chandelier as he walked to the doorway. "Curran's gonna make money off our bettors. It's not like I'm selling him junk bonds. He's gonna make money without doin' any work. That's what he does."

Hazel stood and gathered the papers, putting them in folders as she said, "I know. He's got a good life."

"He sits around," said Chuck, "while Claudel and his wife and this guy Tupps and all his phone guys do his work for him. Hazel, we didn't kill Brian Curran."

"We haven't killed anyone," she said.

CHAPTER TWENTY-EIGHT

Don and Sid did not like living in Don's aunt's apartment building—the aunt lived in a separate apartment on the same floor as Don and Sid with her daughter and the daughter's husband as well as their three kids—on Grant Street, just on the edge of Chinatown. They were entrepreneurs now, and it was time to move out and find a new place, where they could come in late at night and sleep well into the next morning without having to worry about kids and old ladies. But they needed to settle the business with Chuck Holiday and his boss first.

Don sat on the broken side of the couch, which had busted springs and sank down six inches lower than the other side. He looked at Sid, who was on the other side of the couch watching television. Don said in Chinese, "When do you think he'll call?"

Sid loved sitting on the unbroken side of the couch; it was one of the rare opportunities when he was able to look down on somebody when he talked. "I think soon. It's starting to get late," he answered in the same Chinese they'd been trying to avoid, trying to transform into street English, trying to bend into the kind of talk the fat black man used when he had Sid in a headlock at Holiday's apartment.

"How are we going to know what to say to Holiday's boss when it's time to discuss the business?" asked Don, as he adjusted his feet on the cardboard box that he was using as a footrest.

"I don't know what that means," he said.

"I mean that we don't really know much about how to run a gambling business. So how will we make the boss want to let us work with him?"

"We'll make him think that we'll bring him new business from our own community."

Don took his feet off the box and struggled to sit up on the caved-in couch. "But we don't know many people here yet, and I don't think my aunt is going to want to place any bets soon. So how will we bring in the business?"

Sid smiled and said, "He doesn't know that. White people think that we all know each other. They think that we were all packed onto the same boat." He pulled the sides of his eyes and poked out his two front teeth, a parody of himself. Then he sang, "Me Chinese, me play joke, me go pee-pee in your Coke … that's what they think of us."

"Yeah?"

"Yeah," said Sid. "And we also have the restaurant to *clean* the gambling money, like they say."

Don opened the top to the cardboard box. "And why do we need all of these?" he asked as he pulled two handguns out of the pile of weapons.

"Be careful," said Sid. "They're all loaded."

"But why do we need them all?"

"If someone takes my gun again," said Sid. "I want to have another gun close to me, so that I can shoot the man and get my gun back."

"Yes, but all of these?" asked Don, placing the two guns back on the pile and lifting the box up to emphasize his point. The bottom of the thick cardboard sagged with the weight of the weapons, and Don placed it gently back on the warped floor.

"Once we start to build our own business," said Sid, "we'll have people working for us. In this kind of business, it'll be smart for them to have guns too. The guns will not be wasted, I don't think."

"Can I have two?"

Sid was laughing when Don's nephew bounced into the apartment on a pogo stick, counting in English, "… eighty-seven … eighty-eight … eighty-nine …"

Don covered the box with his suit coat and said, "Hubert, you're supposed to knock when you come in here."

"… ninety-three … ninety-four … ninety-five …"

Sid, talking loudly so that he could be heard over Hubert, said, "This is why we must move out of here." He stood up and started to follow Hubert, who was still bouncing across the floor toward Sid's bed.

"… ninety-eight … ninety-nine," said Hubert, and finally, "One-hundred," as he sprung up off the pogo stick and onto Sid's bed, where he rolled onto his back and started laughing.

When Sid reached the side of the bed, he grabbed Hubert by his foot and dragged him off, Hubert protesting, clawing at the old sheets and blankets. Sid tried out some English. "Bring your ass back to your mama," he said, as he snatched up the pogo stick and walked it over to the door, fumbling with it before he tossed it into the hallway.

"Hey, Uncle," Hubert said to Don, "Sid's gonna try out my pogo stick."

Don smiled but said nothing.

Sid said, in Chinese this time, "I'll break the thing over his skull."

Hubert, who only spoke English, heard Sid's Chinese and did a quick impersonation of Sid, which involved crinkling up his face and making a series of obnoxious twanging noises. Then he ran to the door. Before he reached the threshold, he stopped and squinted at his uncle. "What's under the jacket?"

Don put his feet back on top of the box. "Go upstairs and see your mother."

The boy trotted past Sid, who was standing in the hallway like a doorman. Before Hubert bent down to pick up his toy, he stood on his toes and put his hand flat on top of his head. Then he began to move the hand out over Sid's head, as if to suggest that he was taller than Sid.

Sid stepped inside the room and slammed the door. "We can't have that little shit bouncing around in here like a wild animal," he said. "We have loaded guns in here, Don."

"I know. He's eleven years old, and he's trying to see how much he can get away with without getting smacked. I'll talk to his mother."

"And when is that asshole, Holiday, going to call?" he said, as he walked over to the box of firearms and started pulling them out one by one and placing them on the floor in front of the couch. He liked the idea of carrying two guns, and he wanted to pick one that would fit well in a shoulder holster, just like Steve McQueen in *Bullit*.

CHAPTER TWENTY-NINE

As Chuck followed Hazel down the interior stairs of the Curran house, he could hear music playing in the front room, and when they stepped around the corner, he recognized the song. It was Gladys Knight and the Pips doing *Midnight Train to Georgia*.

Andrew Tupps and Gabby Curran were sitting on the couch, and Claudel was standing by the stereo looking at the back of an album cover. Chuck walked by a speaker and noticed the grainy quality of the music. He looked past Claudel and saw a record spinning on the turntable. He hadn't heard a record since he was a little kid, when The Judge used to play country-western songs on his old stereo: Willie Nelson and Wayland Jennings and George Jones.

Claudel acknowledged their arrival. "Check it out," he said and he reached around to the built-in bookshelf, which held a row of old records. He held one up, but from across the room all Chuck could make out of the cover shot was a guy with a big afro and a gal in a mini skirt. When Chuck shook his head, Claudel yelled out, "Ike and Tina, man." Then he lifted another and said, "Otis Redding. Motherfucker sittin' on the dock of the bay and shit."

Chuck smiled at Gabby and Tupps. "Claudel likes the old soul stuff," he said, not sure what he was supposed to be doing. Where the hell was Troy? They were ready to close the deal.

Chuck took Hazel's hand and led her to the loveseat near the fireplace. When they sat, she pressed close, so that they were both sitting on the same cushion.

Claudel said, "Old man Curran gots some good shit in here." He moved his head in a circular motion, trying to read the songs on the spinning label of the record. "Know who this here is?"

Hazel said, "Gladys Knight." Her mouth was so close to Chuck's ear that he winced slightly when she called out her answer.

Claudel laughed. "Hazel know her shit. But lady left out the most important part," he said as he moved into the center of the big room and stood on the Persian rug. "The Pips. Gladys Knight and the Pips." Then he made his hand into a fist, raised it over his head and pulled it down twice as he sang with the record, "whoo, whoo." Then he crossed one foot over the other, paused for a second, and spun like an ice skater, before he stopped abruptly and sang again, "Uh-uh ... no ... uh-uh ... leavin'...."

Gladys was winding down. She'd rather live in his world than live without him in hers when Troy, holding a smoldering cigar, walked into the room and said, "Who's this?" He pointed the cigar at Claudel. "Michael Jackson?"

Tupps let out a booming laugh, and Gabby pushed down on his knee.

"I'm a Pip, man," said Claudel, still doing some moves as Gladys was belting out that she's got to go … she's got to go … on the midnight train. "Don't y'all know a Pip when you see one?" Then he stopped and sat down next to Hazel on the loveseat, the three of them wedged in tight. "Man, Troy, you gots enough soul up in here, you should know what a Pip is. Shit." He was a bit out of breath from his exertions; sweat was beginning to drip down his temples.

Troy threw his cigar into the fireplace and said, "I know what a Pip is. Do *you* know what a Pip is?"

"Just *said* what a Pip is." Claudel was adjusting his big ass on the sofa now, trying to get comfortable without knocking Hazel and Chuck onto the floor. "A dude that dances in back of Gladys. Whoo, whoo."

"Yeah," said Troy, "but do you know what they were named after, what the word pip really means?"

"Thought it was just a make-up name," said Claduel. "Like … shit, I dunno … like Martha Reeves and the Vandellas. Ain't no such thing as a vandella, right?"

"I'm not sure about vandellas, but I know what pips are," he said. "They're the little black dots on dice."

Tupps chuckled.

Claudel said, "No shit?"

"No shit," said Troy.

"God damn," said Claudel. "I like that. Black dots and shit." He slapped Hazel's thigh lightly and said, "Never knew they had a name for 'em."

"A good Scrabble word," said Hazel.

"Yes," Troy said. "You can learn something every day, can't you?"

There was a brief moment of silence. Chuck was wondering if maybe people were thinking about what they'd learned today.

Unable to wait any longer, Chuck said, "We'd like to accept your offer if it's still on the table. We think it's fair, and everybody'll be gettin' something out of it."

"That's what I wanted to hear," Troy said and walked over to shake Chuck's hand. "The kid should be here, Claudel, to see what we did for him. See if you can get a hold of him again. Now I'm startin' to get worried."

"Will do," said Claudel, and opened his phone and punched in the numbers. He waited, and everyone watched him bobbing his head to the rhythm of the Pips. "No luck, boss," he said and put the phone back in his pocket. "I'm driving these here home, though, so we can check out the kid's house, right around the corner from Chuck and Hazel."

"Do it tonight," said Troy.

Chuck and Hazel started to stand, but Troy waved them back onto the couch.

"Stay for one drink," he said. "I like to have a drink after I close a deal."

"Sounds good," said Chuck.

"Tupps," said Troy, "how about bringing in a bottle of that eighteen-year-old Scotch?"

"Sure." He looked at Gabby. "You want something?"

"I'll have some of the Scotch," she said. "This is a big night for Troy, doing something for his big brother's kid and helping Mr. Holiday with his basketball dreams. My husband's a regular philanthropist, looking after the best interests of the thugs and hustlers of the world."

She'd drunk a lot of wine with dinner and her cheeks were pink. She was smiling at Troy as if challenging him to say something, but he was barely paying attention, instead looking at a painting hanging on the wall behind Claudel's head, a seaside landscape, cliffs and sea and sand.

When Troy saw that Chuck had turned to look at the painting, he said, "Marin Headlands. The first body of land on the north side of San Francisco Bay. It's only two miles from the city, but it's a world away, isn't it?"

Chuck nodded, knowing he'd see a similar view when they came out of the Waldo Grade tunnel on the way home.

"That's why I moved over here," said Troy. "Get away from all the nastiness of the city."

"It's nice on this side," said Chuck. "Slower."

"Maybe England'll be the same for you," said Troy.

"I hope so," Chuck said as he accepted a glass from Tupps. He realized he'd been only five years old when the bottle was sealed. "The money from this deal's gonna really help. I appreciate it."

"The money," said Troy. "I almost forgot. Andrew, you wanna bring out the envelope for these guys?"

"Of course," Tupps said and left the room.

"A good man," said Troy, probably loud enough for Tupps to hear over Gladys Knight.

"Sure is," said Gabby Curran, swirling her scotch so that the ice made clinking sounds on the glass.

Troy walked to the arched entrance of the room to meet Tupps and grab the envelope, which he carried to Chuck. He handed over the money and said, "The only thing left for you to do is to notify all your customers, then sit back and collect your juice."

"I'll make the calls tomorrow," said Chuck. "Thanks again." Chuck reached out his hand to help Hazel out of her seat, and, when she was standing next to him, Claudel put out both hands. Hazel grabbed one hand and Chuck the other, and they hoisted him off of the sofa.

"I'll check Brian again after I drop these two off," said Claudel. "Thanks for the eats, Gabby."

She was mixing her drink with her finger. She pulled out her pinky and put it in her mouth. She took a long suck all the way down past the knuckle, and then let it slide off her tongue before she nodded to Claudel.

Tupps walked to the door, opened it, and stood holding the knob as Claudel, Hazel, and Chuck walked out. Chuck almost felt like he should tip the guy. Tupps didn't even look at him as he passed.

Chuck was concentrating on keeping his big feet on the raised stone walkway, so he wouldn't take a header and drop the money. He'd been cool so far and didn't want to blow it in the final moments.

CHAPTER THIRTY

"All that time working for the man and never knew he had Gladys Knight and Ike and Tina," said Claudel as he steered the big car off the private road and started making his way toward Highway 101 south. "Y'know, Tina wasn't no good after she left Ike."

"What do y'mean?" asked Hazel. "She got all those gold records when she was solo."

"Was I talking about gold records?" asked Claudel, looking in the rearview mirror. "Gold records just means lots a folks bought the records. Don't mean nothin' 'bout how good the music is."

"Okay, I'll give you that" said Hazel. "But Ike Turner was beating her."

"I'm not telling y'all that she shoulda stayed with the man. Just said she made her best music with Ike. Know what I'm sayin'? Lady had soul when she was shaking that big booty next to old Ike. Soon's he out the picture, she changes her sound, tries to make like she's a rocker, plays a song with motherfuckin' Brian Adams, whitest cracker around, man. No soul."

"Brian Adams rocks," said Chuck from his seat next to Claudel. Then he started to laugh. "Don't we have other things we gotta talk about?"

"Like how about Claudel's performance in there?" said Hazel.

"Not bad," said Chuck.

Claudel knew he'd kicked ass, had all those white folks thinking he was making phone calls and worried about dead Brian. "Not bad? Shit, I played it a little like Denzel and a little like Samual L. You see me pretended to be not hearing Curran's nephew? That was something I got from the method actor's school, man. Rod Stieger and shit. I was visualizing the whole thing happening while I was talking. Man, I was there in my mind. That shit was real." Then he looked in the rearview mirror at Hazel again. "Denzel ... right?"

"I was thinking more of Cedric the Entertainer," said Hazel.

"Who the ... aw, Hazel that ain't right," said Claudel. Then to Chuck, "You gonna get control of your woman, Goose?"

"I don't know, Claudel. She coulda said Rerun from *What's Happening*. Hey, hey, hey."

"Hey, now," said Claudel. "That ain't right." He liked that they were giving him a little shit. Never got to have fun like that with Tupps and Troy. Only comments they ever made were nigger jokes. Old stale shit. No creativity. "How 'bout when I snuck in the bullshit about the Chinese dudes? That was off the hook."

"Yeah," said Chuck. "That was good. I gotta call those guys right now." He pulled out his cell phone, but before he started to punch in the numbers, he said, "Let's make sure I get this right."

Hazel leaned forward. Claudel could smell her perfume mixed with the odor of the scotch on her breath. If she wasn't Chuck's lady....

Hazel said, "What's gonna work best in terms of the timeline?"

"The sooner the better," said Chuck. "I don't want 'em sitting around getting ideas. We want those guys walking into that meeting with smiles on their faces, ready to do business, start their careers as big time crime lords."

Claudel started thinking about how easy it had been to take the little guy's gun and throw him out of Chuck's house. "Those idiots'll be easy," he said. "I'm worried about gettin' Troy in on this thing without him smellin' the stink, though."

"Let's worry about this first," Chuck said as he made the call. Then, "Don, this is Chuck Holiday. My boss is ready to set up a meeting."

***

Sid was playing with the guns, standing in front of a full-length mirror, looking at himself in different poses, trying to figure out which made him look the baddest. He squinted his eyes like Eastwood and stared at himself in the mirror, tried to scare himself with his own intensity. He was so into it that he almost pulled the triggers when he was startled by the ringing of the telephone.

Don ran over to answer, and Sid placed the guns on the table by the phone. He studied his partner, who sounded relaxed as he worked through his best English.

"That's good news," said Don. "Yes, we are ready to discuss the situation."

Sid tried to imagine what Holiday was saying. He could picture him, towering over his own phone, holding it between his fingers like a miniature toy, saying, "My boss is ready to give you boys a chance."

Don said, "Where should we meet the boss?"

Sid imagined Holiday saying, "The boss would like to meet at the Singing Sow, heard it was a great place for ribs."

But Don's response didn't work. "We would have to go on the other side of the bridge? But we don't know that area."

Holiday must have said that he'd give them directions because Don said, "They better be good because we have not been out of the city since we got here."

Sid didn't want directions. He wanted the meeting to be somewhere familiar. He grabbed the phone from Don and began to speak, but

Holiday had already hung up.

"Why are you letting them pick the place?"

"Why does it matter?" said Don.

"Because they could set some kind of trap and try to take our guns again."

"Why?"

"Because I don't trust them."

"Oh," said Don. "That makes sense."

"It should make sense," said Sid. "Do you remember Holiday and his big black friend throwing us onto the sidewalk? The black motherfucker squeezed my head so hard I thought some of my brain was going to come out through my ears."

"I don't trust them either. But they're not coming to us for a job. *We're* asking them for a job. How are we going to tell them where we should meet?"

Sid knew Don was right, but he was going to be ready for Mr. Chuck Holiday this time. If some kind of funny business was going to happen, Sid was going to be prepared.

He bent down, picked up his two guns, and went back to the mirror.

CHAPTER THIRTY-ONE

Gabby was sitting on the sofa next to Troy, who'd started snoring rudely shortly after their guests had left. Her husband drank like a little kid, couldn't have a couple glasses of scotch without passing out or throwing up. She guessed that was just the way with guys who quit the drinking game but came out of retirement every time they closed a deal. Their brains turned to mush.

And serious Andrew sat across from her, staring at her, loving her. That's what he'd said at the Crescent Moon, that he loved her. Jesus Christ. Like they'd been dating or something. They liked to fuck, nice and simple, and there he was trying to complicate things. And here she was, sitting next to her snoring husband, and she was pretty drunk, too, feeling the booze in her face and her neck, all the way down to her chest.

She felt good but angry at the same time, though she couldn't put a finger on why. She just felt annoyed. But she still felt good, and she was going to do something about it. One of her arms was on the cushion behind Troy, but, with her other hand, she began to unbutton the front of her dress. She stared at Andrew as she did. He didn't move.

When the dress was open down to her navel, she pulled her arm out from behind Troy's head and began to hike up her skirt with both hands.

She closed her eyes, aware of her tongue exploring her own lips, tasting the boozy residue, running over the curve of her bottom lip as if it were ripe fruit. And she was aware that one of her hands was exploring her breast, feeling the swell of soft skin rising up from the lacy surface of the bra. With her other hand, she was feeling the sweat on the inside of her thigh, first with her fingertips, then with her whole hand. And when she opened her eyes, she saw Andrew rise awkwardly and take two steps forward before he bent over and lifted her off the couch, cradled her like a child, and carried her toward his downstairs apartment.

She glanced back at Troy as they left the room.

Spit bubbles. He was snoring and making spit bubbles.

She almost dozed off as Andrew carried her down to his room. She was in and out, drunk and thoughtful, horny and drowsy. When she finally felt herself being placed down on the bed she said, "This is the last time," and she was surprised how clear her voice sounded, neither slurred nor whispered.

"What?"

"This has to be the last time, Andrew. We're going to get caught."

"Doesn't matter. You're going to leave him anyway. We're going to be together."

"No, I don't think we can."

"Why not?"

"Because I don't think I can be with you."

"Yes, you can," he said, angry now, a little scary.

"I'm not going back to work at the Gap, Andrew. I like my life here."

"With Troy?"

"The lifestyle."

"I could support you," he said, sitting on the bed now and putting his hand on her knee.

"Doing what, Andrew?" she said, starting to button her dress now, knowing nothing was going to happen between them.

Andrew stood and walked out of the room. She heard him close the front door of the apartment and a few moments later heard him start the engine of his car, then turn it off again, without putting it into gear.

She took a deep breath and tried to figure out what was bothering her, putting her in this mood, this weird sort of drunk. It only took a few moments to realize that it was Chuck Holiday and his girlfriend. The way they sat next to each other, the way they rolled their eyes at each other when Claudel did something stupid, the way they were leaving together to start a new life. *They* bothered her.

***

Troy didn't know how long the phone had been ringing, but he shook off a wave of nausea and picked it up. "Speak," he said, his voice sounding hoarse and choked.

"That you?" said Claudel's jive-ass voice, clear, like he was sitting in the next room.

"Yeah," said Troy as he began to put together some of the fragments of the evening. The Holiday deal … Gabby's dinner … the scotch … Brian. That's what Claudel was calling about. "How's my nephew?"

"Well," said Claudel. "I don't think he doin' too good."

"What do y'mean?"

"I'm over at his house right now, Troy, and somethin' bad gone down in this place."

"Talk English, Claudel."

"This English enough. Somebody come in here tonight and fucked this place all up. Drawers out, mattress off the bed, broken shit everywhere. Fucked up, man."

"What about Brian?"

"He ain't here, Troy."

"Tell me again what he said to you on the phone tonight," said Troy, and felt his stomach cramp.

"I already said all I heard."

"Yeah, I know, but I don't remember. Tell me again."

"Something about the Chinamens, Troy. I can't remember."

"Are those dogs still down there?"

"Lemme check," said Claudel.

Troy's brain wasn't working the way he wanted it to. He wanted to organize his thoughts and start solving problems, but he kept having flashes, kept hearing his brother's voice asking for help with Brian, the only time his brother had asked anyone for help in his whole life, maybe the only time he needed it.

Claudel was back on the line. "All gone," he said, out of breath, starting to sound panicked.

"What's that mean, Claudel?"

"No dogs," he said. "And no fencing or treadmill or none of that shit was down there like before."

"The Chinamen cleaned the place out," said Troy, mostly to himself. "You see any blood anywhere?"

"Naw, but that garage been hosed out good. Only part of the house that's clean."

"Where do we find these fuckin' gooks, Claudel?"

"Only thing I know's they run a rib joint on West Portal."

"What're a bunch of Chinamen doin' runnin' a rib place?"

"Fuck if I know, but that's what they do."

"Y'think they're open?" asked Troy.

"Mr. Curran, it's motherfuckin' three o'clock in the morning."

"Why'd you wait so long to go over there?" asked Troy.

"I was making calls. Inquiring about your man's whereabouts."

"Well, you need to meet me and Tupps down at the rib place right now," said Troy, as he started to check his pockets for keys. "What's the name of the place again?"

"Singing Sow."

CHAPTER THIRTY-TWO

Claudel didn't have much trouble breaking into the restaurant. He was standing in the big kitchen with Troy and Tupps. Troy looked sick, his hair matted down on one side, and Tupps looked sad, his thick lips turned down at the corners. Claudel was excited, ready to start his Denzel Washington routine again.

"What we lookin' for?" asked Claudel.

"I want these fuckers," said Troy. "So if we can find an address, something that says where they're at, we'll go get 'em tonight and find out what happened to Brian."

There was a desk in the corner next to the ice machine. Tupps sat in the chair and started shuffling through the stacks of papers. Claudel looked over his shoulder and watched the man's surprisingly small, thin hands work through the invoices and phone messages and receipts and supplier order forms, all addressed to the West Portal restaurant.

Claudel reached around Tupps and pulled out the file drawer. He carried it to the long butcher's block table in the center of the room and started emptying the contents onto the table: business cards, pencils and pens, notebooks filled with calculations … nothing with an address. He walked over to a storage shelf and grabbed a bag of potato chips. He opened the bag and started munching, thinking that it wouldn't be bad if they killed those guys tonight. If they sneaked into the dudes' house and shot them, it wouldn't have the drama of a showdown, but it would get the job done, get them off Chuck's back, and ensure that Claudel would get his payments from Chuck. It would also satisfy Troy's need for vengeance. His nephew was dead, and, as far as he knew, the dudes that did it would be dead too, even Steven, eye for an eye—the kind of street justice that would make Troy happy. All would be right in the world.

But that wasn't going to happen unless they came up with an address. Troy was in the front, fucking around near the cash register, pulling drawers but finding nothing but extra napkins and ketchup packets. The man was pissed when he walked back into the kitchen, pacing around and pulling shit off the shelves. He finally sat down on a stack of soda cases. He was pushing his fingers through his matted hair when he said, "We could wait here until morning and ice the fucks when they come in."

"Don't know if they come in and *work* in the restaurant, Troy," said Claudel before he placed another handful of chips in his mouth. "They own the place."

"Whoever does'll probably know where we can find these assholes, right?"

"I guess that's right," said Claudel, little flakes of the chips dropping from his mouth. "But I don't see myself sleeping in this roach motel, man."

Troy didn't respond. He hung his head, and Claudel could hear him breathing through his nose.

Claudel was about to make his planned suggestion that Chuck Holiday might know where to find them, but he stopped when he heard a loud click and then a sliding sound. He turned and saw Tupps opening the freezer, like he was going to find the address on a piece of frozen meat.

"Jesus Christ," said Tupps. "What the fuck are these guys doing?"

Claudel walked over and looked inside. It was packed from floor to ceiling with whole pigs, lying on their sides in layers like a mass grave. "Is this normal? How many you suppose is in there?" said Claudel as he reached out and tried to push one of the carcasses, thinking maybe they were piled up in a single wall and might fall back to reveal a secret treasure behind, but they were packed solid.

Tupps had left the pigs and moved across the kitchen to the walk-in refrigerator on the other side of the bathroom. "Oh, Jesus," he said, his shaky voice echoing from the back of refrigerated space.

Troy rose from his seat on the cases of soda and started to walk toward the sound of Tupps's voice. Claudel followed, having a good idea what might be back there, surprised that he hadn't thought of it before.

Claudel felt the bottoms of his shoes sticking to the floor as he walked closer to the opening of the walk-in. He felt the frosty air on his face as he made the turn around the big door. The room was filled on the side shelves with condiment containers and large packages of Louisiana hot links. And when Claudel looked over Troy's shoulder, he saw what he expected: Brian Curran. And Brian wasn't looking too good. He was missing a big chunk of his shoulder and neck, and his shirt was covered in blood, which looked black in the shadows.

Tupps was holding a tarp which must have been covering the body. Troy was only silent for a moment before he said calmly, "Cover him back up, Andrew." Then he turned and walked past Claudel out of the coldness.

Claudel and Tupps looked at each other. Claudel couldn't quite figure out what it was between them in that dark space, but Tupps almost looked human to him for a split second before he turned back to the body.

Claudel said to Troy, who was back on the stack of sodas, "Shouldn't we take him with us?"

"What're we gonna do with him?"

"Figured you'd want to set up a proper burial and whatnot."

"I can't really worry about that right now," said Troy. "I have to kill these fuckers first."

"Yeah," said Claudel. "Okay. That's right." This was working out pretty well. Troy had already given Chuck the money, and now Troy wanted to kill the two Chinese dudes that wanted Chuck's money. Shit was working out. Almost too easy. "I think maybe Chuck Holiday could tell us where to look for these dudes."

"What does Holiday know about them?"

"I think they met through your nephew."

"No shit?"

"Yeah," said Claudel, rolling now. "I think Brian was gonna sponsor those boys, get 'em in with Holiday."

"So if you think Holiday knows where to find these assholes, why're we breakin' in to the fuckin' Singing Sow in the middle of the night?"

"Didn't say he could *find* 'em," said Claudel. "What may be the case is that my man can get a hold of those dudes, find out where they at."

"Get him on the phone right now," Troy said.

"Middle of the night, Troy."

"Get him on the fuckin' phone right now, Shanks."

CHAPTER THIRTY-THREE

Chuck and Hazel couldn't sleep. They sat on the couch with the envelope of money between them. MTV was doing a show about famous marriages. Madonna and Guy Ritchie were on there; the guy that wrote *Almost Famous* and the good lookin' chick from *Heart*; Pamela Anderson and Kid Rock. After each segment, Hazel would say, "Doomed."

Chuck finally said, "Why?" looking at a still-shot of Kid Rock with his arm around Pam, her boobs nearly jumping out of a little white dress.

"Look at those two." Chuck immediately thought she was talking about Pamela's breasts until she said, "Their marriage is a joke."

"Why do you say that?"

"Because they're both fakes."

Chuck thought for a moment, still trying to get the breasts out of his mind, *couple of fakes*, before he said, "As long as they're not fake to each other, they might be okay, right?"

"Fakers don't make it in relationships," she said.

"But as long as they're not fake to each other, can't they make it?"

Hazel was silent, and Chuck's mind started working. Was she indirectly talking about them? Was she saying that *he* was a fake? Or was she talking about herself, all the bullshitting she did with the tarot cards? He thought their relationship was doing fine, considering they were currently involved in all sorts of illegal activity, the kind of shit that can go hard on a relationship. But they were going to make it. He wanted to reassure her but things like *We'll be fine as soon as we complete the murder cover-up* or *Once the Chinese are dead, everything's gonna be all right* didn't seem to fit.

"I don't want to end up like those sick fucks over there in Marin," she said, nearly in tears.

"What do y'mean?"

"I mean," she said, moving closer to him, "that those people over there ... that marriage was disgusting, Chuck. And that guy, Andrew Tupps—"

Hazel was doing everything in her power to hold the tears back, waiting for Chuck to say something. He reached over and grabbed the back of her neck, pulling her to his chest and holding her. "We're not gonna be like them. We're leaving that behind. In a few days, we're gonna be far away from all that."

"Are we?"

"What?" he said, not sure which point she was questioning.

"Getting away from that life?"

Chuck said, "Yeah, we are," just as the phone rang. He grabbed it and said, "It's three o'clock in the morning."

"Chuck," said Claudel, "Mr. Curran want to have a few words with y'all. Sorry so late, man."

Chuck said, "Well, put him on," wondering if something had gone wrong or if Troy was just eager to find Don and Sid.

"Chuck," said Troy. "Apologies for the late hour, but something's come up and we need to talk to the Chinks that my nephew's been working with on that pit bull deal."

Troy paused, but Chuck said nothing.

"Claudel here says you may know how to get in touch with those guys."

"I know where their restaurant is."

"We know that much."

"I think I have their cell phone number, too," Chuck said.

"You know where they live?"

"I don't," he said, playing dumb, like he didn't have any clue what was going on. "But I could call 'em in the morning and try to find out." He waited, wanting to get just the right timing. He knew Claudel had told Troy about the mess at Brian's house, but he couldn't get a mental picture of where they all were right now. "Did something happen with Brian?" Chuck finally asked.

"Here's Claudel," said Troy.

When Claudel came on the line, he said, "Yeah?"

Chuck knew Claudel had to be careful, so he said, "Claudel, go slow and give me whatever info you can."

"Brian's dead," said Claudel. "Found him in the fridge at the Singing Sow."

"Jesus Christ," said Chuck. To Hazel, "They found Brian's body." Saying those words let the dogs loose in his brain, barking and nipping and sniffing around thoughts that he wanted to put to rest. This was crunch time. He said to Claudel, "Do you want to tell Troy that I think I can get Don and Sid up to his place tomorrow?"

"I don't know," said Claudel, obviously holding back, standing close to Curran.

"Well," said Chuck, "this is it. It's go time. Take a deep breath and try this out. I think it'll work. Just tell Troy that Chuck Holiday says he'll be able to get the Chinese over to his house tomorrow. You don't have to tell how. Just tell him that I'll get a hold of those guys in the morning, and I'll have 'em up there in the afternoon, and Troy can do whatever he wants with 'em."

Silence. Chuck waited a few beats before he said, "Go ahead and tell him that, Claudel. He doesn't have anything to be suspicious about because he thinks these guys killed Brian. Shit, he found the body in their restaurant, for Christ's sake."

"You right," said Claudel. Chuck heard brief mumbling in the background before Claudel got back on the line and said, "Mr. Curran say make it happen, and it'd be much appreciated."

"Good," said Chuck. "Just tell him that Don and Sid are gonna think it's a business meeting. They're not gonna have any idea that Troy is Brian's uncle. They'll have no reason to suspect anything."

"Awright."

CHAPTER THIRTY-FOUR

Troy and Andrew Tupps were waiting on the front patio in the afternoon sun. Tupps was the man for this job. Troy didn't want Claudel fucking it up by using his baseball bat to do work that Tupps would take care of with his Colt. Louder maybe, but not as messy as a couple of guys with their heads bashed to shit. And much quicker. No screaming and begging. Troy didn't have the stomach for that, especially after last night's scotch. He couldn't do it anymore, didn't even know why he kept falling off the wagon. He just didn't get enough enjoyment out of it. Close a deal, have a couple glasses of scotch was a bullshit mantra, and he was done with it. He used to think it was a show of power that he could have a drink now and again without turning back into a drunk, but there were less painful ways to celebrate making money, and who was he trying to impress anyway?

"Does it matter the order I whack these fellas?" said Tupps, adjusting his ankle holster, then practicing pulling his gun out fast.

"As long as they're both dead when Claudel carts 'em outta here," said Troy, "I don't give a shit which one you hit first."

"Sometimes a man wants one of the assholes to have to watch the other one die before he goes," he said. "I guess if you want a man to suffer a little more, you might want him to be scared first and have to think about what's going to happen to himself."

"There might be something to that," said Troy. "But I don't know which one of these two fucks is calling the shots."

"Yeah," said Tupps, leaning back in his chair and crossing his ankle over his knee. "But if you did know, you might want to pick him to go second. It's like I heard one time that if you're asleep when you get in a car wreck, or if you're really drunk, and you hit that windshield before you can tighten up, it's much less painful." He smiled and said, "That second guy that you whack, if you wait a moment before you do it, he has plenty of time to tighten up and really feel that bullet burning through him."

"I don't know about that," said Troy.

"Why not?"

"Well, I don't think those sleeping and drunk guys feel so much less pain. I think it's more that they get fewer injuries for some reason."

"You think that?"

"You ever been shot?"

"Never."

Troy unbuttoned the first three buttons on his powder blue oxford and pulled the shirt back so that his left shoulder was exposed. With his right index finger he pointed at a round pink scar about the size of a quarter just below his clavicle. "I got shot about twelve years ago," he said.

"Who shot you?"

"It's a long story, but that's not the point. It's that I know what it feels like. And y'know what? It don't hurt as bad is you might think."

"Were you tensed up?"

"As a matter of fact, I was. But it still didn't hurt that bad."

"Were you ever shot when you weren't tensed up?"

"This is the only time I been shot."

"Then you don't have anything to compare it to."

"I guess not," said Troy. "But the point's that it doesn't hurt as much as you think it might."

"You know what would be the worst?"

Troy felt like they was playing a kids' game. He wanted to say *having your face eaten by rats*, but he didn't. "What?"

"If you got shot naked."

"Huh?"

"Doesn't it seem," said Tupps, "that it would hurt a lot more if you got shot when you didn't have any clothes on?" "Bullet's coming at you a million miles an hour. You think a thin layer of polyester's gonna cut the pain?"

"I know it sounds crazy, but to me it seems like it'd hurt a lot more if I was naked. Naked and tensed up."

"I don't know about that," said Troy and looked at the curve in his private road, waiting to see those fuckers driving up like they were gonna be making a business deal. He wondered how Holiday was able to set the whole thing up.

And after listening to Tupps, he was wondering if maybe Claudel would have been a better choice for this job after all.

***

Claudel was inside talking with Gabby. He couldn't be outside because the Chinese would know something was up. They'd remember him from Chuck's house, squeezing that little dude's head until he made little squeaking noises.

He had to sit in the kitchen with the man's wife and wait to see if the Goose's plan was going to work out. Chuck already had Troy's money, and it looked like Don and Sid were going to be out of the picture, so Chuck could take his dough and little Hazel and head on over to England, be close to the Rolling Stones and the Beatles, white dudes who started their careers singing black songs, but that's how it was with most of those white boys, including The King. Claudel wondered if Andrew Tupps knew anything about it, sitting out there with Troy, the two of them in dark glasses, trying to look bad.

"What's going on today?" said Gabby, chewing on a piece of See's candy and holding the box out to Claudel, who grabbed two, not caring what was inside. He liked them all.

It was hard to chew and talk, but he said, "I know you think Troy's nephew was an asshole, but they gotta take care them dudes killed him."

"Troy's not gonna kill 'em right here on the patio?" she said, her eyes scared.

"You don't have to worry," he said. "First off, I don't think Troy's gonna be doin' nothin' out there but talkin', and second, he gonna send his house boy Claudel out there to clean it all up after, so y'all got no worries."

"Wait a second. If Troy's just going to be talking, what do you have to clean up?"

Claudel had to pause a moment. She didn't get it. "Yeah," he said, "there gonna be a mess, but Troy ain't gonna lift a finger. That's what he got the Hulk for."

Claudel was surprised to see her face change so much. Suddenly, she wasn't looking so good. "So Troy's making Andrew kill someone for him?"

"That is the plan."

"He's gonna make Andrew a murderer?"

"I don't know much about the arrangement," he said, uncomfortable with the questions now. "But I think this might be part of the job description."

"Well, it's wrong, Claudel," she said, pacing around the kitchen and peeking out the window, leaning her face against the glass, trying to get an angle so she could see Tupps.

"It ain't right that Tupps hate niggers either, but he do, don't he?"

"Claudel," she said, sitting down now at the kitchen table and looking Claudel in the eyes. "That's how he was raised, but he isn't a bad person." Then she was up again at the window before she looked back at him and said, "He's a good person, and Troy's about to change his life forever and turn him into a murderer."

"I assumed the man'd done this sort of thing before, Gabby."

"Well, he hasn't."

Claudel didn't know that she was so snugged up with him, but it was too late. The wheels were already turning. "Well, Troy give him a job to do," he said. "And it look like he intend to do it in a few minutes, whether it gonna *change* him or not."

CHAPTER THIRTY-FIVE

Chuck and Hazel, on the Harley, were on an old fire road that snaked through the hills near Dominican College and looked down on Troy Curran's patio. They had good coverage behind a shrub line, and were close enough that they didn't need binoculars to see the men in the white van pulling onto Troy's private road.

Troy and Tupps sat side by side in patio chairs. They were wearing dark glasses, and had been talking nonstop for the past ten minutes, gesturing with their arms, laughing, Troy even opening his shirt at one point to show Tupps something on his chest. Chuck wondered what they were saying, if they had a complicated plot, or if they were simply going to pop the Chinese as they got out of the van.

Chuck had been in a crouch for about ten minutes, and his knees were starting to ache, so he sat down in the dirt behind the hedge line and poked a hole through the twigs and leaves until he had a clear view of the patio. Hazel knelt down beside him and created her own peephole. "Can you see okay?"

Hazel, who was still breaking twigs and squinting through the opening, said, "I can see Don and Sid's van parking on the road".

"I don't know if I want to watch this," he said at the same time he was pushing his legs into the shrub, so that he could put his face up close to his opening.

"I *know* I don't want to watch this. Why are we here?"

Chuck kept thinking back to those two fuckers flashing their guns at him at Kezar and threatening to do things to Hazel. "I'm responsible for this," he said. "I should *have* to watch it. That's my punishment for getting involved, but I don't want you to watch. You don't have anything to do with this."

Hazel reached over and put her hand on his knee, but she kept watch through the peephole. "You're not responsible for this. This is self-defense."

Chuck watched Sid jump out of his side of the van. He looked even smaller from a distance. Chuck couldn't see Sid's face from his current vantage point, but he guessed that the man was smiling, just loving the fact that he was getting to play with the big boys. "Self-defense?" Chuck said as Don emerged from the other side of the van.

"Yeah," she said, whispering as if someone could hear her from way up there. "If we didn't set them up to be killed, they were gonna kill you … maybe both of us."

"We could have paid them what they wanted," said Chuck, watching

Troy and Tupps rise to shake hands with the men, Troy pointing at the two chairs opposite his and Tupps's. "Then they would have left us alone."

"Maybe. Or maybe they would have killed us anyway." The four men below seemed to be engaging in a cordial conversation. "And we didn't have the money anyway when we started all this."

"We do now," said Chuck and then he saw something out of the corner of his eye, just a slight movement that could have been a leaf falling or a moth fluttering, but it wasn't. It was the back door of the van opening. "What the fuck?"

"What?"

"The van … the van." By the time he looked back to the patio, Tupps was standing and holding a pistol on Don and Sid. Troy was still sitting with his legs crossed at the ankles, as if he were about to watch third round golf coverage.

Chuck saw more movement. The side door to the house was opening. There was too much happening in the picture now. He said again, "What the fuck?"

He looked back at the van and saw the pair of sneakers stretching out of the back door, then the denim pants, and finally the red sweatshirt of either a very small man, shorter than Sid, or a little boy.

Hazel said, "What is *she* doing?"

Chuck turned his attention to the house, where Gabby Curran was running toward the four men. She was wearing a pair of cutoffs and had bare feet, and yelling something, but Chuck couldn't make it out. He checked back on the little kid, who was peeking around the side of the van. Then the kid darted to the open back door and dragged out a duffel bag. He used the van as cover as he placed the bag on the pavement and reached inside. And, God damn it, he was pulling out a gun. Chuck wanted to scream to Troy, but he couldn't. He was too scared to give away his position—and this was a little kid.

He looked at Tupps, who was still holding the gun on Don and Sid, but was taking quick glances at Gabby, who was standing ten feet away from him, her hands on her hips, still yelling. Chuck was trying to make out her words when he heard a sharp pop, not as loud as he'd have expected. Tupps was down.

Troy dove to the ground and tried to get Tupps's gun, but it was too late. Don and Sid both had guns out and were firing on the two men sprawled out beside their chairs.

Gabby was curled up in a ball. Sid walked up to her, pointed, and executed her on the spot. She rolled slowly onto her side as Sid turned toward the door, where Claudel stood holding his baseball bat, as if he'd be able to hit the bullets back at Don and Sid if they decided to try to shoot at him from across the yard, which Sid did, another pop, the sound slightly delayed by the distance between the hedge and the front porch.

Sid's one shot missed badly, breaking a window ten feet away from Claudel. Hazel, still in a whisper, said, "Jesus Christ, why doesn't he get the hell outta there?"

Chuck couldn't talk. He was watching Don running over to the little kid to take the gun while Sid was running toward the open side door. Claudel had disappeared.

"We gotta go help him," said Chuck, who started to stand, thinking he'd be able to see better over the hedge rather than through it.

"How?"

"He's stuck in there," he said, pulling her to her feet.

She had to stand on her toes to see over the hedge line. "I know that. But we don't have guns."

Chuck looked at the duffel bag behind the van, and turned his attention to Don, who'd sat the kid in one of the chairs and was talking to him. Don had a gun in each hand, and he was waving them around as he talked. He kept turning his head to the house, then looking back at the boy. It almost looked like he was scolding the kid, like the kid had played with matches or something. But, shit, the kid had saved his life.

Don ran to the back of the house, holding his guns out in front of him.

Chuck said, "Let's go. We can try to help him."

Hazel closed her eyes for a second. She didn't go into a big theatrical trance like she did with clients, but Chuck could tell she was trying to see something.

"What's up?" he said, watching the little boy pick up the duffle bag.

"I think he's okay," she said, her eyes open but still not quite focused.

The boy was climbing up into the front of the van dragging the bag of guns behind him.

"Who's okay?"

"He's safe," she said.

"Hazel, snap out of it."

"Claudel. Claudel's okay, I think."

"Did you have a vision?"

"Yeah."

"What?"

"It's not really that I see something specific. I see flashes of images and then I get a feeling about them."

"You do?"

"It's like when you went to Brian's to collect last week, I knew something was bad. I saw it."

"Well, thanks for stopping me." He loved her, but couldn't quite make himself fully accept her *gift*.

"You'd already left," she said. "And then Troy Curran came to the house."

"All right, forget it," said Chuck. "What do your images tell you to do now?"

"They're not telling me anything, but I think Claudel can take care of himself, and I think we should get ourselves far away from Don and Sid. Don't you?

FOURTH QUARTER ~ ESCAPE ARTISTS

If the hunter turns his dogs loose
On your dreams
Start early, tell no one
Get rid of the scent.

– C.D. Wright

I never really liked magicians. There's something a little creepy about the "world of illusion." It might be the goofy costumes or the overly choreographed bits and silly music. Whatever it is, I never really got into those acts. But I do like escape artists. No smoke and mirrors there. Just guys getting locked up and trying to figure out ways to get out.

Like Andy Dufrusne in Shawshank. He used that little chisel to break through all that rock and then crawl through a quarter mile of raw sewage before he finally escaped from prison.

That's an escape artist.

But he had time. That made it easier. Patience and time. He picked away at his predicament a little each day. Most escape artists don't have time. In fact, in most scenarios, the clock is ticking. Like Houdini. He had a bunch of escapes where he only had as much time as he could hold his breath.

I've since heard that this is at least partly embellished, but one story about Houdini is that he let himself get handcuffed and locked in a box and then thrown through a hole in the ice into a freezing river. If I remember it correctly, he was under the ice for eight minutes. He didn't hold his breath all that time because he was able to breathe from a thin layer of air between the water and the ice, but he was in that water breaking free and then searching for the hole for eight minutes, a ridiculous amount of time for a human to survive under those conditions.

Escape artist.

Maybe my favorite story of escape took place at Cal, not long before I left. Apparently a bunch of freshmen were taking a science exam in one of those auditorium classes, a couple hundred kids at least. A bitch of an exam. A lot of kids didn't have time to finish. But the professor starts saying to turn the tests in. Time's up.

Well, everyone in the class gets those tests in, a big stack on the professor's table, but one kid keeps working. The professor says, "Son, you have three seconds to place that test on my table, or you will receive a zero."

The story goes that the kid doesn't look up, keeps working on the test but raises a finger up to the professor. Like saying hold on a minute, almost mad that the professor is rushing him.

That's all the professor needs. He says, "That's it. I'm no longer accepting exams." He picks up his briefcase in one hand and he holds the stack of exams in the other. Then he begins walking up the stairs and out of the auditorium.

The kid taking the test slams his pencil down and says, "Finished!" Then he races up the stairs and catches the professor right before he gets to the door. "Here you go," he says, presenting his completed examination.

"You must be joking," says the professor. "I told you thrice to turn in that exam, yet you continued to work."

"So you're not gonna take it?" he says, like he's not believing the guy.

"Of course not," the professor says. "It wouldn't be fair to the other members of this class who turned in their exams on time," he says and takes a step toward the door.

"Wait!" the kid says. "What does this mean?"

"You don't have to be a mathematician to know that getting a zero on the final examination will mean that you have failed this class," he says and stares at the kid. "That's what it means."

The kid squints at the professor and says, "Do you have any idea who I am?"

The professor grins and shakes his head. "I don't have the slightest idea who you are."

"Good," says the kid and with two hands slaps down on the professor's stack of exams. The papers go scattering all over the floor, and the professor looks shocked as he watches the kid slide his paper into the mix, shuffle the stack, and then hand the papers back to the professor. "Have a nice break," the kid says and jogs out into the hallway. I've had friends at other schools tell the same story. Maybe it's an urban legend. Everyone thinks it happened at his particular school. But it must have happened somewhere, right? The story didn't just appear out of thin air.

That kid had to have a good brain and a lot of guts to pull it off.

But there's one other thing that contributes to every escape. Luck. You gotta have some luck. If Andy Dufresne's guards had looked behind his Raquel Welch poster, he would have been toast. If the river's currents carried Houdini's box just a little farther downstream, he wouldn't have been able to make it back to that hole in the ice. And if that professor had put the exams in his briefcase, that kid would have had to repeat the class.

Guts and brains are important, but I'll take the luck anytime.

CHAPTER THIRTY-SIX

Claudel had heard the shots fired, and thought, shit, Gabby had to watch the Hulk puttin' holes in them dudes, everybody *changed* now forever. He also knew he was going to be taking some heavy shit from Troy because he let the lady outside while the man was conducting business. But the chick just hauled ass out of there like she was on fire. Claudel'd been sitting down, and by the time he got out of the chair, she was out the door. He couldn't show himself on the patio. If Don and Sid recognized him, it'd blow the whole deal, scare the dudes into making a run for it. But he knew the shit was gonna be coming now from the Hulk and Troy, especially Troy, who had to have some idea that something was going on with Gabby and the South African, although Claudel didn't know exactly what she was saying when she ran out. He just hoped Troy didn't think Claudel knew something was up with his wife and the Hulk. He didn't want to have to answer to that.

Claudel grabbed his bat and walked toward the door, hoping Gabby didn't say anything too stupid. He smelled something metallic and heard another shot. He looked outside and saw Gabby layin' on the deck, with blood spreading out on her white tube top. And there was that little fuckin' midget standing over her, holding his gun up above his head like some kind of freedom fighter.

When the man saw Claudel in the doorway, he pointed the gun and squeezed off a shot that broke one of the kitchen windows. Claudel was just about to start laughing when reality seeped into his brain. There was a tiny man staring him down, like they were in an old western, *High Noon* and shit, and they were going to draw. Nothing happened for a few seconds. Sid kept staring at Claudel, maybe thinking back to when Claudel fucked him up over at Chuck's. Or maybe he was trying to make the connection between Chuck and Troy and hisself. Or maybe he was just trying to figure out how his aim could be so fuckin' off.

He finally walked toward Claudel, who was thinking that Sid was trying look like Jesse James now, only no spurs and fucking Chinese, man, and getting closer. The little guy wanted to look mean as he got into range to blow Claudel's brains out of his head, and Claudel was standing there with nothin' but a baseball bat. Claudel jumped back inside the house. He locked the door and started to run for the back door, but stopped when he saw the partner's head passing by the row of windows. Don was running around the house to keep Claudel from getting out the back. Then Claudel heard Sid breaking the glass on the side door. Time to make a decision.

He was in the center of the house on the ground floor. The stairs were going to be tough with his bad knee, but he started toward them and tried to take them two at a time. When he got to the first landing, the pain was so great that he started using the bat as a walking stick, hobbling all the way up to the third floor and right to the linen closet.

He pushed open the false door and closed it behind him. Then he sat down in Troy's leather chair and tried to slow his breathing. He rubbed his knee and waited. There was a fire escape outside the little window, but Claudel didn't think he could make it with his knee throbbing. So he waited.

He was able to quiet his huffing and puffing by breathing through his nose and closing his eyes, trying to get into a meditative state, control his heart rate. And once he was calm, he started to play back the last two minutes. He could still see one brain-picture of Sid posed above Gabby Curran, like he was on top of a trophy, and now that Claudel was slowing things down, he was catching flashes of other images. Tupps and Troy down on the ground and Don talking with a little kid. It didn't make sense, but that was what he saw.

Chuck's books were stacked on Troy's desk, and Claudel was coming to the realization that, with Troy dead, the whole deal with Holiday was bust. He'd lost not only his job with Troy, his steady income, but also the monthly percentage from Chuck's former clients that Chuck was going to sign over to him. That was the reason for getting into all this mess in the first place, and now Troy was bleeding all over the fuckin' patio out there.

And he could hear the crazy motherfuckers that did it out in the rooms, opening and closing doors, yelling at each other in Chinese, knocking stuff off the shelves. Neither of them had seen him come all the way up to the third floor, and he was hoping that they would think he got out somehow; otherwise, they were going to rip the place apart until they found Troy's office. And Claudel knew they'd probably torture him a little before they killed him, unless he ambushed the fuckers when they opened the false door, took his signature Adirondack to their heads, maybe his last batting practice ever.

***

Don and Sid were in the living room. Sid was sitting on the couch, and Don was looking through the records stacked around the stereo.

There were dead bodies out in front of the house, a little boy in the van, and a big black man somewhere, but Sid didn't feel the need to panic. He felt invincible.

"How did that fat ass get out?" said Sid in Chinese.

"There's got to be a secret exit somewhere," said Don as he threw Ike and Tina Frisbee-style off the wall, the little black chips raining down over the sofa.

"The older man said he was Brian Curran's uncle," said Sid.

"That's what he said."

"So we were set up," said Sid, looking up just behind Don's head at a painting of cliffs and sea, the Golden Gate Bridge peeking over the hills.

"Holiday."

"Holiday tried to have us killed."

"That's the only way to look at it," said Don, who picked up Gladys Knight and flung her off the wall, the Pips scattering all the way across the room and landing near Sid's feet. "He must have told Curran that we killed his nephew."

"Then we'll kill Holiday."

"We should make him watch us do the girl first."

Sid was surprised that he'd forgotten about the girl. "Good idea. But we have to take care of Hubert before we do anything."

Don was about to throw another record but stopped and said, "What?"

"We have to do something about your nephew."

"He saved our lives."

"I know. But we have to make sure he keeps his mouth shut."

Don sat down on the love seat and said, "How did he get in the van?"

"The little bug must have hid in there when we were getting ready before we left."

"I'm glad he did," said Sid.

"Let's go talk to him," said Don, and started to walk toward the door. He looked tired, and Sid thought that Don was starting to look like an old man.

On the walk to the van, Sid didn't even look at the bodies.

The boy sat in the front, and Sid could tell by his puffy face and red cheeks that he'd been crying. "Why did you hide in the back of the van?" asked Sid.

The boy stared straight forward and said, "I wanted to see what you and my uncle do."

"Do you now know how dangerous it was?" asked Don.

The boy nodded.

"You could have been killed," said Don.

The boy nodded again.

"You can't tell anyone what you saw out here today," he said.

"I won't," said the boy. And then he opened his mouth as if he were going to say something, but he stopped.

Sid said, "What do you want to say?"

"Why did you shoot the lady?"

Sid said nothing.

"She didn't have a gun."

Sid heard Don start the engine. He thought for a moment before he said, "She would have tried to put us in jail." It was all he could come up with. But it didn't seem to satisfy the boy, so he added, "She would have wanted to put *you* in jail too."

The boy turned quickly to his Uncle Don, who nodded slowly and steered the van back onto the private road, away from the bodies. Sid was keeping an eye out for the big black man, hoping that they'd see him on the road and Don could run him over.

The boy cleared his throat and said, "Who was the tall man with the motorcycle?"

Don hit the brakes hard and said, "Where?"

The boy looked scared and said, "A man came and looked at the bodies and then drove off on a motorcycle."

"Where do you think he went?" Don asked Sid.

Sid ignored him and asked the boy, "Did he say anything to you?"

"The girl waved at me."

CHAPTER THIRTY-SEVEN

They rode the motorcycle through Corte Madera and Larkspur, Chuck taking special notice of San Quentin as they moved toward Tiburon and Mill Valley. He felt the cool fog on his face and saw soft mist rolling over the hills to the west when they motored down the Waldo Grade and past the Sausalito exit.

Something about the thickening fog and the Golden Gate Bridge looming in the distance made him take the last Marin exit, which snaked up a cliff that looked out across the bay toward the half-shadowed San Francisco skyline and the darkening cypresses of the Presidio.

Chuck pulled the Harley onto a gravel viewing area. One other car was perched on the lookout, and a man and woman were sitting on the hood, talking to each other in Italian. Chuck got off and helped Hazel by offering his left forearm and taking her around the waist with his right arm.

He kept his arm around her and looked across at all the promise of the beautiful city. He knew that if he leaned out over the railing, he'd be able to see Alcatraz keeping its lookout over the bay, staring in at the piers and Coit Tower but also peering back at its still-functional brother to the north.

Chuck also knew that if he drove up over the ridge and continued down the winding road, he'd find the beach in Curran's painting, those same waves crashing off the white sand. It was hundreds of feet below him, but he could feel it. And he could remember the safety and peace it had meant to Curran, who was now lying in his own blood near his wife and his security man. It was too late for them. He wondered if, in those few moments after the kid had shot Tupps, there had been a blink of time in which Curran became aware that simple geography couldn't always protect him.

Chuck was hoping that if he got far enough away, across an ocean rather than a bay, he could separate himself from the ugliness, that geography *could* save him. Chuck needed to reevaluate his situation. He didn't want to go home. He pictured Don and Sid and the kid waiting in his living room, the kid holding the bag of weapons. Then his mind moved back to the view of the kid sitting in the front seat of the van. When they'd passed by on the motorcycle, Chuck had tried to decipher the kid's blank expression. Did he feel pride that he'd saved the two morons? There were so many other things he could have been feeling. He'd just committed homicide.

"Why did you wave at that kid when we were leaving?" Chuck asked and tightened his grip on Hazel's waist.

"I don't know. I think I felt sorry for him."

"You think he's already partners with those other two fuck ups? You think he's already a gangster?"

Hazel shook her head slowly before she looked up at Chuck and said, "Those guys thought they were making a business deal today. The kid might've been just going along for the ride."

"He seemed pretty comfortable with a gun."

"So did you when you came into the room the other day when I was reading Don's palm. You looked like you'd been using a gun for years."

Chuck didn't tell her he'd had to ask Claudel how to release the safety. "Why did you feel sorry for him?"

"To be that young and already be messed up for life … it's sad," she said and looked at the Italian couple, who were getting back into the car as the fog began to obscure the view.

"You think his life is ruined because he saw what he saw today?" He held her close with both arms, trying to keep her warm as the wind blew in from the Pacific.

"Yeah," she said almost immediately. "He didn't just see it. He was a *part* of it."

Chuck knew she was right, and it bothered him. "We also saw it and were a part of it."

She didn't say anything for a long time. Chuck was looking down at the top of her head and waiting for her to say something that would allow him to keep hoping that they could get out of this. "We're older, and we're trying to get out," she said. She looked at him. There was enough light left for him to see the seriousness in her eyes. "And we're *getting* out. We're going to England, and you're gonna play basketball over there, and we're gonna have a new life and put everything else behind us." He thought he heard her voice starting to crack, but her face was determined, borderline angry. She looked the way she did when they were at the track and her horse was still in the hunt for the home stretch, and she was going to will it to victory.

"But what are we gonna do about Don and Sid and the new little gangster?"

"I have no idea," she said and started to walk back toward the bike. Her hands were clinched in fists.

***

Don and Sid had dropped off the kid in Chinatown and went down to the *Singing Sow.* They pulled the van into the alley behind the restaurant and backed it up to a small loading dock. Don unlocked the sheet metal door and pulled it up, and then he grabbed Sid by the wrist and pulled him up onto the dock.

When they opened the big refrigerator, Don asked, "Should we cut him up?" He'd stopped using English after the shooting, too jumpy still to think about his words.

"No," said Sid, walking over to the body and giving it a kick with his little black shoe. "I want him in one piece for this."

"I think I'm starting to smell him," said Don.

"Not very bad," said Sid. "I wish he smelled worse."

Don didn't want to touch the body. He didn't want to smell it or see it, either, but he knew he would have to. "How are we going to get him in?"

"In the van?"

"Yes."

"We're going to drag it around the corner and slide it in," said Sid. "Why? Do you have some other idea?"

"I'm just worried about the alley," said Don. "What if someone is back there?"

"Nobody will be back there," he said. Then after a moment, "And if there is, we'll shoot him and put him in the back of the van with this one."

Don nodded and walked into the coldness of the refrigerated room. He glanced at the sausages and marinated chicken and ribs so close to the corpse, and he decided that he couldn't eat at the restaurant anymore. Every time he licked his fingers after taking a bite of meat, he'd think of Brian Curran's bloody flesh, that missing chunk of shoulder and neck. He might actually have to become a vegetarian.

"Let's go," said Sid, as he reached down and grabbed the tarp at the foot end.

Don bent down and reached under the tarp, clamping his hands together under what felt like the neck. He could see some bits of hair sticking out the top of the rolled covering, so he looked away and jerked the body up. Sid guided his end toward the back of the room, which forced Don to walk backward with the heavy end of the load.

When he got to the door, Don craned his neck to peek into the alley. It was dark except for a security light, which beamed down near the front of the van. The alley was empty, so Don said, "Okay," and took four quick little backwards steps into the van and dropped the body in the back.

Sid was looking at him as Don hurried out of the van. "Where you going?" asked Sid.

"I'm going in to wash my hands."

Sid laughed.

CHAPTER THIRTY-EIGHT

From the little window in Troy's office, Claudel watched the Chinese drive down the little road in their white van. But he didn't leave right away. He finished looking through Chuck's files, and then he took a look at Troy's. The man was worth a lot of money, and Claudel felt that he deserved a piece of it. He figured that if he took over the business, he'd keep the guys that worked the phones employed, maybe even give 'em a raise, and he could sit back and collect, set up his own secret office and not get involved with any dumbass relatives or Chinese dudes, two good rules to start with.

He filled four boxes with files and audiotapes and notebooks and financial statements. He packed them down to his car, which he'd parked in the garage so that Don and Sid wouldn't be able to see it. He made four trips up and down the stairs from the third floor office to the garage, his knee starting to buckle occasionally and throb constantly. But he got every trace of Troy's sports book operation out of that house. When the bodies were eventually found, he didn't want anyone tracing anything back to him. He was going to walk away with Troy's papers and keep the business rolling. The easy money would help him settle into a nice early retirement.

He drove back to the city and went straight to his apartment, but he didn't call Chuck Holiday right away. Even though that boy was in deep with those chumps, Claudel needed to sit down and ice his knee and not think about anything for a bit.

He put on a pair of gym shorts and sat in his big recliner. He placed a sack of ice on his knee and taped it on with athletic tape. He sat through the first few minutes of pain. Just as the numbness began to set in, he heard a knock at the door. His first thought was that it was Chuck coming to check in and figure out what to do next, but then he started to get a little uptight. Maybe the Chinese had found out where he lived, them being resourceful little gangster wannabes. His final guess came from the aid of the voice at the door saying "SFPD, open up."

That simplified things. It was either the cops or someone saying he was the cops. It wasn't Don or Sid, and he couldn't think of anyone else who would want to ambush him in his own house, so he decided to let 'em knock themselves out. He wasn't opening that door right now. In fact, he sat back and got comfortable while they pounded, this time a different voice saying, "SFPD, open up."

It had been only a few hours since the murders, so it would be tough to find the bodies, then find a judge and get a warrant so fast. No, he'd wait this one out, then call Holiday and find out if the Goose knew anything, though Claudel had watched Chuck and Hazel drive off on that motorcycle while Don and Sid were still searching the house. In fact, he thought he saw Hazel wave at that little kid in the van, but he might've seen that wrong. What would that girl be doing waving to the kid after all that shooting?

There was about a minute where Claudel didn't hear anything. Maybe they'd left to get a warrant or check out some of his hangouts. But then the door heaved in after a loud thump. It didn't come all the way open, but started to splinter near the lock. Then, after another thud, it came swinging off the bottom hinge, and there were three white guys in suits, one older than the other two. The older one was a big fat motherfucker who was probably in his fifties.

They didn't flash any badges, but the two guys who he put in their early forties, looked like detectives with their wrinkled suits and cheap ties. One of them had a cowboy hat and a droopy mustache more like a fireman's, and he stepped forward and said, "Why didn't you answer the door?"

"Can't you see," said Claudel, "I'm laid up with a bad wheel, man?"

"From doin' what?"

"It gets like this in the evenings," said Claudel. "Old injury."

The cowboy moved forward and said, "Maybe I'll take a look at it."

They still hadn't given up their badges or shown guns, and Claudel was about to reach behind the chair and grab his bat, but the older detective stopped the cowboy, saying, "He's telling the truth."

Claudel wondered how in the hell Pops knew about the knee, but he went with it. "Listen to your man there, officer. He knows what's up."

The older dude stepped forward and sat on the arm of the chair. He definitely wasn't a cop. Cops didn't wear nice camel hair sports coats. "Baseball injury," he said. When Claudel looked at him, Pops turned his eyes to the third guy, who had slicked back hair and was chewing gum, and said, "I used to watch this chubbo limping around Big Rec. Slow, but he could hit."

Slick nodded, and then the older guy said, "He actually looked a little like Kirby Pucket the way he turned on that inside pitch."

Claudel liked the compliment, but he didn't know where this was going. "You a baseball fan?" he asked and shifted in his chair. The ice had numbed his knee, but he felt his foot falling asleep.

"I used to play a little ball. But, yes, I'm a fan."

Claudel nodded. What the fuck was going on here?

The old-timer patted him on the shoulder. "You pick up the old stick anymore?"

Claudel shook his head. "Can't do it," he said. "Not with this knee."

The cowboy'd been looking around the room since the moment he pushed past the broken door. Now he moved quickly around the back of the chair and pulled out Claudel's bat. He stepped in front of Claudel and took an awkward swing. "What's this for?" he asked.

"Souvenir," said Claudel.

The old-timer had his arm around Claudel. He said, "It's a funny thing. There was a police report a few days ago, said a guy that fit your description—a fat black asshole—was swinging a bat at some rich guy's knee. Shattered the knee cap."

"That's too bad," Claudel said, not having anything else to offer. Then he thought he might've sounded sarcastic, so he added, "Hate to hear that kind of thing."

"Yeah," said the cowboy. "I'll bet you do." Then he took another awkward swing. He was big and strong, but he wasn't generating any bat speed, didn't know how to use his hips, and his cowboy hat kept shifting down over his eyes when he'd move.

The older one stood and said, "Let's get this going." He took the bat. "Hold him down."

The two younger men went around to the back of the chair and grabbed Claudel by the shoulders. The cowboy bent close to Claudel's ear and whispered, "We all have guns and ain't afraid to use 'em."

"You ain't cops," Claudel said and tested his mobility by trying to sit forward. He had no leverage in the recliner.

"No," said the old-timer. "We just want some information." He reached into his coat pocket and pulled out a shiny little Swiss Army knife. He pulled out the tiny scissors and cut the athletic tape holding the ice to Claudel's knee. He threw the bag on the floor near the broken door. The melted ice splashed out onto the hardwood.

Claudel thought he could feel a pulse in the knee, a rhythmic throbbing. "What the fuck is going on here?" he said.

The old-timer took a couple of practice swings, nice form— quick bat, high follow-through. He said, "I feel loose," and took a swing at a lamp, sending it in pieces toward Claudel's stereo equipment. "I need you to tell me what's going on with Chuck Holiday. What's he gotten himself into?"

"Who *are* you guys?" said Claudel, reaching to his knee to see if he could block the blows if he had to, but he couldn't come close with the two thugs holding his shoulders.

"Does it matter? I'm gonna make it so you can never walk again, and then I'm gonna make sure you go to jail for poppin' the man's knee last week."

"How you gonna get me in jail?"

"I know some folks in San Francisco law enforcement."

"You ain't an ex-cop though," said Claudel. The man had too much style for a cop, nice big ring on his finger, silk tie, shined shoes.

"Even better," the old guy said as he tightened his grip on the bat. "I'm an ex-judge."

It only took a split second for Claudel to put it together. "How you doin', Judge Holiday?"

The Judge smiled. "I'm doing just fine, son. But if you don't tell me what kind of trouble my son's in right now, you're going to be in a good deal of pain."

"Your boy," said Claudel, not seeing many options, "he just tryin' to get rid of the scent, Judge, just tryin' to get his ass outta Dodge."

The Judge flipped the bat in the air and caught the fat end in his big hand. He moved closer to Claudel and started tapping the knob of the bat on Claudel's thigh, and kept tapping, lower and lower, getting closer to the knee, until Claudel was starting to feel little shocks of pain. "You're going to have to do better than that, Claudel," he said, and gave Claudel a hard whack on top of his kneecap.

Claudel bit down hard but didn't yell out as the wave of pain shot through the whole right side of his body. "I got no problem telling y'all what you want to know," he said when he could speak. "But why don't you tell me what you know, and I'll fill in the gaps."

The Judge flipped the bat back around so that he was holding the handle again, resting the old Adirondack on his shoulder like he was posing for a baseball card. "What's my son's business with Troy Curran?"

"Troy don't got a business no more."

CHAPTER THIRTY-NINE

As Chuck jumped the fences in his neighbors' backyards, he felt as if he were in fourth grade again, in the middle of a competitive *kick the can* game. But he had some problems he'd never had in fourth grade. One, it was two o'clock in the morning, and everyone was asleep. Two, he was six and a half feet tall and had trouble hiding behind bushes. And three, there were a couple of killers looking for him. He wanted to get into his house, get his money, and get the hell out of the country.

When he was one backyard down from his own, he peered over the fence at the back of his house. At first, the house appeared to be in complete darkness, but upon further inspection, Chuck noticed through the sheer curtains of Hazel's psychic readings room a faint blue-gray flickering. Since there wasn't a TV in that room, he knew the door must be open and the dim moving light was coming from all the way down the hall in the living room. His initial thought was that Don and Sid were in there watching TV.

He'd made his way around the neighborhood with Hazel, and they didn't see the white van anywhere. But that didn't mean anything.

He took out his phone and called Hazel, who was supposed to be sitting in front of the nearby 7-Eleven. When she answered, she sounded calm.

"What's goin' on?" he said.

"I'm having a slurpee," she said. "What do y'think? I'm waiting to hear from you."

"Yeah," he said, making sure to keep his voice down. "I'm not quite sure what to do. I can tell the TV's on, but I haven't seen any movement in there."

"The TV's on?"

"Yeah."

"Then, at the very least, we know someone's been in the house."

"Yeah, but I don't know if they're still in there or not."

"Wait a minute," she said. "How do you know the TV's on?"

"The door to your room is open. I can see light from the TV."

"Where are you?"

"I'm in the neighbor's yard," he said and looked up at the neighbor's window, making sure he wasn't being watched.

"If you climb over the fence, you can look all the way down the hall and see part of the living room. Maybe you can see who's in there."

"I might be able to see better, but I also might get trapped. At least from here, I have a better chance to get away."

"It's your call," she said. Chuck couldn't get a read from her voice. It was either get in the house and get the rest of their money and at least some of their stuff or get on the motorcycle and drive out of there right now. Hazel needed her driver's license if she was going to get on a plane, and he knew she wanted her tarot cards.

"I'll climb back there and check it out," he said.

She said, "Be careful," and hung up.

Chuck could hear some fear in her voice, but he was going in. He surveyed his own backyard and saw that the fence on the other side was fairly short. From his vantage point, he thought it looked about four feet high, and he thought he could probably hurdle it if he had to. He also spied a fireplace poker that he'd used with the barbeque coals. He could use that if he got into some kind of a fight, although with Don and Sid's preference for guns, it didn't seem likely that the poker would do any good. The short fence was probably his best option.

It was foggy and dark enough where he didn't think he needed to sneak around too much once he was in the yard. He stayed low, but went straight to the window and looked into Hazel's room. It had been ransacked, which meant there was a good chance those fuckers had found the money. The ventilation duct where it was stashed was directly underneath the window, so Chuck couldn't get an angle to see whether or not the cover had been removed.

He cupped his hands and put his face up to the glass to find out if Hazel was right, that he could see all the way down the hallway into part of the living room. It took a moment for his eyes to adjust, but it turned out that Hazel knew what she was talking about. Chuck could see the shadow of the far right section of the couch and half of the middle section. And when he squinted and the lighting from the TV was just right, he could see the silhouette of a person sitting on that middle section. That person was too big to be the little one, maybe even too big for the partner. The person was sitting perfectly still, either really into the show or sleeping. Chuck thought it was a white guy.

He just couldn't come up with anyone it could be. Aside from Don and Sid, no one had a good reason to have broken into his house. There was no other movement or sound in the house. He was about to leave, but he took one more look, putting his hands up to the pane again and squinting through the glass. He wasn't sure if it was a car's headlights or a sudden bright image on the television, but there was a flash, and he finally got a clear image of the man's face. The sight of it brought a sickening tightness to his stomach.

He marched into the alley and used his key to open the side door to the garage. He moved quietly through old boxes of newspaper clippings and college textbooks and Hazel's trinkets that she never bothered to bring into the house. When he got to the kitchen door, he was able to open it without a click, and he walked across the linoleum, making sure his basketball shoes didn't squeak.

He leaned out the kitchen door and peered into the living room, and now he was close enough to the man to confirm his identity. It was Brian Curran, the television light dancing on his blue-white face. As soon as Chuck was able to verify that it was in fact Brian, he immediately started to pick up the smell, which was something like meat gone bad and sewage and mold. Bad enough to make Chuck cover his nose and mouth as he approached the body, which had been propped up on the couch.

Taped to Brian's T-shirt was a paper towel right out of Chuck's kitchen. It said *YOU NEXT* in red Sharpie. Chuck understood that the authors of the note might be in the house somewhere waiting for him with their bad grammar and guns. But he was exhausted, almost to the point of being dazed. He took out his phone and called Hazel.

When she picked up, he said, "We got a new problem."

CHAPTER FORTY

Don had convinced Sid that Chuck wasn't coming back to the house in Gateway tonight, but Sid had the idea of leaving the body and the note to put some more fear into the man for when he did decide to return.

And after that was done, Don suggested that they head back to the Singing Sow and clean up the walk-in refrigerator. Don was disgusted that the corpse had sat there for nearly a week. Sid had agreed to help with the work, maybe coming to the understanding that they needed the restaurant business to remain profitable, as their underworld aspirations were coming apart like slow-cooked pork.

The restaurant was quiet except for the sounds of the buzzing electric lights and the hum of the ice machine. Don was still thinking about his nephew and the image of Sid standing over Curran's wife. He wanted to think of something else, so he said, "What are we going to do with all those pigs in the freezer?"

Sid was standing next to the long table, on which they'd stacked the contents of the walk-in refrigerator, and Don's voice seemed to startle him. "Can we do one thing at a time?" he said. "Grab the hose."

"Why did you take those pigs anyway?" Don asked.

Sid sat down on a stool and rolled the bottoms of his pants up to his knees. Then he walked over and took the hose from Don. "To see if I could do it."

"You *did* it," said Don.

Sid was in the back of the refrigerated room now. "Turn it on," he yelled.

Don did and snatched the mop and a bucket from near the loading dock. This wasn't very glamorous work, but it was a living, and he wanted to forget the other stuff, clean out Brian Curran's residue and get back to the business of running the restaurant.

When they'd cleaned out the refrigerator and replaced the perishables, Don said, "Now what about the pigs?"

Sid shook his head. "I don't know about them," he said and scratched at the beginnings of a thin goatee.

"Should we put some of them in the refrigerator?"

Sid shook his head. "We need to get them thawed and butchered, but there's too many for us to use."

"Could we maybe sell them to someone else?"

"I think we need to get rid of at least half of them," said Sid. "But I don't think there's much call for black market pigs."

Don walked over to the freezer and pulled open the door. The frozen pigs looked like a magnified package of candy animals. Don stood in front of the open door and said, "Fucking pigs."

When they heard the crashing of glass out front, Don was leaning on the freezer door and Sid was standing in the middle of the room with his pants still rolled to his knees. Two men wearing suits and pointing guns walked into the room.

The one with the mustache and a cowboy hat said, "You the Chinamen?"

Don looked at Sid, and then at the desk where both of their guns were resting on top. Don thought about making a run for it, but these men were too close. He'd never make it.

The second man, with his hair combed straight back, must have caught the direction of Don's eyes, because he said, "Don't even think about it, partner. I'll put holes in you."

Don put his hands in the air and said nothing.

The cowboy said, "Word has it you two've been causin' all sorts of problems lately." He motioned with his gun and said, "Have a seat, boys."

Don, with his hands still up, sat on the floor in front of the open freezer, while Sid walked over and sat on the little stool. The cowboy said to Don, "Go ahead and put your hands down." Then he looked beyond Don and said, "The fuck is with all the pigs?"

Don looked at Sid. They were *his* pigs. Sid was hunched over, looking at the floor. The other man said to Sid, "C'mon, junior, what's the story with the pigs?"

Sid looked up and said, "Why? Do you think they're your brothers?"

The cowboy smiled and said to his partner, "Oh, this is a *funny* midget, like Billy Barty."

The other guy laughed and said, "He is a weird looking little fella, isn't he?"

"He's a funny midget," said the cowboy. "Troy Curran got himself killed by a funny midget."

Don could see Sid's face turning red. He wouldn't have been surprised if the little man jumped off the stool and took a bullet while trying to rip out the throat of the cowboy. But the only thing moving was Sid's face, little rumblings at the corners of his mouth and above his eyes.

"You better watch it," the other guy said and pointed at Sid. "He looks like he's getting pissed."

The cowboy moved closer to Sid. "We're not pigs. They'd arrest you. We have no intention of arresting you."

Don was trying to figure out who they were. They didn't seem to care about Curran, and they didn't seem like they'd be connected to Chuck Holiday, either. They looked like cops, bad cops. There was something dark about the way they carried themselves. Their eyes weren't right, too eager. "What do you want?" he asked, his voice cracking. He needed to do something to buy them some time.

The cowboy put his hand up to his chin and squeezed it so that his cleft seemed deeper than it was. He said, "That's a good question. I guess what we'd really like is for you two slime balls to have never been born, but it's too late for that, isn't it?"

His partner nodded and pulled himself up on the butcherblock table. "Yeah," he said, "Can't go back in time and erase 'em, can we?"

Don wondered why they kept finishing their sentences with questions, and he also wondered where his nephew was when they needed him. And why hadn't Sid tried something instead of sitting there looking at the floor? He'd unrolled his pants and straightened his tie, so he looked less foolish when he raised his head and said to Don in Chinese, "We're dead."

CHAPTER FORTY-ONE

Chuck lifted the lid off the vent. "Here we go," he said and reached into the duct. He pulled out the bag and looked inside. "Thank God."

Hazel closed her eyes and mouthed the words, "Thank you, thank you." She put her hand on the bag and said, "Well, at least we have this. If we add this to Troy's money, we're in good shape."

"I know," he said and took a deep breath, thinking that if Don and Sid *had* stolen the money, maybe they'd leave Hazel and him alone. The thought gave him a brief sense of peace. But he would never have been able to live with that, either, those two weasels walking around with their guns and his money. He looked at Hazel and said, "What's next?"

"Can't we just go right now and get a hotel room near the airport, then get a flight out tomorrow?"

"We gotta get Brian outta here, or I'm gonna be the first suspect when someone reports the smell, and I'll be extradited back to the U.S."

"Can you bury him in the backyard?" she said with a shiver.

"I thought of that, but I don't want Don and Sid coming back here in the next few minutes and throwing me in the hole before I can get Brian in it." He knew it was going to sound absurd, but he said it anyway. "We gotta get that fucker on the back of the Harley and bury him somewhere else."

Hazel started to chew on her fingernail. "How're you gonna get him on the motorcycle? Are you gonna put the helmet on him and tell him to hold on?"

Chuck shrugged and shook his head.

"And what am I supposed to do while you're out joyriding with Brian?" She raised her eyebrows. "Wait for the little lizard man to come back here?"

Chuck walked into the kitchen and grabbed his backpack off the table. He placed the bag of money inside and said, "Come here."

When Hazel, holding her nose, walked into the kitchen, Chuck said, "Turn around." When Hazel complied, he put the straps on her shoulders and said, "Go back up to 7-Eleven."

"With all this money?" she said.

"Do you want me to drive around with the money *and* the dead body? If I get caught, at least you'll have the money."

"I don't know," she said, sounding angry. "I don't want to stand in front of 7-Eleven with all this money at three o'clock in the morning."

"Who's working tonight?"

"The fat guy,"

"The Mexican or the bald white guy?"

"The bald guy."

"Good," said Chuck. "That guy knows me. He bets college football. Tell him you're waiting for me and he'll let you sit inside. Buy a magazine or something. I won't be long."

"I'm going out through the garage." Just before she opened the door, she said, "Hurry up." She closed the door, but opened it up a few seconds after. "Don't get caught, Chuck."

***

Chuck brought his motorcycle into the garage and dragged the body down the steps. He moved the Harley so that the rear wheel was flush against the garage door. After fifteen minutes of propping Brian up, dry heaving, watching him fall off, then propping him up again, Chuck finally got it. Brian's stiff, slightly wet body was straddling the bike and leaning against the door. With bungee cords, Chuck attached Brian's body to his own. The smell and the feel of the corpse against his back were overwhelming. Chuck didn't know if he was going to make it.

His plan was to take side streets to Skyline, near the top of John Daly Boulevard. It was only about a mile from his house, and there was an old, closed road up there, where parts of the old highway were gradually falling over the eroded cliff to Thorton Beach below. He'd drive on the road for a few hundred yards and then take the body into the trees and bury it in the soft, sandy soil. He slid a little Army spade inside the bungee across his chest. Then he turned the Harley around, reached over and pushed the button for the automatic garage door opener. He swayed a bit to the right and to the left to check the efficiency of the bungee, and then pulled out of the garage and coasted down the street.

It was getting close to four o'clock in the morning, and the streets were empty and quiet. A heavy fog was hovering just above the lampposts and throwing out a light mist over the neighborhood, making visibility difficult. But he did see two headlights making the turn in front of him. It was bad luck, but if he just kept moving, nobody would notice anything strange. It was too dark, too foggy. He and Brian just looked like two guys on a motorcycle.

However, as he was passing the vehicle, he was pretty sure he knew who it was. It was a white van. Chuck couldn't see the driver, but he still accelerated around the turn. Over the rev of his engine, he heard the screeching of brakes. He'd have to get to Skyline well before the van, or they'd see him make the turn onto the closed highway a quarter of a mile north. And if they saw him make that turn, he'd be trapped, because the road eventually crumbled into broken asphalt, then gravel, and finally fell off into the Pacific Ocean.

It was difficult to make turns because of Brian's shifting weight, but Chuck hit the first turn hard and then shot down toward that section of the little highway with the *Road Closed* sign and the long bar across the old opening. As he approached, he slowed so that he'd be able to get the correct angle and squeeze through the pedestrian opening without having to stop. The gap between the end of the bar and the post on the other side of the path appeared to be about four feet, plenty of room for a motorcycle to pass through without having to slow down too much. However, the closer he got, the smaller the gap appeared. Chuck panicked and slammed on the brake.

The ground was wet and mixed with sand that had blown up from under the ice plants. The bike fishtailed and threw Chuck and Brian over the bar. They stayed attached in the air and twisted before they crashed to the sandy pavement, Brian's body cushioning the blow, before the bungee snapped, and the two men and the shovel tumbled apart.

Chuck never lost consciousness, but he did lie on his back for a moment to take stock of his injuries, which seemed minor. What hurt most was his pinky, which he held up and saw in the illumination cast by the motorcycle's headlight. It was dislocated, but before he could set it, he realized that he had to go cover that light before it gave away his position.

When he stood up, he felt stings and aches and throbbings that sent him back to the pavement. On his hands and knees, he scrambled to the motorcycle, which was on its side in front of the pole. Chuck put his whole body on the headlight while he reached for the ignition key, but it was too late. He could hear the van make the turn and saw the two beams of the headlights brightening the area around him, getting closer. His demise approached like the waves crashing on the beach below him, just as inevitable … just as inescapable.

But when the doors opened, he didn't see Don and Sid. Chuck rubbed his eyes in disbelief. He was looking at a white man with long mustache, a suit, and a cowboy hat. The way his mustache was curved up on one side made it look like he was half-smiling when he said, "You okay, kid?"

Chuck rolled off the Harley and sat on his butt, his bony knees wishboned out in front of him. He nodded but really had no idea whether he was all right or not.

The man opened the back doors of the van, and he said, "Did you think we were *these* guys?" He moved to the side.

Chuck leaned forward and squinted into the back of the van, where two shadowy figures were seated on the floor. He was still apprehensive about getting any closer, so he grabbed the handlebars of the motorcycle and tilted them so that the headlight lit up the inside.

Don and Sid. Both of them had been shot dead, their foreheads like miniature Japanese flags, dark red circles against their pale skin. Both of them had their eyes opened, but neither looked scared. Their expressions were of men disgusted with themselves, maybe a bit ashamed at their predicament.

"Who are you?" asked Chuck, standing up now but still keeping his distance.

"We're friends of your old man."

Chuck looked deeper into the van to see another man sitting in the driver's seat, smiling and waving.

Of course they worked for his dad. "What does he want you to do with me?"

The guy in the cowboy hat said, "Get you on a plane."

"What about all these guys?" asked Chuck, motioning to Brian, then Don and Sid.

"We'll take care of all that. You're supposed to start concentrating on your jump shot."

"Is that what The Judge said?"

"Why don't you help me get this one up in the van."

"And the Lord spake unto the fish, and it vomited Jonah upon the dry land."

- Jonah

When I was four or five, we were across the bay at Marin Town and Country Club. Only a few kids had water wings back then, and I wasn't one of them. There were a hundred kids in the pool, and most of us were in the shallow end. For some reason, I was jumping around very close to the rope that separates the deep end from the shallow end, and somehow I went underwater and came up on the wrong side.

I remember that I didn't panic at first. I was holding my breath down at the bottom of the pool and thought I could simply walk up the slight grade until I could stand up. But that didn't happen. After a couple of steps I lost traction, and I was walking on nothing, my feet spinning like I was on a stationary bike.

That's when I started to panic. I opened my mouth to yell and ended up swallowing some water. I was kicking and flapping my arms like some kind of mad bird, but I couldn't keep my head above water. I fought it for a few moments before I ran out of gas. I was just a little kid, and the panicking sucked all the energy out of me. I remember thinking I'd let myself sink down until I had enough energy to push myself back up again, but when I started to sink, I knew I didn't have anything left. I had my eyes open, and I was looking at the legs of the bigger kids, bouncing around just a few feet away from me.

When I look back on that day, it makes me want to cry because I'm pretty sure I was thinking that I was never going to get to be a big kid, that this was it.

Then there was an explosion in the water, and I was surrounded by bubbles and hands. Eventually, I was yanked over to the shallow end. I couldn't see anything because I was coughing and had my eyes closed, but I could feel myself being pulled through the water. Before we got to the stairs, I opened my eyes and threw up into the water.

By the time I was carried out of the pool, the lifeguards were blowing their whistles and telling everyone to get out so they could clean up my chunks, bits of hot dog and potato salad colored pink from Kool-Aid. I could hear kids whining about it, pissed off that the pool was closed. Then I was placed on the grass near my mom's lawn chair.

"Well," I heard my dad say to my mom. "Here he is. Your little angel just lost his cookies in the pool."

When I looked up at him, he was soaking wet, his T-shirt stuck to his body and his Bermuda shorts sagging down past his knees. There was also some of my puke on his arm, but I don't think he'd noticed yet. The oddest sight was the wet cigar hanging out of his mouth. "And he ruined one of my Cubans," he said.

"How did you find me?" I asked and my voice sounded odd, throaty, an older person's voice.

"I was watching you the whole time," he said and threw his cigar into some bushes behind my mom's chair.

"Why'd you wait so long?"

"If I got you right away," he said. "You wouldn't have learned a damn thing."

And so, for the next twenty years, I survived because of and despite my father.

CHAPTER FORTY-TWO

The Judge was going in for back surgery, so he asked Cunningham to pick up the kid and bring him to the airport, and Cunningham asked if he could bring along his girlfriend. The Judge didn't give a shit, so Cunningham borrowed The Judge's car and took Marta over to Gateway to pick up Chuck and his girl.

When they got to the house, Cunningham noticed a sign out front for palm reading and said to Marta, "You ever have someone tell you your fortune?"

"My fortune?"

"Your future. You ever have your palm read?"

"Why would I want to know my future?"

"I don't know," said Cunningham. "People like to know their future."

"Not me," said Marta. "That takes the fun out of it." She started waving out the window. Chuck and Hazel were carrying their suitcases down the front walkway. Cunningham popped the trunk.

Chuck opened the door for the girl, who slid across, and then he angled his body in after her. "Thanks for getting us to the airport, Mr. Cunningham," he said and patted Cunningham on the shoulder. "This is Hazel."

Cunningham made eye contact with her through the rearview mirror and said, "Nice to meet you." Then he put his arm around Marta and said, "This is Marta. She's gonna take a ride with us today."

Chuck and Hazel nodded, and Cunningham pulled a U-turn and took The Judge's car out toward 87th Avenue, so they could eventually hook up with 280 and then switch over to 101 right after South City. "Are you guys all set up with a place to live over there?" he asked.

Hazel said, "No idea." When Cunningham glanced in the rearview mirror, he saw that she was smiling.

Marta said, "I didn't know where I was going to live when I came to this country." Cunningham looked at her and winked, not sure why she was sharing this information. "But if I had a place to live, it might have led me somewhere different than where I am now, and then I never would meet with Dan," she said, and it was quiet for a moment. Then she said, "So I think it's nice that you don't know where you are going to be. Maybe you'll meet some people that will change your life."

"I like the way you think," said Chuck.

"So do I," said Hazel.

Then The Judge's kid leaned forward in his seat so that his head was between Marta's and Cunningham's. "What did you do with them?"

"You sure you wanna know?"

Looking in the rearview mirror, Cunningham watched the kid lean back now and look over at Hazel, but she was staring straight forward, looking at the back of Marta's head.

"Why not?" said Chuck.

"Why not?" said Cunningham. "Because you don't need to know if you don't wanna know." Cunningham could picture the kid waking up in his bed in England after having a bad nightmare about those dudes in their frozen state.

Chuck looked at Hazel one more time, but she wasn't giving him anything. "We can take it," he said.

Cunningham peeked in the rearview just in time to see Hazel give the kid a quick look before she shifted her gaze forward again.

If he wanted to know, Cunningham didn't give a shit. Let him see the mess he got himself in. "The two Orientals and Troy's nephew are in the walk-in freezer of the barbeque place down on West Portal," said Cunningham and watched Chuck's expression freeze like all those pigs' faces. "We swept the Curran kid's house for anything that might incriminate you. Then we did the same thing to the other guys' place." Cunningham smiled as he thought about the little kid who tried to pull a gun on him and Vince when they were at the apartment in North Beach. "You're clean, Chuck," he said and tried to smile at the kid in the rearview, but Chuck wasn't looking

Chuck was staring out the side window. "Clean," Chuck said, but in a way that made it sound like the word didn't have any meaning.

***

They had to wait two hours before their flight, but Chuck was glad to be sitting in an airport bar at SFO. He was tired of running, and it was nice to be able to have a beer and talk to Claudel, who wanted to see them off and had picked this particular watering hole, a fake sports bar, decorated with San Francisco sports memorabilia: a framed Joe Montana jersey; black and white photographs of Willie Mays, Rick Barry, Y.A. Tittle; beer tap handles with Niners, Raiders, A's and Giants helmets—all very clean and new, with none of the character of a neighborhood place.

"Love airport bars," said Claudel, leaning back and unzipping his leather jacket. "No one hangin' around thinkin' he a *regular*, wantin' special treatment. No happy hour bringin' in the riff-raff. No Jagermeister girls rubbin' they titties on you, get you horny so you buy a shot." He took a sip of his vodka and soda, smiled and said, "Just folks tryin' take the edge off 'fore they go up."

Chuck shook his head. "Everything's kinda plastic though," he said. "Not a lot of personality."

"Why you want personality?" said Claudel. "Alls you want's a drink, right? You got all the personality you need sittin' right here." He nodded and bit down on his lower lip, and, with his thumbs, he indicated that he was talking about himself. While he was still nodding, he said, "That reminds me of a joke." He smiled at Hazel and said, "You don't mind none if it's a little dirty, right?"

"I'm just flattered that you're asking," said Hazel.

Claudel pointed at her and said, "Here it is: What has two thumbs and likes blow-jobs?"

"Tell us," said Chuck.

Claudel made a big production of taking off his jacket and pushing up the sleeves on his mock turtleneck. He put both hands up like a hitchhiker who didn't know what direction he was going. Then he rotated his wrists, wiggled his thumbs and started pointing them toward his own chest. He let out a big laugh. "Two thumbs and likes blow-jobs," he said and laughed again.

"Where did y'get that one?" said Chuck, smiling but not laughing out loud. Too tired.

"That's old school," said Claudel. "My daddy used to tell that one."

For some reason, Chuck had never thought of Claudel as having a father. The guy just seemed like he'd been put together from spare parts: short legs, giant arms, barrel chest, flat nose, high cheekbones … a science experiment.

"How 'bout this one," said Chuck. "A woman's working in the kitchen. Her husband walks in, and he's carrying a sheep. He says, 'This is the pig I've been sleeping with.' So the wife says, 'You jackass. That's not a pig. It's a sheep.' The husband looks at his wife and says, 'I wasn't talking to you.'"

It took Claudel a second, but he got it. Laughed and said, "Your dad might like that one. Seemed like the man might have a sense of humor."

"Yeah," said Chuck. "That's his joke. How do you think he found out?"

"He been watching you, Chuck," said Claudel. "Got dudes working for him, keepin' they eyes out. They know who you hangin' with."

Chuck was quiet. He'd always had a feeling, but finally knowing for certain had him thinking back to everything he'd done since he left Cal. Were there surveillance cameras? Phone taps? Why didn't The Judge stop him when he first started booking bets? And how much of a role had his father played in manipulating his life? "You think The Judge had anything to do with me getting this chance with the BBL?"

Claudel smiled and said, "Who cares?"

Maybe he was right. It didn't really matter.

Hazel asked, "So what're you gonna do now that Troy's gone?"

"Gonna run the business," Claudel said. "Trim it down a little, but still make the sweet coin."

Chuck smiled. "You sure you wanna stay in the business?"

"What else am I gonna do?" he said and took a sip of his drink.

Chuck had a series of funny images run through his head: Claudel as postman, Claudel as short order cook, Claudel as gardener. "You'll do great running the business," he said.

"Yeah," said Claudel. "And I wanna get you that original deal back."

"What do y'mean?"

"You were promised a percentage every month for the sale of your franchise," said Claudel. "I'd like to make good on that."

Chuck thought about it, the nice extra money coming in and no work required, but he looked at Hazel before he turned back to Claudel and said, "Naw, man, we're out."

Hazel grabbed Chuck's hand and said to Claudel, "We're gonna get a fresh start over there, try something new."

"I know where you comin' from," Claudel said. "And you got nothin' to worry about in terms of your dealings with Troy Curran and the law, 'cause I got all your shit outta there before the cops started they investigation. You clean."

That was the second time in an hour that Chuck had been told that he was clean. "Thanks for everything, Claudel," he said, and raised his beer.

Claudel finished his drink, stood and shook Chuck's hand, gave Hazel a kiss on the cheek and said to both of them, "Y'all gonna stack asses over there." He walked out of the bar, his leather jacket swinging behind him as he worked his limp into a modified pimp-walk.

When Claudel moved out of view, Hazel smiled at Chuck and said, "What does *stack asses* mean?"

He smiled back and thought for a moment. "Maybe it means that we'll kick so much ass over there that we'll have to stack them up to store them."

"Why would we want to store the asses?" she asked, her smile getting bigger.

"You'd have to ask Claudel," he said, feeling playful, excited, and weary at the same time, like he used to feel after a big game, knowing there'd be a party later.

"Let's let Claudel go," she said.

"That's a good plan," he said.

About the Author

Tim Reardon has taught writing at St. Ignatius College Prep in San Francisco for the past twenty-five years. He lives in the Ashbury Heights neighborhood with his wife, Gina, and his three daughters, Kate, Claire, and Lizzy, and their border collie, Annie. *Part of the Game* is his second novel. His first novel, *Shadow Lessons*, was published in 2010.

ALL THINGS THAT MATTER PRESS

FOR MORE INFORMATION ON TITLES AVAILABLE FROM
ALL THINGS THAT MATTER PRESS, GO TO
http://allthingsthatmatterpress.com
or contact us at
allthingsthatmatterpress@gmail.com